KU-247-642

NEW WORLD

www.kidsatrandomhouse.co.uk

Also available by Chris Priestley,
and published by Random House Children's Books:

The Tom Marlowe Adventures

Death and the Arrow

The White Rider

Redwulf's Curse

NEW WORLD

CHRIS PRIESTLEY

CORGI BOOKS

NEW WORLD
A CORGI BOOK 978 0 552 55235 6

Published in Great Britain by Corgi Books,
an imprint of Random House Children's Books

This edition published 2007

1 3 5 7 9 10 8 6 4 2

Set in 12½/15pt Bembo by
Falcon Oast Graphic Art Ltd.

Corgi Books are published by Random House Children's Books,
61–63 Uxbridge Road, London W5 5SA,
a division of The Random House Group Ltd

Addresses for companies within The Random House Group Limited
can be found at: www.randomhouse.co.uk/offices.htm

THE RANDOM HOUSE GROUP Limited Reg. No. 954009
www.**kids**at**randomhouse**.co.uk

Mixed Sources
Product group from well-managed
forests and other controlled sources
www.fsc.org Cert no. TT-COC-2139
© 1996 Forest Stewardship Council
FSC

A CIP catalogue record for this book is available from the British Library.

Printed in the UK by CPI Bookmarque, Croydon, CR0 4TD

For Chris

Route of the 1585 Virginia Expedition

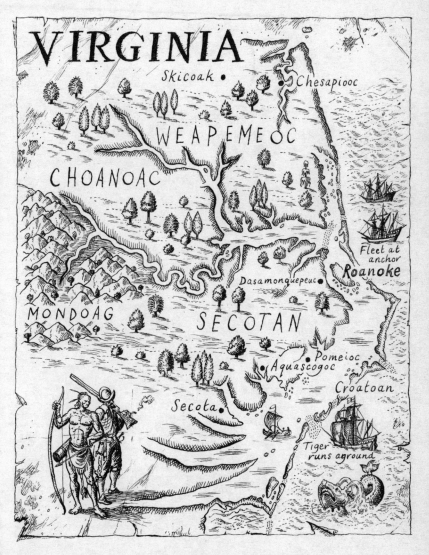

Virginia 1585

Part One
London, 1584

Chapter 1

A roar gathered strength in the crowd, surging like a wave hitting a shingle beach. The soldiers were coming! The bright morning sunshine flickered across their helmets and spear tips, the breath of their horses rising up like smoke in the cold air. Someone leaning from an upstairs window shouted, 'God save the Queen! God save Queen Elizabeth!' and a mighty cheer went up.

Onlookers jostled for position, pushing and shoving, standing on tiptoe, slithering about in the churned-up mud and yelling like the audience at a bear-baiting. Children who had strayed into the street were pulled back, giggling and clapping their hands with glee. Older boys searched for stones.

Here was a treat indeed for London's poor. For on this day they were not the lowest of the low. On this day there were men whom even *they* could sneer and spit at. Bound to hurdles and dragged behind horses, two Catholics – Jesuits, crippled by the rack, bruised and bloody from the journey – were on their way to the gallows at Tyburn.

Bursting through the crowd, just in front of the soldiers, came a fourteen-year-old boy running as if his life depended on it. He hurled himself into the crowd at the other side of the street, squirming and elbowing his way with all his might.

The leading horse snorted and skittered sideways, knocking a lady sprawling into the filth – to the amusement of everyone but the lady herself. Moments later, a second youth burst through the crowd just where the boy had emerged from.

'Stop! Thief!' he yelled before following his prey into the crowd.

The boy he was chasing ducked into the courtyard of an inn and, looking anxiously over his shoulder to check whether he had been followed, careered straight into a group of men, knocking one of them over – a big man wearing a leather jerkin. He begged their pardons and was trying to lift the fallen man to his feet as his pursuer entered the yard.

'Stop that boy!'

The man who had been knocked over got to his feet and grabbed the lad round the throat. The boy struggled to break free, but the man's grip merely became tighter still.

'You have made a grave mistake, lad!' the man said, and he slowly began to lift the boy into the air. The man had close-cropped hair and a neck that was almost as wide as his jaw, and his hands and face were etched with old scars and more recent injuries. His captive guessed with a sinking heart that he was in the hands of a soldier.

'Ah, many thanks,' said the boy's pursuer. 'You have apprehended the rogue. I have chased him—'

But the bull-necked soldier ignored him, his attention on the boy in his grasp.

'Sir,' said the boy's pursuer, moving a little closer. 'We must let the law take its turn.'

'You may do whatever you wish – once I have finished with the lad,' said the man without turning round.

But Kit's pursuer grabbed his arm. 'I must insist!' he said.

The man's two friends put their hands on their sword hilts.

'You dare to stand in my way!' shouted the soldier.

'I do!' said the pursuer, then he announced that the boy had stolen from his employer, Walter Raleigh of Durham House on the Strand, and that he alone should decide what happened to the thief. The man smiled, then after a moment's hesitation he reluctantly loosened his grip on the boy's throat and the lad leaned forward, gasping like a cat with a fur ball.

'Take him then,' he said with a grim chuckle. He turned to his friends saying, 'He has more to fear from that devil Raleigh than he ever would from me! I served in Ireland with that killer.'

'Come on, you,' said the pursuer, drawing a dagger

and grabbing the boy by the scruff of the neck. 'We are away to Durham House. And do not try to escape if you set any value on your life.'

'After that black-hearted rogue Raleigh and his band of wizards and heathens have finished with you,' shouted the man, 'you'll be dreaming of the beating you'd have got from me!'

The boy was shoved along the street, muttering and mumbling to himself, until his captor turned, looked behind them and said with a grin, 'We're in the clear, Kit. They haven't followed us.'

Kit whistled and laughed. 'You were a bit enthusiastic with the shoving today, weren't you, Hugh?' he said, clipping his arm with the back of his hand.

'You are going to get yourself killed!' said Hugh. 'He was an evil character, that one. You've got to learn who to crash into and who not.'

Kit tutted. 'It all turned out fine, didn't it? Don't be such a nag. I have to say that the Raleigh touch was a stroke of genius. Did you see the look on his face?' They both laughed.

The two boys were a team; a pair of magpies. They were as sharp-witted as any court mathematician and they needed to be. They had seen others caught and cruelly punished and they had learned to be clever. They did not stick with one method too long. That was a sure way to lose your ears at the stocks. The trick was to be adaptable, and they were.

Both boys were skilled pickpockets and could ply

that trade alone if necessary. They could work a con too, and they could do it well. Most of all, they looked out for each other and if the worst happened, as it had this day, and one of them – in this case Kit – was about to be caught, the other would immediately fall into one of the many pre-arranged gambits to get them out of it.

Kit had been spotted picking the purse of a man watching the procession to Tyburn, and Hugh had yelled, 'Stop! Thief!' The owner of the purse was too old to chase Kit himself, and everyone else was only too pleased to let Hugh do his public duty and risk being stabbed.

This ploy had the added benefit of allowing both Kit and Hugh to crash into people, which gave them easy pickings from the men and women they jostled. If anyone actually bothered to grab Kit, Hugh would simply trot up, take possession of him and march him off to the constables. Or so the onlookers would think.

The two boys walked for several minutes before they felt able to stop and talk properly. It was always as well to get some distance between themselves and the deed in case they were followed or someone recognized them. Thieves were strange beasts: as keen as foxes when on the chase, and then as watchful as deer in the forest when the job was done. They were predator and prey in one body.

As they came to a halt in an alleyway, Hugh asked Kit what he'd managed to thieve.

Kit produced a pearl earring and the purse of the man who had grabbed him. 'How about you?'

Hugh fumbled about inside his jerkin and brought out a gold ring and a brooch, polishing them on his sleeve and squinting at them. 'Oh, and a purse with . . . not a lot in it. Not much, is it?' They heard a latch lifting on a nearby door and their stolen goods were hidden in their pockets by the time the old man emerged.

'It's not bad,' said Kit when he had gone. 'How much do you think Tooley will give us for them?' They walked into the busy street.

'Not a lot,' said Hugh. 'I hate that man, Kit.'

'Who doesn't?' Kit grabbed a pie from a stall with a magician's sleight of hand. 'But we need him, don't we? There ain't no point in stealing things if you ain't got someone who'll buy them from you. We're stuck with him.'

'*You* might be,' said Hugh.

Kit slapped his arm with the back of his free hand while he took another bite from the pie. A dog began to follow them, hoping for crumbs. 'You're just out of sorts because we didn't get much of a haul, that's all.'

Hugh didn't answer and neither of them spoke for a few minutes. Kit held out the half-eaten pie but Hugh shook his head. He tossed a piece of crust to the dog which, in a flash, caught it and ran away.

'Kit,' said Hugh finally, sitting on a low wall, 'I've got something to tell you.' Kit grunted in response, taking another mouthful and sitting down next to him.

'I'm giving it up.' Kit carried on eating as if he hadn't heard. 'Did you hear me, Kit?'

'Giving up what?' asked Kit in a bored tone, pulling a piece of gristle from his mouth, examining it and then tossing it away with a grimace.

'This,' said Hugh, waving his hands around. 'Thieving. You know very well what I mean. I've told you enough times but you just don't want to listen.'

Kit sniffed, flicked crumbs off the front of his jerkin and asked Hugh if he was going to beg instead. Hugh said that he was planning to take up acting.

Kit nearly choked. 'What? You're giving up thieving for *acting*? Have you no shame?'

'Keep your voice down, Kit, for God's sake!' Hugh hissed.

'But, *acting*?' said Kit. 'What kind of a life is that? Dressing up as women and reciting all kinds of rubbish.' He clasped his hands over his heart and looked up adoringly. 'O dearest love, o tender heart. Thou art more beauteous than a horse's arse!'

But Hugh looked away and simply said that his mind was made up. He had been offered a place with a company of players – something he had always wanted – and he was going to take it.

'Well take it then!' Kit shouted. 'I don't need you anyway!'

Hugh rose to his feet, his lips clamped tightly together as if by the effort of stopping himself from responding. 'Goodbye, Kit,' he managed eventually, holding out a hand. 'Don't hate me for this. Sooner or later we're going to get caught. Do you want to get branded? Or lose your ears. Do you want to *hang*?'

'Do you know, I think you're going to make a really convincing woman,' said Kit bitterly, turning away from his friend.

Hugh sighed. 'I love you like a brother, Kit, but you think of no one but yourself,' he said, 'and you're not the only one who's had it hard. Well, take care of yourself, and come and see me if you can.' He smiled sadly and turned away.

Only then did Kit look round. He watched the only friend he had in the world walk into the distance until he disappeared from sight among the crowds, and he tried very hard to stay angry enough to keep the tears at bay.

Chapter 2

Without Hugh to partner him, Kit was forced to accept that a more direct route was going to be called for in his thievery. It was safer to work as part of a team, but thieving was the only living he knew, so he would just have to take the risk until he could find someone to replace Hugh.

It would not be easy. Thieves were not ones to trust lightly, and yet trust was everything between partners, for a breach of that trust could mean a stint in the stocks, a flogging or worse. Within a week, the last of the money he and Hugh had 'earned' was gone, so until he could find another partner whom he could trust with his life – like Hugh – he would have to return to the more solitary (and dangerous) life of the lone pickpocket. Here, patience was everything; it could mean the difference between life and death.

After nearly half an hour of watching the crowds of shoppers on the Strand, Kit saw his man. His intended victim was an elderly gentleman whose purse was dangling from his belt. Kit walked backwards into him, almost knocking the old man over. He apologized profusely, readjusting the man's cloak while the gentleman cursed and pushed him away. He had ducked down an alleyway with the man's purse before he heard the inevitable shout of 'Stop! Thief!'

Kit had chosen the old gentleman because he would be unlikely to chase him, but he had not bargained on the man's son – a very fit and burly young man – being with him. The son had been inside a shop when the theft had taken place, but had emerged in time to see Kit sneak away. He dashed after him.

Kit heard the footsteps first and turned just in time to see the brewer thundering towards him, teeth clenched and eyes blazing. Kit only narrowly missed being grabbed there and then but he had by no means escaped.

A chase ensued, one which was even more dramatic than the ones that he and Hugh had arranged, as this one was genuine; Kit faced the very real prospect of being branded or worse. And as he began to tire, his pursuer was catching him up.

Just as the son was about to lay his hands on Kit's shoulders, though, a dog broke free from its owner and decided to set about the leg of Kit's assailant as though it were his favourite meal. The man screamed in pain and anger and Kit made his getaway down an alley.

He slowed to a walk now so as not to draw attention to himself, chuckling with relief. He turned into the courtyard of an inn to count his takings, but cursed loudly when he saw that the purse was practically empty.

'Well, well, well,' said a man nearby, grabbing Kit by the scruff of the neck and lifting him onto the tips of his toes. 'What have we here?' With a sinking heart, Kit realized that it was the same crop-haired soldier he had knocked into the week before. 'And how are things at Durham House?'

'I . . . I . . .' For once, Kit was lost for words. Two Kentish farmers in town for the market threw some coins onto the table and made themselves scarce.

'Master Raleigh seems to have spared your ears,' said the man, lifting up Kit's curls. 'And you still have both hands. He must have been in a very forgiving mood.' Without warning the soldier struck Kit across the side of the face, making him stagger backwards into another man. 'You made a fool of me, boy,' he continued, his smile disappearing like the sun behind a cloud. 'You will regret that. You will regret that most painfully. Now, where is my purse, you louse?'

'I don't have it. You can have this one, though,' croaked Kit, shaking his head from the blow and handing him the purse he had just stolen.

The soldier grabbed the purse and weighed it in his hands, noting how light it was. 'I don't think so,' he said.

'I'll get you the rest,' said Kit.

The man laughed. 'Of course you will,' he said, taking out a large dagger. 'Of course you will. But how about I cut your pizzle off instead? Hold him, Skelton. Hold him good and tight.'

Kit now saw his own startled eyes reflected in the blade. He had been in many tight corners before, but none that had seemed so without chance of escape. He could hear his breath coming short and fast – like the panting of a dying dog he had once found lying in the shadow of a cart. He had stroked the dog until the panting had stopped. Was it his turn? Was Death now coming for him?

'Come,' said a quiet voice behind them. 'He is but a boy.'

Everyone, including Kit, followed the sound of the voice to find a thin man in his thirties with mouse-coloured hair and a pale straggly beard, well-dressed without being fashionable. He seemed to take half a step back as the men turned.

'What business is it of yours?' said the soldier holding Kit.

'Well,' said the newcomer, 'I am an Englishman and I will not stand idly by and watch you kill this boy, I shall tell you that.'

The soldier turned and cocked his head to one side, smiling grimly. 'I don't see you making any great effort to stop me.'

'Now listen here. My name is John White, sir. I am a servant of the Crown. I am on my way to Durham House where I—'

The men all broke into laughter, drowning out the rest of his words.

'We've heard that one before, my friend,' said the

soldier. 'You need to learn a new trick. You're another accomplice, ain't you? Grab him, Aston.'

White yelled in outrage as a third man grabbed his arms, but held his tongue when a dagger was waved in front of his face. Kit saw his chance. While his attackers were distracted, he stamped with all his might on the foot of the man holding him and then bit deeply into his hand, making him loose his grip just enough for Kit to break free and sprint out of the courtyard.

He ran without looking round, thanking his lucky stars, but then suddenly he skidded to a halt, turned round and looked back towards the inn. No one had followed him. But although every sinew in his body was quivering with the urge to keep on running, something now held Kit prisoner. He hung his head, remembering Hugh's words about only caring for himself. Perhaps he was right. This stranger had put his life in danger on Kit's behalf, and here he was running away. He cursed loudly and turned to head back towards the inn.

This newfound attack of conscience had not entirely extinguished Kit's natural instinct for self-preservation, however. Even as his feet took him back to the inn, his mind was burning with doubt. How exactly was he supposed to help this stranger against three armed men?

But just as he reached the entrance to the lane in which the inn stood, Kit heard the sound of bleating and turned to see a huge flock of sheep trotting towards him, being driven to market by three shepherds. An idea popped into his mind and he grinned.

He ran just past the entrance to the inn courtyard – near enough to hear the voices of his attackers as they taunted their new victim – and, as the first of the sheep approached, grabbed a nearby cart and pulled it across the narrow lane, blocking their route. Then he jumped up, waving his arms and shouting.

The sheep panicked, running away from Kit and into the courtyard, bleating and leaping over each other in panic. The irate shepherds followed, torn between chasing Kit and rounding up their precious flock.

Kit dodged the nearest shepherd as he lunged at him and followed the sheep into the courtyard. They were quickly filling up all the available space, jumping over tables and benches, and the men who had grabbed him were now completely surrounded, waist high in a woollen torrent, cursing and shouting at the shepherds as they were jostled and butted.

Kit saw his chance. Dropping onto all fours, hidden by the flock of sheep, he squeezed through to White. He tapped him on the leg, then, as White looked down, startled and pale, Kit put his finger to his lips and nodded with his head towards the back of the inn, where he had spotted a window in the wall near the kitchens. Signalling with his hand for White to follow, he crawled off and White began to shuffle sideways over to the window. The soldiers were now arguing with the shepherds and a fight looked likely to break out at any moment. Hissing at White to hurry, Kit stood up to open the window.

It clearly had not been opened in some time and the frame was jammed. Kit heaved at it with all his might but it would not budge. As he gave it two hefty blows with his fist, he heard a voice he dreaded behind him.

'Hey!' the bull-necked soldier was shouting. 'That thieving brat is back and they're getting away!'

Kit desperately struck the window once more and this time it opened. As White climbed out, the three soldiers were wading through the sheep towards them, the one who had first grabbed Kit drawing his sword. Jumping through the window himself, Kit heard the blade sing past his ear; as he hit the ground, the soldier was already at the window, his head and shoulders pushing through, his sword jabbing. Then there was a loud thud and the soldier slumped forward unconscious. Kit turned to see White standing beside him with a heavy wooden bucket in his hands.

'Nice work,' said Kit with a chuckle. 'Come on. His friends will follow for sure.'

White needed no further persuasion to walk briskly away from the inn, following Kit's every step in and out of alleyways and courtyards until they stood on the banks of the Thames, a fresh wind cooling their sweating brows.

Kit stared off towards the Tower. 'Sorry,' he said, almost too quietly to hear, 'that I ran off and left you. What with you stepping in to help me and all. Not that I needed any help, of course.'

'No, no,' said White. 'I could see that you were managing very well.'

Kit grinned despite himself. 'You're all right,' he said.

'Thank you,' said White. 'I shall take that as a compliment.'

Kit grinned and bade White farewell, but as he began walking away, White called after him.

'I have need of some assistance in my household,' he said casually.

'Sorry,' said Kit, stopping and turning round. 'I don't have much to do with servants. But if I hear of anyone looking, I'll send them your way. Master White, wasn't it?'

'John White of Cheapside,' he replied. 'And I was rather thinking you might be interested.'

'Me?' said Kit, poking himself in the chest with a look of amazement. 'A job? *Me?*' He burst into hearty laughter, doubling up and slapping his thigh. 'Oh, I don't think you'd want *me*.'

'I am serious,' said White.

Kit frowned and looked about him, stepping forward to whisper conspiratorially. 'The thing is,' he said. 'The truth is . . . Well, the truth is . . . I'm a thief. That's why the oaf back there grabbed me.'

'I realize that,' White whispered back. 'And I do not condone thievery. But I do not believe you were born a thief and I thought that maybe you might like to *stop* being a thief. It does seem a rather dangerous profession.'

'Nah,' said Kit with a shrug. 'I ain't no servant. I'll stick to what I know, thanks all the same.'

'As you wish,' said White. 'Come and see me if you change your mind. Remember – John White of Cheapside. Ask for me and someone will be sure to point the way to my house. For now, farewell, lad.'

'Aye, you fare well too, Master White,' called Kit as he walked away once more, swallowed up by the London crowd within seconds.

Chapter 3

After a troubled sleep, Kit woke the following morning to the sound of water dripping onto the floorboards by his head. He sat up, bleary eyed, and looked at the ceiling where the plaster was sagging and cracking. Suddenly there was a groan and a creak and then chunks of sodden plaster rained down on him, followed by the mass of rainwater that had been building up overnight.

'Of all the——!' he shouted, covering his soaking head with his hands until the final piece of plaster had bounced off and joined the rest strewn across his bed.

Kit got to his feet in a fury and stormed across to the door. Flinging it open, he yelled at the top of his voice: 'Mrs Milliner! Mrs Milliner!'

There was a scratching and clunking as locks and bolts were drawn on a door on the landing below. The door opened and a woman emerged, squinting and blinking slowly, like an animal emerging from hibernation. She stood in her nightgown, fists on hips, and peered up at Kit.

'What is it, Kit?' she said with a yawn. 'What's with all the godforsaken howling? A girl's got to have her sleep now, ain't she, boy? You're disturbing my other lodgers.'

'There's water pouring in through the ceiling! Look at me! Look at me!'

Mrs Milliner leaned forward and opened her eyes. 'Oh dear me,' she said with a giggle. 'Oh dear, oh dear.'

'It is *not* funny!' shouted Kit, water dripping from the end of his nose, plaster dust caked to his face.

'You want to be standing where I'm standing, sweetheart,' Mrs Milliner laughed.

At this moment, there were footsteps on the stairs below and Kit could see that a well-dressed young man was approaching. Mrs Milliner loosened her grip on her nightgown and ran a hand through her hair, smiling as she did so.

'Well what have we here?' she called down. 'What can I do for your lordship?'

'Hugh Palmer, madam,' the man said with a bow. 'I am looking for a young friend of mine . . .'

Kit recognized Hugh's voice immediately. 'You're no friend of mine any more!' he called out. 'Stop saying you are because you're not! I ain't got no friends no more!' But as he looked down, he was dumbfounded to see a barely recognizable Hugh, dressed in clothes so fine he looked as though he had just jumped off the royal barge from Greenwich.

'Ah,' said Hugh grandly. 'Here is the young prince now. Have I come at an inconvenient time?'

'Yes!' Kit shouted, his scowl quickly returning. As if it was not bad enough that Hugh had left him in the lurch, now here he was turning up in all his finery to gloat. 'Mrs Milliner!' he continued. 'I want to know what you are going to do about my room!'

'Well, dear,' she said. 'That all depends.'

'All depends? On what?'

'On whether you are intending to pay the rent, you good-for-nothing little magpie!' Mrs Milliner yelled these words at the top of her voice and Kit saw Hugh wince. She looked sideways at him and smiled, lowering her voice to its previous simpering level. 'He would try the patience of a saint, he really would.'

'Quite so, dear lady,' said Hugh as Kit yelled a volley of curses at no one in particular. 'But he is young, and youth must be forgiven its excesses.'

Why was Hugh talking in that ridiculous way? Kit was getting more and more angry by the second.

'The young must have some respect for their elders, though, must they not?' said Mrs Milliner testily.

'Elders?' said Hugh, throwing up his hands in dismay. 'Why surely, dear lady, you cannot be but more than a few months older than my friend there.'

Mrs Milliner blushed and turned her face away. 'I fear you might be surprised to know how old I really am,' she said.

Hugh raised an eyebrow and flicked a glance at Kit, who was staring open-mouthed at the newly coquettish Mrs Milliner.

'I cannot believe, my lady, that any surprise you may have to offer could be anything other than delightful,' Hugh continued as Mrs Milliner fluttered her eyelashes. 'How much does the lad owe?'

Mrs Milliner's eyelashes immediately stopped fluttering and Kit's eyes widened in surprise. 'You are offering to pay his debt?' Her tone had become instantly more business-like.

'I am,' said Hugh, taking out a purse and jangling the contents as if it were a hand bell. 'Will this cover it?'

Mrs Milliner weighed the purse in her hands and smiled. Kit's annoyance was giving way to bafflement.

'Well, there is the damage to his room to consider,' she said, looking hopefully at Hugh. Kit opened his mouth to speak but Hugh held up a hand to silence him.

'And there is the damage to the poor lad's clothes to consider,' he said, taking the purse away. 'He will have to have new clothes now, will he not?'

Mrs Milliner caught hold of Hugh's hand. 'I should never be in business with my soft heart,' she said. 'But I'll take your little bag of coins and we'll say no more.' Her hand scuttled through the air like a crab and took the purse.

'You are a shining example of your kind, dear lady,' said Hugh with a bow. 'Come on, Kit, don't just stand there dripping like a halibut. We have urgent business.'

'What urgent business . . . ?' Kit asked suspiciously. But all the same he squelched down the stairs towards Hugh, eager to discover what his old partner would do next.

'But you're not leaving?' cried Mrs Milliner.

'I fear I must, dear lady,' said Hugh. 'The Queen calls and I must answer.'

He turned to leave, but Mrs Milliner caught his arm. 'The Queen? You are at the court?'

'I have that honour, dear lady,' said Hugh. 'Come, Kit, we must away.'

Again Mrs Milliner caught his arm. 'But how on earth does a gentleman like you come to know a cockroach like this? If you don't mind me asking?' she said, twisting her face up as she looked at Kit.

Hugh leaned towards Mrs Milliner. 'The Queen must have eyes and ears in every part of her realm,' he whispered, tapping the side of his nose.

'Hah!' she snorted. 'You don't mean to tell me that this tick here is on the Queen's business?'

Hugh put his finger to his lips and leaned even closer. 'His disguise is convincing, is it not?'

Mrs Milliner looked at Kit, twisted her top lip and frowned. 'Very,' she said. 'But even if he was an ear or a nose or whatever else of the Queen's, why is he here? What is he spying on me for?'

'On you, dear lady?' said Hugh. 'Why, I'm sure there is no more loyal subject in all the land . . .'

Mrs Milliner smiled and nodded. 'I would do anything for Her Majesty, sir, everyone knows it,' she said. 'Anything I have is hers for the asking.'

'The Queen will be most gratified to hear it, dear lady,' Hugh replied. 'So many of her subjects think only of themselves. It will be a genuine pleasure to be able to tell Her Majesty of someone who did not solely concern themselves with profit.' He looked casually at the purse full of coins which Mrs Milliner had taken from him. She frowned and then hurriedly handed it back. Kit had to stop himself gasping in admiration. 'There is no need, dear lady,' Hugh said, taking the purse from her.

'No, no,' said Mrs Milliner, suddenly flustered again. 'It is my duty . . . That is, I would never . . . You will speak kindly of poor Mrs Milliner, won't you, lad?'

Kit opened his mouth to answer, but Hugh spoke first.

'Of course he shall,' he said. 'But I need not tell you of the mortal danger the Queen faces from those who would aid her enemies . . .'

'Catholics!' hissed Mrs Milliner and made as if to spit, then thought better of it and swallowed with a shudder.

'Worse,' whispered Hugh.

'Spaniards!' she said in a strangled whisper.

'Quite so,' said Hugh nonchalantly. 'Kit, we must be going.'

Kit, who had been staring at his friend's performance in a trance-like state of admiration, followed Hugh down the stairs.

'I'm impressed,' he said when they were out in the street and away from Mrs Milliner's beady gaze. 'Truly impressed. Maybe this acting lark isn't so foolish after all. But what is all this? Why were you looking for me?' His face suddenly lit up as if struck by sunlight. 'You've changed your mind! You've decided to carry on thieving.'

'No, Kit,' said Hugh, shaking his head. 'I just didn't want us to part on bad terms.'

'What about that purse full of coins you were offering old Milliner?'

'Stage money, Kit. Worthless. We're performing nearby and I thought you'd get a laugh out of seeing me dressed in these duds. I was rehearsing and thought I'd come by and see how you were. It looked like you could do with some help . . .'

'I don't need your help,' said Kit sulkily.

'I'll take that as a thank you.'

'I didn't need no help,' Kit insisted forcefully.

Hugh sighed. 'Let's not argue again, Kit. Come on, we're playing at the inn just over the bridge. You can change into a costume while your clothes are drying and tell me what you've been up to.'

Kit took a deep breath and nodded. The two friends walked through the tangled knot of alleyways before emerging into the busy traffic going to and from London Bridge. Kit hated – dreaded – using the bridge but he could never have explained why to Hugh, so he simply followed after him, a cold sweat greasing the palms of his hands.

The cause of Kit's distress loomed above them: the Great Stone Gateway. The bridge was the only way across the Thames apart from by ferry boat. It was London's front door and as such was seen as a fitting place to display a warning to anyone who might be harbouring treasonous thoughts.

Kit kept his eyes firmly focused on the ground in front of his feet, but he could hear the ravens croaking above him as they perched on the severed heads of England's enemies, partially boiled and tarred by the executioner to protect them from the elements.

With the sound of the ravens' croaking and the rhythmic heartbeat of the waterwheel pounding below, they passed through the gateway and into the tunnel-like gloom of the bridge, its shops and houses piled up above them. Livestock lowed and bleated its way to market, the noise competing in volume with the chatter of travellers and shoppers, the clatter of horses' hooves, the creak and rattle of carts and wagons.

Kit followed Hugh off the bridge, up a steep alleyway that smelled of fish and on to an inn he did not know. Set back from the river, the inn's courtyard was being readied for a play. Hugh shouted hallos to his new friends and Kit felt a pang of jealousy, but whether he was jealous of these friends or of Hugh for having them, he could not have said.

They sat on a bench and, with a little prompting, Kit told Hugh about crashing into the soldier again and how a stranger had stepped in and tried to help him. Hugh was surprised enough that a gentleman would come to the aid of a thief, but this was nothing to his amazement on hearing that Kit had actually returned to the inn to help this Good Samaritan. Kit was a little hurt by Hugh's expression, but let it go for fear of starting another argument.

Kit told the story of being offered a job as though it was a joke, but Hugh did not laugh. He repeated the tale, wondering if his friend had missed some vital part of it.

'And what would be so wrong with being a servant?' said Hugh. 'It would be safer. You'd have a decent roof over your head; food in your belly.'

'I do all right,' said Kit.

Hugh shook his head.

'Can you see me as a servant? Honestly?'

Hugh had to admit it was rather difficult to imagine, but he told Kit that this was a chance that might never come along again; a chance to get off the streets and live a better life.

'But I'd get so bored!' complained Kit. 'It's all right for you, you're doing something exciting.'

'It might be dull at first, but you never know,' said Hugh. 'What does this fellow do who's offered you the job?'

'I never asked,' said Kit with a shrug.

Hugh shook his head. 'Well I wish you'd take it, whatever the work is,' he said.

'I'm doing all right,' Kit said again, stubbornly.

A group of actors erupted into raucous laughter at the other end of the courtyard. Hugh smiled and looked towards them, but his smile was dimmed when he looked back at Kit

'Course you are, Kit,' he said. 'Course you are. But for how long? You're living by your luck, Kit . . . and luck runs out. I don't want to see you hanged.'

'Well, thanks,' said Kit with a grin. 'I'm not too keen to catch that show myself.'

'Seriously, Kit,' said Hugh. 'You know I'm right. We've seen it happen enough times, haven't we? Remember Tom Quick? And what about Dead-Eye Jenny? And there's—'

'Yes, yes,' said Kit, holding up his hands. 'Don't go on.'

'Sorry, Kit.' Hugh dropped his voice once more. 'I worry about you, that's all.' He looked down at his shoes.

'It's all right for you,' said Kit forlornly, looking at the actors rehearsing nearby, laughing and joking. 'You're doing something you've always wanted to do. Why have I got to be the one who does the boring thing?'

'It might not always be boring,' said Hugh. 'It's better to be bored but safe, isn't it?'

'Is it?' said Kit.

Neither of them spoke for a while then Hugh sighed. 'I'm sorry, Kit,' he said. 'I must get on. I have to rehearse. Look, why don't you borrow a costume and dry your clothes? You can stay for a time if—'

'No,' said Kit, getting up. 'I'd better go.'

Hugh knew Kit well enough to realize that he should let the matter of the servant's job rest. They embraced and wished each other luck, both pleased to be parting on better terms. As Kit left Hugh thrust some coins – real ones, this time – into his hand and refused to listen to his protests or to take them back.

An actor called for Hugh and Kit told him to go. But as he walked out into the alley, his heart ached with a renewed sorrow for the loss of Hugh's company and with a longing for his life to be more than simply a matter of survival.

Chapter 4

Kit returned to Southwark by boat, happily paying the penny charge rather than cross by the bridge again. He walked towards his lodgings, kicking a stone ahead of him. A blood-curdling cheer sounded from the bear-baiting pit.

A memory of his own fear-crazed eyes reflected in the soldier's dagger came back to him and he gulped dryly, as if choking on a piece of stale bread. Hugh was right. One day, and it might be soon, he was going to run out of luck.

As he reached the foot of the rickety stairs leading to his room, he noticed a bundle lying in the dirt. He was just stepping over it when he recognized it as his blanket and realized that the little pile of belongings were his own. He bounded up the stairs.

'Mrs Milliner! Mrs Milliner!' he yelled.

Mrs Milliner appeared on the landing and blocked his way. Two men were standing behind her. Kit had seen them before. They were her sons and their appearance usually meant trouble for somebody.

'Why have you thrown my stuff in a heap outside?' Kit asked, trying not to look at the sons.

'I ain't having no spies in this house.'

'I'm no intelligencer,' snapped Kit.

Mrs Milliner raised an eyebrow. 'The gent what was here earlier seemed awful sure you was,' she said.

'Look,' said Kit, 'he was just . . . He was . . . I don't even know him.'

'Don't know him? Do you hear all this, boys? Do you see the kind of lying and trickery and knavery I have to put up with?' The sons stared malevolently at Kit. One of them was rhythmically clenching his hand into a fist.

'Look, I've got nowhere else to go,' said Kit forlornly. The street had suddenly lost its appeal.

'Oh bless his heart,' said Mrs Milliner with a queasy smile, her face whiter than her teeth. The smile vanished as quickly as it had appeared. 'See him out, boys.'

'You old witch!' yelled Kit. He turned on his heels and made a mad dash for the stairs. The sons struggled to get past their cursing mother on the narrow landing. By the time they had squeezed past her, Kit had jumped down the last few steps and was in the courtyard below.

Mrs Milliner leaned over the railings, her face distorted by rage. 'How dare you call me *old*, you little dungheap!' she shrieked.

Kit ran out of the courtyard, not daring to look round

when he heard an almighty crash and groan as might be made by one large son falling through the rotten staircase and the other falling heavily on top of him.

Within minutes, Kit was looking breathlessly at London across the grey water of the Thames, which that day was as choppy as the open ocean. The wind had picked up and was bringing with it a freezing rain that was falling like spittle as it turned to sleet.

Suddenly the prospect of spending the night under a cart did not seem as easy as before. Cheapside, and John White, it would have to be then. Kit looked once over his shoulder at his old life, then whistled to a boatman.

When he got to Cheapside, Kit asked a bellman where John White lived. The old man pointed out a house at the corner of a narrow lane.

'What business do you have with John White?'

'He has offered me employment,' said Kit.

The bellman looked Kit up and down and raised an eyebrow. He leaned forward and Kit could smell the beer on his breath. 'Be on your guard, young fellow,' he whispered.

'Why?' said Kit. 'He seems a good man.'

The bellman snorted and, after looking each way up the street in a comically exaggerated fashion, leaned even closer. 'Wizard,' he hissed.

Kit laughed, but the old man was clearly not joking.

'Wizard,' he repeated. 'As God's my witness.' Then he tottered off down the street, leaving Kit to wonder if he should walk away while he could. Wizards and witches, conjurors and cunning men – they all gave Kit the shivers.

But he felt tired – and he was running out of options. He took a deep breath, walked towards White's door and rapped the knocker. A maid answered and took some persuasion to fetch her master.

'Ah,' said White with a smile when he came to the door. 'It is my young friend from the inn, is it not?' The maid stood behind him, looking at Kit as though he were a particularly filthy stray dog.

'Yes,' Kit replied, then after a moment's thought he added, 'Sir.'

'Well, come in, come in,' White said. 'So you are in need of work after all. That will be all, Annie.' The maid sniffed and walked away.

'I don't know, sir. That is, I suppose so, sir. I never had much cause to work before. Not what you'd call real work anyway, sir.'

White sighed and smiled despite himself, but then his expression became more serious. 'You should know that I will not abide theft of any kind, lad. I am no fool. If you steal from me it will be the end of us, do you understand?' White said these words in such a gentle and kindly way that Kit could see nothing to say and simply nodded in agreement.

'Now then, lad – I think it is about time I knew your name.'

'Kit, sir.'

'Well, Kit, I suspect you must have had a hard life to turn to thievery. You have no family?'

'I am an orphan, sir,' said Kit.

White nodded. 'You have lived wild on London's streets and I know that many die of less,' he said. 'Now, if you are willing to learn, and willing to work fairly and act truly, then you shall find me a good master, I hope. Can you read?'

'No, sir,' said Kit after an almost imperceptible pause.

'Never mind,' said White. 'That is not important to begin with; there are many tasks I require an assistant to carry out for me.' He looked at Kit with such an expression of expectancy that Kit felt almost as though he were interviewing White and not the other way round. 'Right then,' he continued. 'I'll show you where you can sleep. I do not have a great deal of room, as you can see, but we shall manage.'

He led Kit through to the kitchen and showed him a straw mattress on the floor near the fire. White then asked Annie to bring them some bread and cheese and a jug of beer. Kit's life on the street had taught him to eat whenever food was available and he tucked into this supper as if he had not eaten for days.

White said that as it was late, he would explain Kit's duties to him the following day. It was all the same to Kit as he had no intention of staying there longer than he had to. He was tired and happy to hear that White was going to bed.

Kit took to his mattress, and no sooner had he pulled

the blanket up around his ears than he was asleep, and no sooner was he asleep than he fell to dreaming and in his dreaming mind began replaying the events earlier in the day when he had followed Hugh over London Bridge. But the dread Kit had felt in the real world was now doubled in this nightmare one.

He was once again walking with Hugh under the Stone Gateway of London Bridge. A raven took to a loping flight and called out, 'Kit! Kit! Kit!' As Kit walked nearer to the bridge he heard voices from above. To his horror, the spiked heads above the gate were also calling him. 'Kit! Kit!' they cried. Kit put his hands over his ears and ran after Hugh, who was walking on, oblivious.

The waterwheel at the bridge was turning and beating out its rhythm on the river. 'Kit! Kit! Kit!' it seemed to chunter. 'Kit! Kit! Kit!' over and over again. The chatter of the passers-by seemed to have only one word: 'Kit!' and that same word was yelled by hawkers and shop boys.

Kit followed Hugh into the gloom of the bridge, but it was so dark inside that he could barely see at all and he suddenly found himself pinned up against a door. He fumbled for the latch and entered a hallway he knew did not belong on the bridge; it was the hallway of his childhood home in Westminster.

Kit walked across the tiled hallway towards the staircase. This was a dream he had dreamed many times over the years and he knew its course by heart. Here was the blackened oak newel post at the base of the banister with its carving of Adam and Eve and the Tree of Knowledge, the serpent in its boughs; polished by the hands of all those who had climbed the stairs as, in his dream, Kit now did himself.

As the staircase turned back on itself, there was a painting of St Sebastian which his father had bought in Italy. Kit was, as always, fascinated and repulsed by it: the pale flesh of St Sebastian bound to the pillar, the arrows protruding from his side, his chest, his thigh; the Roman soldiers preparing to fire again as he looked up to heaven.

Kit walked on, climbing the stairs to his parents' bedroom; aware as he did so that he was no longer fourteen, but now inhabited the body of his eight-year-old self.

He was running now, but quietly, caught up in the excitement of a game and looking for a place to hide. He looked behind to see if anyone had followed him up the stairs, then ducked into his parents' bedroom and climbed into a huge empty linen chest by the window seat.

The only light inside the chest came from a keyhole; if Kit leaned forward this became a tiny window. But as soon as he put his eye to the keyhole, something passed in front and made him recoil.

A vague blackness swept back and forth, intermittently blocking Kit's view. Then, on the other side of the room, he saw a figure cloaked in black, crouching down, its back to the linen chest and Kit.

CHRIS PRIESTLEY

Kit could hear the hollow drumbeat of his heart quickening as the scene played itself out to its inevitable conclusion. To his mounting horror, the figure seemed to hear something outside and turned as it always did – turned to show a hideous, jet-black, horned and hollow-eyed devil mask . . .

Chapter 5

Kit awoke abruptly and started at his surroundings, confused at first, the devil-faced man still clear in his mind's eye. Annie the maid was bustling about and came in to light the fire, eyeing Kit suspiciously every now and then.

'Morning,' said Kit blearily. She snorted and left the room. He curled his lip and muttered to himself, getting up slowly, stretching and yawning.

Annie came back in with a shawl wrapped round her head. 'I've got to go out and get bread and such like,' she said. 'The master is out and says you can be left, though I think it's madness, but there you are Keep your hands off what ain't yours or I'll have you put in the stocks myself,' she finished, raising her head and looking down her long nose at Kit. Then she tutted loudly, turned and left. Kit could hear her muttering even when she was in the street outside and caught the words, 'We could all be murdered in our beds.'

Kit smiled at the maid's tetchiness. She could not

have been that much older than him. She did have a point too: White did seem to be too trusting. He and Hugh used to go searching for easy pickings from men like White and then laugh about their foolishness. 'Soft heart, soft head,' they used to say.

The cook, who Kit learned was called Mrs Fisher, and who looked at him with the same undisguised suspicion as Annie, set to work stirring a huge pot of porridge. Kit's stomach clenched with expectation, but the breakfast was not served until Annie's return.

Kit attacked his bowl of porridge with such animal enthusiasm that both Mrs Fisher and Annie sat open-mouthed, staring at him. When bread was put on the table, he snatched as many pieces as he could and held them close just as he would have done on the streets to prevent anyone grabbing them.

Annie was tutting disapprovingly as White walked into the kitchen. He raised an eyebrow when he saw Kit alternately gnawing on the bread and noisily shovelling porridge into his mouth.

'Come along, Kit,' said White. 'We do not have all day.'

'Sir?' said Kit, tucking greedily into another spoonful of porridge. 'Why, sir?'

White stared at him. 'Because we are off to church, lad,' he said. 'It's Sunday.'

'Sunday? Church?' spluttered Kit.

'Yes, church,' said White. 'You do go to church, I hope?'

'Me? Church? But I . . . I mean, I . . . Well . . .' began Kit.

'Excellent,' said White. 'Are those the best clothes you have?'

'They're the only clothes I have.'

White exchanged glances with Mrs Fisher. 'He will need a bath.'

'Aye, sir,' said Mrs Fisher. 'The water's already on.'

As White nodded and left, Annie went outside and dragged in a huge tub half full of water, which she set down on the kitchen tiles before going out to the well to fetch another bucketful.

'A bath?' said Kit. 'I don't need no bath. I don't want a bath.'

Mrs Fisher ignored him, and as Annie poured another bucketful of water into the tub, the cook called to the girl to help her with a massive pan of boiling water and they heaved it together across to the tub and poured that in too.

'I don't need no bath!' shouted Kit.

'If the master says you're having a bath, then a bath is what you're having.' Before Kit had time to say another word, Mrs Fisher had him in a vice-like grip. 'Let's have them clothes off.'

'I don't think so!'

'Take 'em off,' said Mrs Fisher. 'Or I'll get Annie here to cut them off.'

Kit turned to see Annie standing with a large grin

and an even bigger knife. 'Not with her here!' he said, sensing defeat.

Mrs Fisher signalled to Annie to leave and Annie whined and stomped off.

Kit began to get undressed. The last time he had been naked was when Hugh and he had gone bathing in the Thames some months before, and there had certainly been no females watching then.

Mrs Fisher clucked as if she were encouraging a mule. 'Come on, come on,' she said. 'You ain't got nothing I ain't seen before. Get a move on or I shall have to call Annie back.'

Kit stripped and stood shivering, hands clasped over his genitals. He felt horribly vulnerable and a little tearful all of a sudden. Mrs Fisher led him towards the tub and made him get in. He was about to complain about the heat of the water when the cook, who had arms like a bull's thighs, pushed him down into it with so much enthusiasm that he was almost completely submerged.

She began to scrub at Kit's back with a brush. At the third pass of its stubbles, Kit felt as though the very skin was being taken from his flesh and he howled in protest, wriggling around, trying to escape her grip. But she merely let go of his shoulder and moved her huge hand to his head, grabbing a fistful of hair instead.

Cries of pain seemed to be interpreted as words of encouragement as Mrs Fisher chuckled to herself and renewed her efforts with increased vigour, humming a little tune to herself. Kit felt as if he were being flayed alive. When she had finished, she handed him a length of muslin to dry himself with, then whisked it away to leave Kit standing there shivering and cursing to himself.

'Such language,' tutted the cook. 'Really.'

Just as Kit was recovering from the scrubbing, his whole body glowing as if it had been cooked, Mrs Fisher advanced towards him with a pair of shears.

'What are you going to do now?' he said, backing off.

'Haircut.'

Kit had lost any will to resist and stood as quietly as a lamb while Mrs Fisher cut his hair, humming all the while, her mighty bosom shaking as she danced around him. He hardly even winced when she nicked his ear.

'There now,' she said triumphantly. 'All done! And not such a bad job neither.' She swept up the hair and, picking it up at arm's length, threw it on the fire. 'That's the lice done for anyway.'

Kit put his hand to his head and felt only stubble. He looked around. 'Where's my clothes?'

'Annie popped in and took them.'

'Well she can give them back,' said Kit, wondering with a blush exactly when Annie had come back in.

'Can't. They're burned by now.'

'Burned?' exclaimed Kit. 'You can't just burn another person's clothes!'

'It's done, lad,' she replied, putting another clump of Kit's hair on the fire. 'It's not worth getting in a fuss about. They were crawling with ticks and goodness knows what.'

Again Kit found himself struggling against tears as he stood there naked, wisps of hair tickling his back and chest. The door opened and Kit thought that his misery was going to be amplified by a giggling Annie, but instead there stood White holding a bundle of clothes.

'These were the best I could do at such short notice,' he said gently, seeing the beaten look on Kit's face. 'The hair will grow back.'

Kit took the clothes without a word and hurriedly got dressed so that at least his ordeal of nakedness could end. The new clothes itched with an unfamiliar cleanliness and he did not recognize his own body when he looked down. Mrs Fisher brought him a looking glass and Kit peered into it, puzzled by the boy looking back, so different from the filthy, mop-haired urchin he had caught glimpses of reflected in darkened windows and ditch water.

'You ain't so bad-looking scrubbed up,' said Annie.

'Maybe you ought to try it,' said Kit, dodging the inevitable slap.

Chapter 6

Kit had not been to church for as long as he could
remember – not once through all his four long
years on the street – but this did not seem to be the thing
to say to a law-abiding, God-fearing master like White,
so he had no real choice but to do as he was bid.

Kit and White walked up the hill to the church, Annie
and Mrs Fisher behind them. The bells were ringing out
to the congregations, who now formed a steady stream
through the gates of this and every other churchyard
in England, for if faith did not move you, the fine of
£20 a month for non-attendance surely would. Anyone
who wanted to live a respectable life in London had to
go to church. If you did not go, then questions would
be asked as to why. Maybe you had something to hide.
Maybe you were a non-believer. Maybe you were even
a Catholic. Only street-dwellers like Kit were able to
absent themselves – the churchgoers did not want his
kind around decent people anyway.

As they took their seats, Kit looked around. The

whitewash on the church walls was beginning to fade after twenty-odd years and the ghosts of ancient wall paintings were beginning to show through where people had brushed past them as they walked towards the altar. Kit could just make out a faint image of St Michael's foot standing on the devil's throat.

And the devil was the theme of the sermon. The devil and his agents: the Jesuits and Catholics, who – the minister reminded them – were waging an evil crusade against the good people of England.

'Has any person here forgotten that some fifteen years ago the then so-called Pope, whom the Catholics called Pius the Fifth, did order the excommunication of our own dear Queen?'

There were shouts of 'No!' and 'Shame!'

'Well, I say God bless the old sinner!' cried the minister to much gasping and murmuring. 'For he has shown the true way of things between us. He told the Catholics in this country that Queen Elizabeth is but a *pretended* Queen.' There was angry muttering among the congregation, and a man behind Kit growled like a dog. 'He told them that no true Catholic should support her; that to murder her would be no sin. He even gave encouragement to Mary, the one-time Queen of Scots, who would be Queen of England! Her own people do not even want her and now she sits imprisoned, but alive still, in a castle in Staffordshire; waiting like a viper at the bosom of this blessed land.' At this the muttering became cries and shouts and the minister raised his hands to silence them.

'And the present Pope is no better,' he went on. 'He reissued that vile order five years ago, and ever since then this realm has been rotten with all manner of Jesuit and Catholic vermin bent on murdering our Queen and tearing our people away from the true faith!'

There were shouts of 'Aye!' and the growling man behind joined in enthusiastically. Kit could feel his breath on the back of his neck. Again, the minister held up his hands.

'We need to be on our guard, each and every one of us,' he said. 'We have a duty unto God to protect our Queen from Catholic plotters and assassins. We will keep Her Majesty in our prayers and keep watch in our taverns and warehouses and marketplaces for those who would do her harm. God bless Her Majesty!'

'Are you all right?' asked White, looking at Kit's pale and troubled face.

'Me?' said Kit nervously. 'Why wouldn't I be?'

'I am sure I do not know,' said White quietly.

'Well then, I'm fine,' said Kit. 'Sir.'

But in truth, Kit was far from fine. This was the first time he had set foot in a church since he had lived with his aunt many years ago. But it was not this lapse in church attendance that troubled Kit. Breaking the law was hardly an issue for a thief, and he had felt little need to attend church over the years. If there was a God, he had decided, he seemed to have little concern for Kit, one way or another.

No, it was something else entirely that caused Kit's discomfort. Kit was a Catholic; or at least his parents had been Catholics and he had been brought up a Catholic until their deaths had seen him sent to live with his aunt. This alone was enough to make him nervous, with Londoners seeing Jesuits behind every woodpile and the Catholic Spaniards, rich with Inca gold, just across the North Sea in the Low Countries. The Spanish were not going to put up with Protestant England for ever. War was coming. Kit knew it. Everyone knew it. The merest taint of Catholicism was enough to arouse suspicion.

But Kit was not uncomfortable merely because of his childhood Catholicism. It was the manner of his father's death that was his darkest and most uncomfortable secret.

For Kit was the son of a traitor. His father, Sir Richard Fulbourn, had been executed at the Tower of London for his involvement in a plot to kill Elizabeth. His father's head had sat atop a spike on London Bridge, decorating the Great Stone Gateway. His mother, never strong, had not recovered from the shock and humiliation as their lands and property were seized by the Crown and gifted to more loyal subjects. She died two months later, leaving Kit orphaned at the age of nine.

Though Kit knew that he could hardly be held responsible for the actions of his father, he knew also that such logic did not always apply in these times.

But it was not fear alone that made Kit secretive; he felt a burning shame that his father could have done such a thing. Kit might have been a thief and a wastrel, but he cheered the exploits of Drake and Hawkins and feared and hated the Spanish like any other English boy.

The Queen was England in human form for Kit, as she was for many English folk. Whatever he might think of her, an attack on the Queen was an attack on England. His father was a traitor through and through – letters found in his possession revealed his part in a plot to kill the Queen and he had confessed his guilt. Kit could not even think about it without being overwhelmed by the shame of it. He did not blame the *Queen* for executing his father; he blamed his *father* for his treachery, for the death of his mother and for taking away the life he could and should have had.

Taking his mother's name of Milton, he had been sent to live with the maiden aunt – his mother's sister – who had taken Kit in out of duty, not love. His mother's family had enthusiastically embraced the Protestant religion when England had made its break with the Pope, and Kit's aunt had been appalled when her younger sister had married a Catholic and saw everything that had happened thereafter as a judgement from God. Kit, as the son of a traitor, she saw as a taint on her own family and she took out her rage on the boy, beating him regularly for his supposed sins. Kit had hated her and he had run away to live as a thief on the streets of London – a life he had lived ever since.

Kit and White came out of the church and Annie and Mrs Fisher bustled ahead of them, Kit's ears still ringing from the sermon.

'They say them Catholics are poisoning wells,' said Annie.

'Hsssh, you silly goose,' said Mrs Fisher. 'That's *Jews*.'

'No,' protested Annie. 'They say Catholics is doing it now.'

Kit felt as if he were walking in the midst of a pack of wolves; at any moment they might sniff out his true identity and tear him limb from limb. As they were leaving the churchyard, a cracked voice yelled Kit's name and he flinched. He stopped and turned to see a mop-haired boy of about fifteen, waving and running towards him.

'What's all this? What's all this?' said the boy, dancing about in front of him and tugging at Kit's clothes. 'I nearly didn't recognize you, Kit.'

'Are you not going to introduce us, Kit?' said White, looking down his long nose at the new arrival as if he were looking at a new species of fish.

Kit took a deep breath while the boy grinned, clearly enjoying the spectacle as much as if he were at a puppet show. 'This is Blind Peter,' he said. 'Blind Peter, this is Master White.'

'I'm very pleased to be making your acquaintance,' said Blind Peter. Then, moving closer and edging between Kit and White, he whispered, 'So what's the game?'

'There is no game, as you put it, I am afraid,' said White.

'That's good,' said Blind Peter. ''E's good, ain't he? Sounds like a right proper gent.'

'Look, there's nothing going on here,' said Kit. 'I ain't working. I'm just coming out of church, that's all. I work for Master White now.'

'Just coming out of . . .' said Blind Peter. 'Church? Work? You?' Then he took a step back and frowned. 'Oh, I get it. You just don't want me squeezing in on your act. That's it. Understood. Don't have to get all frosty. I thought there must be something on when I see you with this here gentry cove.'

'Yes,' said White. 'You've guessed it. Now we must be getting along. Come on, Kit.'

Kit stared at White, shrugged at Blind Peter and followed White down the hill.

'Sorry, sir,' said Kit after a while.

'Sorry?' said White. 'What for?'

'For Blind Peter. He was what you might call an associate of mine in my previous life.'

White nodded and smiled. 'He did not seem in the least bit blind, your friend,' he remarked.

'That's because he wasn't working,' Kit explained. 'You see him working and you'd swear on your mother's life he couldn't see a thing.'

'I see,' said White.

Kit laughed, thinking White was making a joke, but his master simply looked confused.

'And he's not a friend of mine,' Kit added.

'I'm pleased to hear it,' said White.

'I ain't got no friends.'

'I'm pleased to hear it,' said White. 'That is . . . Oh, never mind.'

Chapter 7

Kit lay awake that night and tried to think what he would do next. Staying at White's house had only ever been a temporary measure in Kit's mind; shelter and food until something better came along. He liked White well enough, but sooner or later he would have to return to his old trade. Bumping into Blind Peter had been a stroke of luck. Maybe he needed a partner.

With this in mind, the following morning, after breakfast, he thanked White for the food, got up from the table and explained that he had some matters to attend to. Before Kit had reached the door, however, White explained – in a surprisingly forceful way – that he would be requiring Kit to stay and do some work.

The whole notion of work was a novelty to Kit – as was the idea that he would do as he was told. For the last four years he had paid no heed to anyone apart from Hugh, and had certainly never been expected to be reliable in any way. His first instinct was to give White a piece of his mind, but he managed to stop himself just in time. With no clear plan of action, the reality was that he had no certain place to go to and, with the nights getting colder, he realized that he did not welcome the idea of sleeping in a barn or on a rubbish heap if it did not work out with Blind Peter. For the moment, he thought it wise to smile and meekly return to his seat at the table.

'Mrs Fisher will give you some work to do,' said White. 'I have some business to attend to at Durham House.'

'Durham House?' said Kit nervously. 'I thought you just said that to impress those soldier boys. Are you Raleigh's man then?'

'He appreciates my talents, I hope,' White replied. 'You do not sound as though you approve of Master Raleigh. What can he have done to deserve your displeasure?'

'Me?' said Kit. 'I don't know. No one likes him, do they? He's rich and he flaunts it, and no one likes that, do they? They say he keeps a coven of wizards and—' Kit suddenly remembered the bellman's warning about White and did not finish his sentence.

White shook his head. 'I know that there is a lot of nonsense spoken about the man. I am just surprised that a clever lad like you listens to it,' he said. 'But there we are. I must be away. Do as Mrs Fisher bids you. I advise you not to annoy her.'

After the experience of being scrubbed clean by the powerful Mrs Fisher, Kit had no intention whatsoever of annoying her and followed meekly as she led him to the brick-paved courtyard behind the house.

Mrs Fisher gave him a brush and told him that she wanted him to sweep the yard until it was spotless. Kit heaved a sigh, but did not argue. Whilst on the streets, he had seen thieving as his profession and had been proud that he had 'earned' his living, rather than simply scrounging or begging. Now, in return for the roof over his head and the food in his belly, he saw it as fair that he should do something in return.

Kit had not been sweeping long before he saw something twinkling beside the low roofed wall that surrounded the well. He looked round to see if he was being watched, then leaned forward. There was a gold earring lying in the dust. He picked it up and put it in his pocket.

When he had finished, he rapped on the kitchen door and Mrs Fisher came out, her big hands in fists, her knuckles pressed into her wide hips. She looked around, smiling and nodding, clearly surprised at the effort Kit had put in. Kit reached into his pocket and took out the earring.

'I found this,' he said, holding it out on the palm of his hand.

'Oh,' she said, taking it off him and holding it up to the light. 'Master White's daughter, Mistress Eleanora, said she'd lost an earring. She will be pleased.'

Kit smiled and cocked his head, raising an eyebrow. 'You put that there on purpose, didn't you?' he said.

The cook grinned. 'You're not as daft as you look, are you?'

'What would you have done if I hadn't given it back?'

'I'd have taken it from you and kicked your sorry backside all the way down Cheapside.'

Kit laughed. 'I believe you would.'

'Good. Then we'll get along fine.'

Mrs Fisher said that he deserved a piece of bread and Kit sat eating at the kitchen table while she busied herself with the washing. As she carried a bundle of wet clothes outside, she called out to him that he wasn't to think he was finished and that as soon as she'd done with the washing, she'd give him a mop and bucket and he could wash the yard he had just swept.

While Mrs Fisher was singing to herself out in the yard, and with Annie gone to the market, Kit decided to take a chance and have a quick look around and see if he could find out who or what this John White was. He was clearly not a rich man: the house was not large, though it was comfortable and was in a respectable area. What exactly did his master do?

Listening out every now and then to make sure he could still hear the cook in the yard, he went on a rapid tour of the house. Everything seemed reasonably normal until he reached the workshop at the back, which had a small brick oven in it that stank dreadfully of something Kit could not place, but was certainly not food of any kind. He remembered the watchman and his whispered voice hissing 'Wizard!' and shivered slightly.

Eventually there was only one door that Kit had not opened. It was at the top of the house. His thief's sixth sense could tell even before his thumb hit the latch that it was locked.

He looked about for a key, but he had a feeling that White would have it with him. He dropped down to look through the keyhole, but the shutters must still have been closed because it was as dark as night inside and he could see nothing. The sound of singing stopped suddenly and Kit bounded down the stairs. By the time the cook returned to the kitchen, he was back in his seat at the table, bread in hand. Even so, Mrs Fisher eyed him suspiciously.

'Come on,' she said. 'Stop trying to make that bread last all day. There's work to be done.'

'Yes, Mrs Fisher,' said Kit, standing up. 'Whatever you say.'

Chapter 8

White apologized to Kit for Mrs Fisher's little honesty test the following morning, but Kit could see that he was clearly delighted that he had passed it.

He was on his knees scrubbing the tiles in the hall when a messenger arrived at the door and White went to speak to him. Kit was blinking away the sweat that trickled down his face, and thinking to himself that scrubbing floors did not seem much like an assistant's work. He was beginning to wish he had not lied about being able to read. Maybe White would have given him something more interesting to do if he had told him he could read and write. But the lie had been instinctive – a legacy of his years on the street.

White came back a few moments later and held a key up in front of his face. It was as if he had been reading Kit's mind. Kit knew straight away what lock the key opened.

'There is a room at the top of the house,' said White with a smile. 'When you have finished your work, go and wait for me there. I will not be long. And don't touch anything.' Kit took the key and White left with the messenger.

Annie shook her head and muttered to herself, and Kit asked her if she had something to say.

'Don't think I don't know a filthy little thief when I see one,' she said. 'I've seen your type; cutpurses and coney-catchers. I've seen it all before.'

'I bet you have,' said Kit.

Annie flushed. 'Why, you cheeky little—'

'Master White knows what I am and he don't seem to mind,' said Kit. 'So leave me be.'

'Listen to me, thief,' she said, prodding Kit in the chest. 'Master White took me in when I was only a girl and he's been a good master to me. There's many a father who wouldn't have been so kind as he has been to me. I won't see him ill-used. Not by you, nor anybody else neither!'

And with that she turned on her heels and left the room, her nose in the air. Kit couldn't help smiling.

When he had finished the floor and Mrs Fisher had given it her seal of approval, he held up the key he had been given and climbed the stairs.

He felt strangely more nervous now that he had been given permission and had the key than when he had been sneaking about the house on his own. The lock worked smoothly and the door opened without a creak.

He had been expecting a dark and gloomy room but the shutters were open and it was light and airy. It was in the corner of the house and lit by windows on two sides, one of which was open. Kit could hear a woman singing in the courtyard below; he walked over and looked out to see Mrs Fisher hanging out more washing.

Kit turned back to the centre of the room where there was a huge table on which lay a large piece of marble. There were bottles filled with powders, grains and crystals of different colours. There were jars of oil, a pestle and mortar, a set of scales. There were strange instruments and devices Kit had never seen before. It was very clear to Kit what all this meant and he backed away nervously towards the doorway, only to find that White was standing in it.

'You *are* a wizard!' said Kit, looking about him in panic and seeing that White stood in front of the only exit. 'I knew it!'

'I assure you I am not,' said White.

'I'm no fool!' Kit exclaimed. 'Don't think I am, because I'm not!' He was not easily frightened, but wizards and witches made his flesh creep and the room seemed to be closing in on him.

'I am sure you are not,' said White gently.

'What's all this stuff in these bottles?' asked Kit. 'If that isn't wizardry or alchemy or some such, then what is it?'

'They are pigments.'

'Pig's what?' said Kit, looking again at the rows of glass-stoppered jars and bottles.

'Pigments,' repeated White with a shake of his head.

'Colours for painting with – and various other materials that I need in my work.'

'And what is your work? Why are you so secretive about it.'

'I am a proud member of the Guild of Painter Stainers,' said White. 'I intended, when I was young, to earn my living painting portraits. But, alas, I am no Hilliard.' Kit frowned in puzzlement. 'Nicholas Hilliard,' White explained. 'The famous portrait painter. You have not heard of him?'

'No, I haven't,' said Kit suspiciously.

'Well in any case,' said White, 'the life of a court painter was not for me. I want to travel in uncharted areas. I want to paint things that no man has ever painted before. I want to record the world, not pander to the vanities of courtiers.'

'So what are these if they ain't demon's marks?' asked Kit, waving the sheet of symbols in the air.

'They are calculations,' said White. 'They are measurements. It is mathematics, that is all.'

Kit stared and backed away. 'I knew it! You are a wizard.'

White laughed.

'They say mathematics is the devil's work!' Kit said.

White laughed again. 'It sometimes feels that way,' he replied, nodding and chuckling to himself. 'But an intelligent lad like you should not be swayed by foolish talk like that.'

Kit pointed to the map. 'What's that then?' He was starting to feel a little foolish.

'As well as being a painter,' explained White, 'I am a maker of maps.'

'Maps? What kind of maps?'

White paused before replying, seeming to weigh the words in his mouth before saying them. His fingers knitted together as if in prayer. 'Maps of lands that interest the Queen and servants of the Queen,' he said at last.

'You mean like Ireland?' said Kit.

'Ireland, yes.' White nodded. 'And other places.'

Kit took a deep breath. He looked long and hard at his master, looking for any sign that he was lying to him.

White put his hand against his chest, over his heart. 'I assure you that I am no conjuror,' he said. 'I wish I was. I would get my work done more quickly.'

Kit nodded and a half-smile played across his face. 'You're not a wizard?' he asked. 'Truly?'

'I am not,' said White. 'But all the same, I must ask you to keep anything you might hear or see in this house to yourself. The work I do involves information that may one day be of great value to England and those who love England. It may therefore also be of value to those who hate England. Do you understand?'

'That's no problem,' said Kit. 'I don't know anybody.'

White smiled; but only with his mouth. 'You must not speak of it to anyone, Kit,' he said softly. 'Whether it be Blind Paul or any other of your acquaintances from your previous life.'

'Blind Peter, sir,' corrected Kit. 'And no one I know cares one way or the other about some colony in Ireland. The Queen could plant a colony on the moon for all Blind Peter would care about it. When you're on the street, you're more interested in trying to fill your belly, sir, if you see what I mean.'

'Even so,' persisted White, 'I must ask you to keep it to yourself. Can I trust you on this?'

Kit was flustered for a moment and could feel himself blush a little. The notion that anyone would trust him seemed almost ridiculous. He was simultaneously embarrassed at how untrustworthy a wretch he was, and surprised to feel a sudden tearfulness at the thought that White was prepared to trust him at all.

'Yes,' he said finally. 'Yes, sir, you can.'

Chapter 9

The promise to keep quiet about what he saw in his master's study was easily kept for Kit saw nothing worth mentioning, even if he had ever bumped into any of his old acquaintances. The maps and charts that White worked on were always rolled up and locked away in a chest at the end of the day and the glimpses Kit caught of them were meaningless to him in any case – Kit knew nothing about maps and would not have recognized a map of London had he ever had cause to see one.

White had once left a map open on his desk while he was called away, but Kit could make nothing of it. It clearly showed a coastline because White had scribbled in waves, but there were no towns or villages marked. The only thing that grabbed Kit's attention was the head and tail of a sea monster that White had drawn rearing out of the waves. It could have been a map of the moon for all Kit knew.

White had a steady stream of visitors to his house and study. A gaunt, po-faced man who suddenly appeared like a ghost one day turned out to be a young man called Thomas Harriot, whom White described as the 'cleverest man in all England.' Kit could see that Harriot would have blushed if there had been sufficient blood in his deathly face.

Harriot said that if he were indeed the cleverest man in England it was only because Dr Dee was not in the country at the present time. The mention of Dr Dee sent a chill through Kit's bones. Everyone had heard of Dr Dee. He was the Queen's pet wizard and Kit knew some of those who had formed the mob that ransacked his house when he had left the country.

Harriot – like Dee – was a Durham House regular; one of Raleigh's strange band. He made no effort to even acknowledge Kit, let alone speak to him, and whenever he visited – which was often – Kit would be sent out of the study on some errand or other and he would hear the map chest being unlocked and the study door being bolted behind him.

The same was true of the other visitors from Durham House. Harriot might have been as cold as a codfish and almost certainly some kind of magician – but in Kit's eyes he at least had the redeeming feature of being English. The same could not be true of either Simon Fernandez or Joachim Ganz.

Fernandez was a Portuguese pilot – an experienced navigator. He was arrogant and loud, but White seemed to find his rudeness amusing rather than irritating and told Kit that it was just Fernandez's way. White said that he knew the Atlantic Ocean as well as Kit knew London.

But Kit was not at all convinced. Being Portuguese was a little too close to being Spanish as far as he was concerned. Surely if the maps and plans were so important, it was a mistake to involve a foreigner, no matter how good a sailor White said he was.

The same went for Joachim Ganz in Kit's opinion. Ganz was a mineral man; an expert in ores and metals, according to White. Kit was not sure where Ganz came from, except that it was not England. He was short and pale and Kit imagined that he had recently come blinking into the daylight from an underground lair like some troll from a fairy tale.

He was as taciturn as Fernandez was talkative, dour and unresponsive. Kit had barely heard him speak, and never seen him smile. Even White struggled to be complimentary about this humourless man, save to say that he was highly thought of.

Happily, though, these men were not the only visitors to John White's house. His daughter, Eleanora, and her husband, Ananais Dare, were frequent visitors. Though Ananais clearly viewed Kit with great suspicion, Eleanora seemed to take an instant shine to him and always made a point of coming to see him when she visited.

Kit liked Eleanora. She looked so different from her father that Kit supposed that she must be a kind of mirror of her poor mother, so little of John White seemed to be visible in her. She welcomed Kit into her father's household without question and, like him, accepted his past without prejudice.

Whilst Ananais talked to his father-in-law, Eleanora would come into the study and chat to Kit, teasing him gently about his work or his clothes. She made Kit feel part of the household; as if he belonged there. Even Mrs Fisher and Annie seemed to have accepted him, although Kit noticed that wherever he went, Annie still watched him like a hawk.

John White's house was beginning to feel like home and Kit was content to leave things as they were. He felt in no hurry to return to his old life of thievery. Blind Peter would get along fine without him.

Chapter 10

Some weeks after arriving at White's house, Kit left the city by Bishopsgate, heading for Shoreditch. The rough streets beyond the city walls were lined with hawkers working the crowds. There was a change in the atmosphere, a subtle shift in temperature. It was that little bit more dangerous here than in the city and Kit grew more alert; like a fox near a farmstead.

Men were yelling and handing out printed handbills and pamphlets, some telling of shows and fairs, others of the exploits of Hawkins and Drake. There were prints depicting the horrors of the Inquisition or showing in hideous detail the many atrocities of the Spanish in the Low Countries.

Stout pie-men sold their wares from rickety carts, and red-cheeked country girls stood with baskets of apples, singing out to their customers, winking at the young blades on their way to the tavern or the theatre; holding out their apples like so many Eves.

Kit noticed a ragged boy was following him about

three paces behind. He stopped to look in the window of a cobbler's shop, then smiled as he felt a very slight movement at his belt. Quick as a flash, he grabbed the boy's arm.

'Get off!' squealed the boy.

'Not bad,' said Kit. 'Not bad at all.'

'Please, sir,' said the boy. 'I ain't never done nothing like this before. I won't never do it again.'

Kit laughed. 'You haven't got to be that good without a bit of practice,' he said, 'you lying little tick.' He let the boy go. 'Just thank your stars it was me who caught you.'

The boy stood there, looking at Kit with a baffled expression. 'Ain't you gonna beat me then or hand me in to the constables?'

'Not unless you want me to,' said Kit. 'Now be off with you before I change my mind!'

As the boy vanished into the crowds, Kit headed for the Curtain Theatre, feeling a growing wariness. He very seldom felt nervous on the streets, except at times like this when he was heading into unknown territory. He had seen travelling actors perform at the fairs but he had never actually been inside a theatre before.

His nerves disappeared as soon as he realized that the theatre was not so very different from a bear-baiting pit, other than that the crowds who elbowed him and shoved him and stood on his toes in their urge to get to the front were a little rowdier.

The other difference was that Kit was now standing

in the pit where the bear would have been, along with hundreds of other people, all still jostling and jabbering and shoving themselves into a better position in front of the stage.

The ladies and gentlemen in the seated galleries surrounding the pit were no less rowdy, for all their finery, and they too had to squeeze themselves into their seats.

The play finally began, accompanied by loud cheers and the stamping of feet. A 'lady' appeared on stage, with red cheeks and startled eyebrows drawn onto her forehead. She flounced across the stage, fluttering her eyelashes to much whistling and cat-calling. Kit chortled with laughter when he realized after a few minutes that 'she' was Hugh.

Howling with laughter, he stuck his fingers in his mouth and gave Hugh a long lewd whistle. As the audience laughed, Hugh turned to face his heckler and saw Kit's face beaming up at him. His face cracked into a wide smile until he realized he was supposed to say the next line, and he returned to his role looking flustered.

Kit enjoyed the play immensely and followed the action with a broad grin. He felt a pang of sadness when he saw how good Hugh was, because he realized that their life as it had been was truly over. But the sadness soon passed.

There was a fight scene where the hero of the play took on three of his enemies and despatched them all one by one with expert flourishes of his sword and dagger, while the crowd oohed and aahed. When the play was over, the audience yelled and whistled but none more so than Kit, who shouted till he was hoarse. The actors took several bows and Hugh signalled to Kit to wait.

Kit could see now that Hugh's life as a thief had been good preparation for a life on the stage. He and Kit had been acting under far more exacting circumstances on the streets: if they had failed to convince they could have paid with their lives. Kit stood near the stage and let the crowd disperse without him. They left as raucously as they had entered. It was as if the theatre had sucked in a swarm of bees and was now spitting them out into the street. In no time at all, the theatre was all but empty; a trinket box without trinkets.

After a little while the actors, in various states of undress, reappeared and began to gather up the few coins that had been thrown and the props and costumes that were left on the stage. Hugh was still in make-up, but without his wig or dress.

'What do you look like?' said Kit.

Hugh laughed. 'It was terrible, wasn't it?' he said. 'Sorry.'

'No,' said Kit with a smile. 'It was good. *You* were good.'

'Truly?' Hugh could not hide his surprise at receiving a compliment from Kit and Kit felt a little hurt.

'Truly. I haven't laughed so much since you tried to steal that old lady's purse in Fleet Street and she caught you and walloped the merry hell out of you with her stick.' He spluttered with laughter and slapped his thigh.

'She had a grip like iron,' said Hugh. 'The old witch.' They both chuckled at the memory, then paused, caught each other's eye and laughed again. 'I'm glad you came, Kit,' Hugh went on, slapping him on both arms and grinning.

'Me too,' said Kit.

'So how goes it? What is it like being a servant?'

'Oh, you know,' said Kit. 'As it happens it's not so bad. Could be worse.'

'So I see,' said Hugh, stepping back and looking him up and down. 'If you've got the spare change to buy new clothes. And is it the bad light or have you had a wash?' Kit blushed. 'And a haircut?' Kit screwed up his face – partly in embarrassment, and partly at the memory. 'So, what is it that you do exactly?'

'This and that,' said Kit with a shrug.

'This and that?' said Hugh suspiciously. 'What exactly?'

'Can't say. The gent I'm working for – I am his *assistant* – has asked me not to talk about it.'

Hugh laughed at first, but then saw that Kit was serious and gave him a searching look. 'You don't trust me?' he asked, sounding a little hurt.

Kit rolled his eyes. 'It's not that,' he said. 'It's that he *trusts* me. No one's ever done that before.' Hugh did not seem impressed by this and refused to look at Kit. 'It

72

ain't my secret to tell,' said Kit finally. 'But I will tell you one that is.'

Hugh turned to face him. 'What's that then?' he asked sulkily.

'I'm not who you think I am,' said Kit.

'Who are you then? Mary, Queen of Scots?'

Kit took a deep breath and, after checking that there was no one in earshot, told Hugh the story of his short life, of the arrest and execution of his father, of the death of his mother, of the cruel aunt and his escape onto the streets, where he had been befriended by an older boy who had taught him to survive by his wits.

'You saved my life as sure as if you pulled me from the river,' said Kit. 'But you might regret that now you know who I am and what I am.'

''Course I don't regret it, you fool,' said Hugh.

'But I'm a Catholic. Leastways my parents were,' protested Kit. 'And you hate Catholics.'

'Do I?'

'You know you do,' said Kit. 'Everybody does.'

Hugh grabbed Kit by both shoulders. 'Well I don't hate you,' he said. 'You're like a brother to me, Kit. I can't blame you for what your father did. And as for hating Catholics, there are two of them in our troop and I don't hate them. Not all of them want the Spanish to rule over us, Kit.'

Kit could not answer for fear that he would break down sobbing. He had carried his secret for years and the relief of telling it was like the unloading of a crippling burden.

'Thanks for telling me, Kit,' Hugh continued. 'It must have taken a lot, and you know I'll never tell anyone, don't you?'

Kit nodded. 'I know.'

For a little while, neither could think of anything to say.

'Were you there?' asked Hugh. 'When they arrested your father? Do you remember it?'

'Not much,' said Kit. 'I think I've spent so long not wanting to think about it that mostly I can't remember. They were having a masked ball at our house. It was Twelfth Night. I was playing hide and seek with some cousins and I hid in a linen chest and—'

'What?' said Hugh.

Kit shook his head. 'It doesn't matter,' he said.

'So you were rich then?' said Hugh eventually, clearly having some difficulty imagining Kit as the son of a courtier.

'Aye,' said Kit with a sad smile. 'I suppose we were. Our house and money were confiscated when my father was executed. The Queen gave everything away as gifts to her favourites.'

'Did you ever go to court? When you were a boy, I mean?'

'Aye,' said Kit nodding. 'But I can't really remember it. We went to Hampton Court, I think. But I was only young. I played in the gardens mostly.'

Hugh shook his head in amazement at the thought.

'My father was even at Oxford with Raleigh, for all the good it did him,' said Kit.

'I can't quite believe it. Raleigh? Really?'

'Really,' said Kit. 'Raleigh.' They both laughed.

The parting was awkward, with neither friend wishing to be the one who turned away, but eventually they embraced and Kit headed back towards the city gates. Two men ahead of him were looking at something on the ground. As Kit approached, one of them tapped the other on the arm and they hurried away, looking about furtively as they did so.

When Kit got to the spot where they had been standing he saw what it was they had been looking at. There in the dust – like a heap of rags – was the body of the boy who had attempted to rob him earlier. The boy's clothes were wet with blood, his eyes open and staring.

'Bastards!' yelled Kit, and he picked up a stone and hurled it towards the two men. 'Bastards!' he shouted again. He knelt down and closed the boy's eyes. There was nothing more he could do. Figures nearby avoided his gaze, not wanting to get involved.

Twilight was drawing all the decent people of London back to the safety of the city. The gates would be closing soon. With tears in his eyes Kit left the boy and walked towards Bishopsgate, reaching Cheapside just as the bells rang for curfew.

Chapter 11

One Sunday after church, White suddenly clapped his hands, making Kit jump and almost knock a bottle of ink to the floor. Kit had been bored into a sleepy stupor by a particularly long and dull sermon and hurriedly tried to blink himself awake. White was standing in front of him holding a bow.

'This is for you, Kit,' he said.

Kit raised an eyebrow and mumbled a thank-you, taking the bow from his master as if it were a poisonous snake.

'It must be rather dull for a spirited lad like yourself, so I thought we might go over to the butts and shoot a few arrows today, Kit!'

'Arrows?' said Kit. 'Me? I ain't never shot an arrow in my life, sir.'

This was not strictly true. Kit's father had given him a bow when he was six years old and they had had a target in their garden. If he were to ever allow himself fond memories, Kit would have had them of their shooting together. But that had been in another life and not one he was going to share with White.

'But it is the law!' said White with a touch of exasperation. 'I must have a bow for myself and every boy must have one from his father or master. It is our duty to practise.' Kit snorted and shrugged. 'It is the law!' his master repeated.

'I know,' Kit said with a grin. 'But no one takes any notice of that.'

White closed his eyes and, sighing, launched into a long speech about the great tradition of English bowmen from Robin Hood to Agincourt. Kit had never seen him so agitated about any subject before. He railed against the rise of the crossbow and against the pastimes Londoners chose to pursue instead of the bow.

'Skittles!' sneered White. 'Cards, dice. Even those who should know better seem more interested in playing bowls or tennis. Skittles and tennis will not save England if the Spanish invade these shores.'

'Very well, sir,' said Kit finally. 'I'm sorry. I'm sorry. I'll go to the butts with you if the whole of England is depending on it.'

White stopped in mid flow, a little embarrassed at how worked up he had become. He went to fetch two quivers full of arrows, handed one to Kit, then smiled and led him out into the hazy autumn sunshine.

They walked up through the bustling city and out of Moorgate towards Finsbury Fields. Here, windmills creaked lazily in the breeze and the ceaseless hum of the city died away and was replaced by the twitter of birds in the hedgerows as they hunted for berries. It was cold, frost still glistening in the shadows.

The archery field was busier than Kit had expected and they had to walk for a little while before they found a vacant target – a large wicker roundel in front of a grass bank to catch any misfired arrows. Kit watched with barely disguised boredom as White carefully selected an arrow and took aim.

It seemed an age before his fingers let go. Kit heard the thud of the arrow and turned to look at the target, surprised to see that White had hit the bull's-eye.

'Hey!' he said. 'You're good at this, ain't you?'

White blushed a little, but was clearly pleased with the shot. 'It is all about practice,' he said.

Neither of his next two shots were quite as good as the first, but both hit the target and both were fairly central. Kit was impressed and gave White a round of applause as his master pulled the arrows from the target.

White bowed and handed Kit the arrows. 'Now you,' he said.

Kit raised his eyebrows and looked about a little sheepishly. White showed him how to grip the bow and how to hold the arrow so that the flights rested against his cheek, and he looked along the arrow's shaft towards the target. He let go the arrow and cursed as it thudded into the ground halfway between him and the target.

'Really,' said White. 'We must do something about your language, lad.'

Kit sulkily tried to give the bow to his master but he refused to take it.

'Try again, Kit,' he said. 'And don't jerk at it. Release the arrow and it will fly on its own.'

Kit sighed but went through the procedure again, bracing his arm as he pulled back the bowstring, feeling it cutting into his fingers as he did so. He looked along the shaft to the arrowhead and the target and then let go, cursing once more as the arrow fell ineffectually to the ground. A youth nearby chortled and Kit turned to face him with such anger that the boy, though older, turned away and refused to meet his gaze.

'That was better, Kit,' said White calmly. 'Try again.'

Kit took a deep breath and snatched the arrow his master held out to him. He pulled back the bowstring and looked down the arrow shaft. And then something strange happened. All the chatter of the other archers died away. Even White's gentle encouragement faded. The cheeping of birds fell silent. Everything around him blurred into a strange nothingness. The only things that were in focus were the arrowhead and the target. Then Kit let go.

The sound flooded back in as the arrow thudded home, in the dead centre of the target. White looked on, amazed, then he slapped Kit on the back and Kit smiled back, groggy as if coming out of a faint.

'Beginner's luck, Kit,' said White.

But it was not beginner's luck, or at least not entirely. Every time Kit managed to find that trance-like state of concentration, he hit the target and the bull's-eye. He had some gift for archery and no one could have been more amazed than Kit himself.

White only managed to partially disguise his jealousy that Kit seemed able to shoot as well as he with a mere hour of practice, and said that perhaps it was time to get something to eat. They packed their arrows away and set off back towards the city. They had barely walked through Moorgate when someone called White's name.

'Master Wylam,' said White with a rather forced smile. 'What a pleasant surprise.'

Kit turned to see a fashionably dressed man in his late twenties, his hair long and coal-black. His clothes were satin and velvet and spun with gold, and he had a fur cloak over one shoulder. Pearl earrings dripped from his ears, glinting on either side of his handsome face; a wide and generous smile framed by a well-groomed moustache and beard. He looked every inch the dashing court fop.

'Master White,' said Wylam. 'A pleasure to see you as always. You have been to the butts, I see.'

'Yes,' said White. 'My servant and I were just on our way to an inn so we shall bid you—'

'I am about the same business. Perhaps I could join you?'

'Well I . . . Yes, of course . . .' said White without conviction. Kit had to stop himself smirking at White's obvious discomfort.

'Excellent!' said Wylam with a clap of his hands.

'Then let us away, my friends, for I could eat a horse with the rider still aboard!'

White led them off in the direction of an inn he knew in Milk Street. He introduced Kit on the way and Wylam bowed to him as grandly as if he had been an ambassador from the Ottoman Empire, grinning from ear to ear when Kit tried a clumsy bow of his own in return. White sniffed irritably and quickened his pace, disappearing round a corner ahead of them.

When Kit rounded the corner himself, he was amazed to see the long lane ahead of him empty – White seemed to have disappeared into thin air. But then he heard voices nearby, and as he followed the sound and entered a stableyard, he could see White being held by one of three men. The man turned at the sound of Kit's approach and showed himself to be – to Kit's horror – the soldier who had twice attempted to do him grievous harm.

'And here is the other!' cried the man with the joyful expression of one who has found not one but two silver coins. He head-butted White, who slumped to the floor with a groan, then strode towards the terrified Kit. Before he reached him, however, Wylam had stepped between them. Kit froze but Wylam looked unconcerned.

'This is private business,' said the soldier.

'Come now, friend,' said Wylam. 'He is but a lad and the gentleman there would hardly give you any sport.'

The soldier poked him in the chest with his finger. 'I don't recall asking for your opinion on the matter, *friend*,' he said.

'True, true,' said Wylam, gingerly taking hold of the other's finger as if it were a loose thread or a hair and dropping it. 'Nevertheless I see no need for us to lose our good humour over such a trifling matter.' He took out a pair of pale grey kid gloves from his belt and put them on.

'There you go again,' said the man. 'I say I do not seek your opinion, and yet still you do not hold your tongue. Perhaps we should have some sport with you instead.'

'I apologize if I have caused any offence,' said the newcomer, holding out his gloved hand. 'Henry Wylam. I merely wish to—'

The soldier ignored Wylam's hand and drew a dagger, prodding him in the chest with his finger once more and holding the blade a few inches from his face.

'Are you a simpleton?' he asked. 'Do you not understand when to shut your mouth? I can just as easily deal with you *and* the boy, as well as this "gentleman" on the ground.' He gestured towards the still-groggy White.

Wylam smiled. 'Calm yourself, friend,' he said. 'I have no desire for trouble. I do worry, though, that you may damage your finger with all that prodding.' The man squinted at him and then turned to his friends, grinning.

'Do you hear that?' he called. 'He's worried about my finger.'

'No, truly,' said Wylam. 'A man once broke his

finger prodding me in the chest.' The man holding Kit laughed.

The man raised his eyebrows and grinned even more. 'He broke his finger, did he?' he said, renewing his prodding of Wylam. 'Poking you in the chest? And how might . . . ?' Quick as a flash, Wylam grabbed the man's finger and flicked his wrist. Kit heard the snap and the man yelled as Wylam grabbed the hand holding the dagger and lifted it high in the air, bending the hand back until the man was forced to drop it. Wylam then brought his knee up into the man's stomach and as he doubled up in pain, Wylam brought his elbow down on the man's back and he dropped to the ground gasping for breath.

All this happened with such speed and violence everyone – including the soldier's two friends – stood staring, frozen like statues. One of them came to his senses and drew his sword.

'Put down your sword,' said Wylam. 'I have no argument with you. You may fancy yourself in a tavern brawl, friend, but this is my living.'

The man hesitated, but then snarled and lunged at Wylam with the sword. Wylam sidestepped it easily, grabbing the man's sword arm with his left hand and pulling the man on, then thudding his right elbow into his throat. As the man staggered backwards, choking, his sword dropping to the ground, Wylam kicked both his legs away and he smacked backwards onto the brick-paved floor of the courtyard and lay groaning.

His friend then grabbed Wylam round the neck from behind, but Wylam simply bent forward and sent him sprawling over his shoulder onto a cart, which collapsed under the force of the blow. As the assailant tried to get up, Wylam kicked him round the side of the head and the man slumped into unconsciousness.

The soldier with the broken finger had recovered his breath by now and scrabbled for his dagger on the floor, but Wylam put his boot on the man's wrist as one might upon the throat of a snake.

'Unless you want a broken wrist to match your broken finger, I advise you to leave go,' he said. The man let go and Wylam reached down, picked up the dagger and threw it away. 'Excellent,' he concluded. 'And now we will bid you gentlemen good day.'

Wylam helped White back to his feet, then turned to lead them away, but he had taken only three steps when Kit saw the soldier pull out a smaller dagger and hold it up to throw at Wylam's back.

'He has a knife!' Kit shouted. Wylam lunged swiftly to one side and the dagger landed with a thud in one of the wooden columns supporting the balcony.

Wylam examined the dagger and pulled it out. 'That's a pretty dagger,' he said, examining the decoration on the blade. 'Italian, I'd wager. Nice weight to it too.' He mimed throwing it in the direction of its owner, then walked back towards him smiling, juggling the knife with amazing dexterity, tossing it from one hand to the other and twirling it between his fingers. The soldier on the floor stared up, as spellbound as Kit. 'Whoops!' said Wylam, tossing the dagger into the air above the man, who looked up in panic as it came plummeting towards him point first. When it was about six inches from his forehead, Wylam caught it by the hilt. The soldier let out the air he'd been holding with a gasp.

'I have been practising,' said Wylam with a grin. The dagger's owner stared at him with a mixture of horror and disbelief, then Wylam punched him in the jaw and the man slumped to the floor alongside his friends.

A stable lad emerged at that point and surveyed the scene with bewilderment, looking from the bodies on the ground to the unlikely trio standing nearby.

Wylam took out a purse and thrust a handful of coins into the boy's hand.

'Run to the City Guard at Moorgate and tell them that Henry Wylam has ordered the arrest of these three men and wants them evicted from London by curfew. If he asks by what authority, tell them Sir Christopher Hatton. That ought to move them. Do you have that?'

'Aye, sir,' said the stable lad. 'Henry Wylam. Sir Christopher Hatton. Kicked out by curfew.'

'Good lad,' said Wylam. He turned to Kit and White, smoothing his hair back into place. 'We should go.'

They left the stableyard and wove their way through the lanes until they stood by the Stocks Market. White thanked Wylam for coming to their assistance and Wylam offered to buy them lunch, but White said that he had now lost his appetite so he and Kit would return home and eat there later. Wylam bowed and bade them farewell, Kit staring after him in awe.

'Come along, Kit,' snapped White, dabbing at his nose with the back of his hand. 'If you stare any harder, your eyes will fall from their sockets.'

'I've never seen anyone fight like that,' said Kit in admiration. 'Did you see the way he broke that oaf's finger?' He whistled, but White was already walking away up the hill. 'I don't understand, sir,' he said when he'd caught up again. 'Why don't you like Master Wylam?'

White came to a halt. 'Because there is a difference between fighting for your life or fighting for your country – and fighting because you *enjoy* fighting. Master Wylam fights as much for his own amusement as anything else.'

'So would I if I was as good at it as he is,' said Kit. 'Besides, he did rescue us, didn't he?'

White smiled. 'You are right, of course,' he said wearily. 'And I am being ungracious. There is something about Master Wylam I do not like. I cannot rightly say what it is. Come along – let us see what Mrs Fisher has in the larder.'

Kit nodded and followed his master towards Cheapside, but he could not stop thinking about Wylam and the three men lying sprawled out in the stableyard. If he could have had one wish granted and magically become anyone in the world, at that moment, Kit would have become Henry Wylam, whatever White might say.

Chapter 12

The days passed slowly but pleasantly in White's study. Kit had initially told himself he did not owe White a thing, and when he had somewhere better to go, then go he would. But the truth was, Kit had begun to change. Not dramatically, and not overnight, but little by little the hard shell he had grown on the streets was being eroded.

Telling Hugh the truth about his background had changed him too. Although he still had to guard his secret past from those around him, the fact that someone knew the truth had released some of the pressure. He felt lighter, freer. He slept better. The nightmares that had plagued him for years came less frequently.

Life with White was not boring at all, as he had thought it would be. Despite all his best efforts, Kit had begun to enjoy the work he did for White and he had grown to like the man too. No two days were alike. One day he would be preparing pigments, the next he would be accompanying White on a shopping expedition for parchment or paper.

Kit became more and more of a genuine assistant to his master. He still felt a little like a sorcerer's apprentice as he ground the pigments in the mortar or tipped them into small heaps of colour: the warm red-brown ochre from Siena in Tuscany; brilliant crimson from the crushed cochineal bugs of Peru; saffron from the crocus fields of Saffron Waldon in Essex. He was fascinated by these piles of coloured dust, and the strange names and the distant lands they came from: the beautiful, deep blue ultramarine made from the semi-precious lapis lazuli; the violet blue of smalt, made from ground cobalt glass; the hot red cinnabar that White created himself in his workshop at the bottom of the house by heating mercury with sulphur until devilishly vermilion smoke puffed out of the clay oven.

There was chalk white and lead white; lamp black and bone black. There was charcoal made from burnt willow and black graphite from the mines of Borrowdale in Cumbria; there was soot ink, and iron-gall ink, distilled from the little galls formed when parasitic wasps laid their eggs in the buds of oak trees.

Kit also learned about the bottles and jars full of the resins and gums and oils needed to bind these pigments: the bone glues and rabbitskin glues, beeswax and honey, linseed oil and turpentine. In a matter of weeks, he had become such a part of White's workshop that White could scarcely believe he had ever managed without him.

The study was also like a schoolroom, with White

showing Kit how to look at a map and see the land the spidery drawing described. Kit learned more in a month with White than he had in the previous five years – or at least, he learned more *honest* things.

White showed him the instruments of navigation and how to use them: the cross-staff, which was used to measure the sun's height and thus the latitude, or the position relative to the equator; the astrolabe, which was a dial, hung from a cord with its pointer turned until it was directed towards the sun or the Pole Star.

These tools were used together with the mysterious compass. Kit had never seen one before, so he was fascinated when White brought out a small wooden box and opened it to reveal the round face of the compass and its magical lodestone, persistently pointing north as if alive. He stared at it in wonder and it rekindled his suspicion that whatever White called himself, there *was* a kind of sorcery at work here.

In fact Kit was wondering yet again what exactly it was that White and Harriot got up to together at Durham House when he returned one day with a new batch of quills to find an unannounced visitor standing over the map table in the study. Kit challenged him and the man turned with a broad grin.

'Master Wylam!' said Kit. 'What brings you here, sir?'

'I am in the employ of Sir Christopher Hatton,' Wylam replied, fiddling with a large ring of twisted silver he wore on the little finger of his right hand. His voice made it clear that he would rather be doing almost anything else. 'Sir Christopher likes to keep abreast of all Master Raleigh's various schemes. The Queen is very interested in Master Raleigh, and whatever interests the Queen interests Sir Christopher.' Wylam smiled. 'He is with Master White in his workshop downstairs. Goodness knows what they're up to.'

Kit was overawed for a few moments, then he began to burble. 'The way you . . . that fight . . . the men in the stables. I ain't never seen anything like it.'

Wylam smiled. 'I was lucky.'

'It didn't look much like luck, sir,' said Kit. 'Where did you learn to fight like that?'

'In places you can be thankful never to have seen, lad,' said Wylam, his smile ebbing.

'I ain't always been a servant,' said Kit defensively, worried that Wylam thought him some soft house boy. 'I've been in some scrapes too.'

Wylam's smile returned. 'I am sure you have, Kit,' he said. He sniffed suspiciously at a jar of pale green verdigris and picked up a map, squinting at it with a sour expression. 'What is a normal lad like you doing amongst all this . . . this . . . whatever it is?' he queried.

Kit laughed. 'I like it here,' he said.

'Really?' said Wylam, astonished. 'Truly? Well, each to his own. Each to his own.' And he left, shaking his head.

Chapter 13

'It appears we have been summoned to court,' said White one day.

'We, sir?' said Kit with a smile, putting down a jar of rich brown burnt umber.

'Well, it is true that the summons does not mention you by *name*,' said White, returning the smile. 'But all the same, I think it is only right that you accompany me. I think you deserve it, after all the work you have done for me.'

'I . . . I . . . don't know,' said Kit.

'Would you not like to see Hampton Court Palace – such a great house? King Henry lived there, you know. It has a rich past. Are you not a little curious?'

'I suppose so,' said Kit in an odd, flat voice that made White give him a searching look.

Part of Kit was indeed excited by the idea of going to Hampton Court, but not for any reason White could imagine. He had a hazy, dreamlike memory of the place from his childhood, when he had been taken there by his parents, but might it bring back memories of that past happy life and the pain of its loss? Hampton Court belonged to the world of Christopher Fulbourn, not Kit Milton.

'You are a strange one, Kit,' said White, looking at his worried expression. Then he looked at the boy's clothes and pursed his lips. 'But we will have to get you some new clothes. These will never do.'

So Kit was taken to buy a new suit of clothes, with White dithering endlessly over buttons and breeches until Kit could barely stay awake with boredom. Then, on a freezing cold day in late October, they took a tilt boat from a jetty near the bridge and set out for the palace.

The wind was bitter and snow clouds sat deep and dark to the north. Ice was forming where the river was still and clogged the ditches and marshes that lay beside it. Ducks made their unsteady progress across the ice on their way to running water. A blue-white frost lay on every rooftop and smoke rose from every chimney.

The boat they sat in grew colder and colder as it took on the temperature of the icy water around them, and Kit hugged himself against the gnawing chill and wrapped himself up in his cloak, but by the time the turrets of Hampton Court appeared above them, he could no longer feel his toes.

Kit followed close behind White as they walked up from the river to the entrance to the Palace. Armed guards, pikes at the ready, stood at the gatehouse. A gentleman walked forward and greeted White, waving them through. The guards stared blankly ahead.

Beyond the gatehouse, the full scale of Hampton Court opened up to them, the palace buildings standing in huge grounds, with formal gardens immediately around and hunting forest beyond. It was an impressive sight by any standard and White smiled at Kit, seeing what he took to be a look of awe on Kit's face.

But it was not amazement he saw; it was anxiety. For no sooner had Kit walked through the gatehouse than he had felt an urge to turn on his heels and get back in the boat. The palms of his hands began to sweat and he felt as though his legs were dragging weights. He *remembered* having been here before with his parents.

He recalled walking these paths as a small boy, and the memory of it came back foggily in the smell of the grass and the noise of the gravel underfoot, echoing against the high walls of the palace. He had the faintest sensation of his mother's hand enclosing his own, and then it was gone. It was not so much a memory as a taste, a taste that was now tainted and bitter.

It was not just these hidden memories that caused the turmoil, but the realization that he was now in among the people who had been responsible for the deaths of his parents – both those who had drawn his father into treachery, and those who had turned their backs upon his mother.

White looked at the troubled face of his young companion and, mistaking it for nerves, put a comforting hand on Kit's shoulder as they walked into the house itself.

Kit's recollection of Hampton Court Palace had been indistinct; so ephemeral that it was in effect no more real to him than a story his nurse might have told him. Even now, as he entered the palace wide awake and full of wonder, the sight was still otherworldly.

Everywhere he looked the walls shimmered and glistened. The tapestries that decorated the rooms twinkled with pearls and jewels and gold thread and the ceilings above his head were encrusted with carved wooden foliage, smothered in gold. It was like being inside a gigantic, gleaming jewellery box.

Where there were no tapestries, the walls themselves were painted in such rich colours and with such clever trickery that they looked exactly like marble or hanging cloth until Kit came close enough to see the illusion, shaking his head in disbelief.

The ladies and gentlemen who peopled the rooms were no less decorated as they moved about, chattering and whispering, the ladies' dresses swishing and rustling. It was like a theatre set, alive with fabulously costumed actors. Everything was artifice and trickery.

Kit watched these exotic creatures sway back and forth and his mood slowly changed from wide-eyed amazement to something darker. He had seen wealthy people before, many times; the Strand was full of wealthy people. But here at court they seemed different somehow. Here their wealth was shouted out, safe within the confines of the palace; here these peacocks could cover themselves in jewels without fear of theft.

White pointed out several well-known faces to Kit. The Queen's most important counsellor, Lord Burghley, the Lord Treasurer, stood on his own looking bored. His face was pale with heavy-lidded eyes and his white beard fell over his lace ruff.

The Earl of Leicester stood nearby. Kit was momentarily transfixed. The Earl was one of the most famous – or infamous – men in the country. He had known the Queen since they were both young and some said they had been lovers. Some said they still were. Some also said he had killed his first wife.

He looked older than Kit had imagined, quite red-faced, with a large paunch straining at the buttons of his doublet. But Kit could feel the power that emanated from him as if it were heat from a fire. He was a survivor and had even managed to work his way back into the Queen's favour after secretly remarrying. He might be an old lion, but he was still a lion.

Then White pointed out Walter Raleigh. This was the first time Kit had seen him and though he knew he had been a friend of his father's, he had no recollection of having met him then. Here was the man who was the subject of so much gossip and rumour; the scourge of the Irish, favourite of the Queen.

Though he had no title, he was dressed like a prince in pale silks with pearl buttons and earrings. Kit thought he must be about thirty years of age, and his high-browed face with its neatly trimmed moustache and beard wore a quick and cunning, fox-sharp expression. He was more handsome than Kit had imagined, but there was something of the Devil in that pointed beard and arching eyebrow.

'Master White,' said a voice behind them. They both turned and Kit found himself facing a tall man in black, a skullcap on his head and his long-fingered hands clasped at his chest. His face was sallow and he had the look of a rather strict abbot.

'Sir Francis,' said White. 'It is good to see you again, sir. How is Dame Ursula?'

Sir Francis? thought Kit. It was certainly not Sir Francis Drake – there was no way this man had captained a ship.

'My wife is very well, thank you, Master White. She is here somewhere, catching up on court gossip no doubt.' He turned his attention to Kit, who felt himself wither slightly under his gaze.

'Ah, this is my young assistant, Kit, Sir Francis,' said White, nudging Kit. 'Kit, this is Sir Francis Walsingham.'

Kit froze.

'I am told that Master White has taken you in from the streets. I trust you are a loyal servant,' said Walsingham.

Kit did not reply.

White stepped in nervously. 'He is, Sir Francis,' he said.

'Very well, then. Good day, Master White.'

'Really, Kit!' whispered White as soon as Walsingham

was out of earshot. 'You must learn some manners. It does not do to upset people like Sir Francis. It does not do at all.'

'That was Sir Francis *Walsingham*?' said Kit finally, almost in a daze as he watched the man walk away through the crowd. 'Him that hunts down Jesuits and such?'

'Traitors of all kinds, Kit,' corrected White. 'The Queen calls him her "Moor" on account of his sallow skin and dour appearance. But how on earth did he know about you? It is extraordinary. His intelligencers are everywhere.'

But Kit already knew that. It had been Sir Francis's intelligencers who had trapped his father; trapped him and racked him and led him to the executioner's block.

Kit suddenly felt stifled, as if the whole sumptuously decorated scene were closing in around him, smothering him like a giant embroidered cushion. He left White, pushing his way through the spangled mass of courtiers to the hall and then following the light until he emerged outside, panting like an anxious dog.

Kit walked out into the gardens. The sun glimmered dimly behind a curtain of low cloud and mist, and the morning's dew still dripped from the leaves of the plants and hedges. Holly and bay leaves shone as if polished, and a rich scent rose up from the damp box hedges.

Kit shrugged against the cold and damp and shivered. His nose had begun to run and he wiped it on his sleeve before looking round sheepishly to see if anyone had seen him. Behind the hedges and rising up above him, he suddenly saw a long pole, on top of which was a carved wooden dragon, crouched and snarling with wings like a bat. It had been painted, and its claws and the flames coming from its mouth were covered in shimmering gilt. Kit walked over to the hedges, the gravel path crunching underfoot.

There was a row of these strange beasts on poles – lions, unicorns, griffins, leopards – trailing away towards the palace, and Kit saw that his interest in them was shared by others. Only a few yards away, on the other side of the hedge, Thomas Harriot was standing staring up at a gryphon. With him were two very oddly dressed men, though Kit's view of them was mostly obscured by the hedges. He heard footsteps on the gravel and saw Walter Raleigh walking along the path towards them.

'Ah, gentlemen,' said Raleigh. 'Is everything to your satisfaction? You must come inside. The Queen wishes to meet you.'

Two ladies-in-waiting walked past at this moment, stared in amazement at the men with Harriot and Raleigh, then collapsed into giggles and ran hurriedly away. Raleigh raised his eyes to the heavens. 'How do you like the gardens, gentlemen?' he continued. 'The Queen employed a French fellow at huge expense. What is wrong with English gardeners, heaven only knows. They are fine, though, are they not?'

The two men looked about them as if they had not noticed the gardens before.

'Where is the food?' said one in a deep voice and in an accent Kit had never heard before.

'The food?' said Raleigh, looking puzzled. 'Are you hungry? There is no finer food served in all England.'

'No,' said the man. 'Why is there no food growing?'

'Oh I see, food, yes. Well, there is a kitchen garden, of course, and there is a fine orchard, but these gardens are for pleasure, not for food.'

'And these? These are magic spirits?'

Raleigh followed his gaze to the carved beasts and laughed. 'Not magic, no,' he said.

'If no magic, then what for?'

Kit could see now that the foreigners were dressed in brown taffeta costumes, almost as if they were actors on a stage. They had dark skin, but they were not Moors or Ethiops, or even fairground Egyptians, and their hair seemed to be cut in a very strange fashion with a kind of topknot. Kit had never seen men like them before.

'They are not *for* anything,' said Raleigh with a swirl of his fingers.

The men had a brief conversation in a foreign language and then shrugged, clearly unimpressed by Raleigh's explanation.

'Do we go see her now? Weroanza Elizabeth?' asked one of them.

'Weroanza?' repeated Raleigh.

Harriot smiled a crooked smile. 'It means big chief, sir,' he said. 'A female big chief.'

Raleigh chuckled. 'Does it really?' he said. 'Oh,

that's very good.' He turned back to the strangers. 'Remember when you approach her, bow and do not get up until she gives her permission.'

The two strangers looked at each other and nodded. Harriot then led them towards the palace. Kit stood to one side as they approached him and it was then that he saw the full strangeness of these foreigners. He could see clearly now that the sides of the men's heads were shaven as closely as his hair had been by Mrs Fisher; however, a section had been spared on the crown so that it grew like a crest or the comb of a cockerel. He stared open-mouthed, wondering if these strangers were men at all, or some kind of daemons conjured up by the Durham House wizards.

As the group walked past, one of the strangers stopped and looked at Kit, smiling.

'Do not worry, little English,' he said in a deep voice. 'Wanchese will not eat you.'

Then he chuckled and was joined by his companion, and even the normally grim-faced Harriot seemed to enjoy this joke. Raleigh too laughed heartily as he walked past. In fact everyone seemed to find it amusing – everyone except Kit, who stood staring after them, chilled by more than the October air.

Chapter 14

A couple of days after their visit to Hampton Court, White said he had something to finish in his workshop and left Kit alone in the study. For only the second time since he had begun working there, White had left a map on his table. Kit edged across to look, casting wary glances at the study door.

It was a version of the same map he had seen before, only this time it was more detailed. Now the unknown stretch of coastline had small features drawn across it. There were trees and hills, and masts of wrecked ships poked through the sea near the shore.

Peering closer, Kit could see that White had added some writing too, but the words seemed like a drunken jumble of letters – *Paquiwoc*, *Wokokon*, *Roanoke*. The only word Kit could decipher was the name across the top of the map – *Virginia*.

He was baffled. Where was this place? Kit was sure that there were many lands in the world he had not heard of and certainly would not recognize from a map, but surely this one had to be English with a name like Virginia. Elizabeth was called the Virgin Queen after all. It could not surely be a coincidence?

Kit knew that the English were attempting to colonize Ireland. Maybe this was some part of Ireland?

Then he had a revelation: the strange men at Hampton Court, the visits from the pilot, Fernandez – could this be a map of some part of the *Americas*?

Suddenly Kit heard White's footsteps on the stairs. In his eagerness to return to his usual place, he knocked over a jar of chalk dust, spilling some over one corner of the map. He cursed and blew the dust away, but it flew up in a fine choking cloud and he was still coughing when White opened the door to find him hard at work with the mortar and pestle.

White went to his map desk and Kit saw him gently run a finger across the table's surface and lift his whitened finger. Kit looked down to avoid his gaze.

'Kit?' said White.

'Yes, sir?'

'Could you pass me one of those empty jars behind you,' said White. 'The one labelled "Alizarin Crimson".'

Kit breathed a quiet sigh of relief and fetched the jar, handing it to White.

'Why did you tell me that you could not read, Kit?' White frowned suspiciously.

Kit was about to say that he could just tell what jar it was, but he knew that would not work. The jar was empty and identical to the others – save for the label.

'It's hard to say, sir,' he said slowly. 'On the streets you don't have anything but what you have in here . . .' Kit patted his head. 'And here . . .' He tapped his chest. 'You don't give anything away if you can help it. You might be giving away something that will give you an edge one day. Do you know what I mean, sir?'

White nodded. 'It's not so different at court, you know,' he said, smiling. 'But no more secrets. Agreed?'

'Those . . . men . . . with Master Raleigh,' Kit asked. 'What were they, sir?'

White smiled and put his fingers together, clearly weighing something up in his mind. 'I think you may have already guessed that they are from the Americas,' he said finally. 'Now that Raleigh has paraded them at court, it is hardly a secret. An expedition was sent to the Americas earlier this year and those natives – Manteo and Wanchese – were brought back in one of the ships. Master Harriot is learning their language.'

'What for, sir?' said Kit. 'They already speak a little English.'

'It will be of invaluable help to us should we return. Instead of treating the natives as animals as the Spanish do, we will be able to talk to them, to parley with them, to befriend them.'

Kit curled his lip. The savages did not look like anyone he would be eager to befriend. And there was something else that did not make sense. 'I thought the New World belonged to the Spanish?' he said.

White frowned. 'So they and the Pope would have us

believe; but our fishermen and whalers have sailed the waters of the northern part for many a year.' He took a blank sheet of paper and drew some lines. 'This is England, Kit,' he said. 'And this is America. To the south, here, are the fabled lands of Mexico and Peru, wherein the Spaniards have become so rich. Their control extends to the islands of the West Indies and up into the land of Florida above. In the far north, the French have begun exploring. England must act soon, or this new land will be entirely in the hands of our enemies. Look, do you see here?' He pointed. 'Here on the east coast, between the Spanish and the French. This land is known as *Norumbega*. John Cabot, sailing for Henry the Eighth, landed somewhere about here.' He pointed again. 'A place we call Newfoundland. That was in fourteen ninety-seven, Kit – only five years after Columbus arrived in the Bahamas. But I have spoken to Bristol men who believe that Englishmen had reached these lands many years before. We have a right to these lands, Kit, be sure of that. And in any case, Cabot was given leave to explore whatever land had not already been possessed by Spain. I myself have sailed to America—'

'You, sir!' gasped Kit.

'Aye, lad,' replied White, tapping his sketch map with a piece of graphite. 'I have sailed to the northern lands where there is ice in the sea . . . great floating mountains of ice, Kit. Can you imagine that?'

Kit tried but failed.

'It was back in seventy-six, when you were but a

little boy. We set sail with the Queen waving us off as we floated past her palace at Greenwich; we were looking for a passage to Cathay, north of the Americas.' White chuckled to himself.

'And did you find the passage?' asked Kit.

White raised his eyebrows. 'Well of course not, boy,' he said with a laugh. 'Or we'd all be as rich as Spaniards. Though we did think we had found gold.'

'And had you?'

White chuckled and shook his head. 'No,' he said. 'But I shall tell that tale another time. I have already perhaps said too much. It is enough to say that the licence to explore the eastern coast of North America granted to Cabot has now passed to Raleigh, and he has named this tract of land *Virginia* in honour of Her Majesty the Queen.'

'He plans to start a colony!' said Kit, wide-eyed.

'One day,' said White. 'Perhaps. But for the moment, Kit, I will say no more about this map or the natives at Durham House. One day I will tell you everything you want to know, but for now I think it safest for both of us that you know no more, and I would ask you not to speculate about what you have seen. Is that understood?'

'Yes, sir,' said Kit. 'Of course.'

Chapter 15

One day White had asked Kit to go south of the river to a leather worker in Rotherhithe to collect a large bag he was having made to carry his equipment. Kit had barely taken two steps when a hand reached out and dragged him into a narrow alleyway.

'Hey!' shouted Kit. 'Who are you grabbing?'

'Be still, friend,' said his attacker, 'or I shall have to silence you myself. And you would not like that.'

The man was dressed completely in black apart from a small white lace ruff at his throat. Jet buttons fastened his black doublet, and inky curlicues of embroidery coiled up and down the black jerkin he wore over it. He had short hair and a thin beard and moustache. He had no weapon that Kit could see, but there was something about the way he spoke that stopped him from struggling.

'What do you want with me?' he asked.

'I am an agent of the Crown,' said the man. 'You may call me Gabriel. My master wishes to see you.'

'Your master?' said Kit. 'And who's that?'

'All in good time, Master Milton. Come on.'

'How do you know me? Where are we going?'

'Rest your tongue and move your legs,' said Gabriel. 'You'll find out where soon enough.' He paused and smiled. 'You may be thinking that you can escape when my back is turned. Can I advise you against that? You may indeed succeed in getting away, but that would simply mean that I would have to come and find you again. Such a delay would not please my master – and it is in no one's interest to annoy him, as you may learn. Is that understood?'

Kit nodded and Gabriel smiled, then led him through the tangle of streets that led down to Fish Wharf. As Gabriel had predicted, Kit was filled with an urge to run, but felt shackled by a dread of being caught again.

'We are about to shake off the filthy grime of the city and venture upriver,' Gabriel said over his shoulder, clapping his hands and rubbing the palms together briskly.

'Upriver? Where upriver? It's freezing!' Kit looked about him apprehensively.

Gabriel whistled to a boatman who was drinking from a keg. 'Will you take us to Barnes, my good fellow?'

'I'll take you to the New World if you've got the ready cash, guv'nor,' said the man, putting down his keg with a thump and wiping his lips with the back of his hand.

'Barnes will do,' said Gabriel. 'Get in, Kit.'

107

'Barnes?' said Kit. 'Why are we going to Barnes? It's miles away!'

Gabriel frowned and stepped to one side as he gestured to Kit to climb aboard the tilt boat, then he followed him on board and the boatman whistled to another man, who climbed on and took the other set of oars. A third boatman loosed the mooring rope and pushed them off. The ferrymen caught their oars and began to row them out into the middle of the river.

'You'll never guess who I had in the back of the boat the other day, sir,' said the boatman nearest to them. Gabriel did not respond. 'I said, you'll never guess who I had in the boat the other day,' the ferryman repeated.

'I do not suppose we will,' said Gabriel in a bored voice.

'Only Sir Francis Drake, that's who,' said the ferryman, ignoring Gabriel's tone.

'No!' said Kit excitedly. 'In this very boat?' Drake was a particular hero of Kit and Hugh's and they had followed his adventures with avid interest. They had both travelled to Tilbury and squeezed through the crowds to see Drake knighted by the Queen aboard the *Golden Hind* after he had circled the globe.

'Where *your* arse is now, his was then,' said the ferryman. 'Damn me as a liar if that ain't God's truth. He weren't stuffy like some of them.' He looked swiftly at Gabriel and then back at Kit. 'No, he was like you or me, really.'

'And what had he to tell you then?' asked Gabriel, adjusting his black lace cuffs.

'All kinds of things, sir,' said the ferryman. 'You know – about his voyages and that.'

'What *exactly*?' asked Gabriel. 'Please. I'm intrigued.'

'Well, sir,' said the ferryman, making a small adjustment in his grip on the oars. 'For one thing, sir, he told me them Spanish sailors are all cowards and no match for us English lads, sir.'

'That certainly *sounds* like Sir Francis,' said Gabriel. 'And it's just as well really.'

'What is, sir?'

'That the Spanish are such cowards,' said Gabriel, looking off towards the riverbank. 'Seeing as the navy will be putting all you rivermen to your country's service if there is a war.'

'A war, sir?' said the boatman nervously. 'Is there to be a war?'

'Sir Francis would be in a better position than I to say,' said Gabriel. 'Perhaps he could have told you himself had he not been in Devon this last month.'

The boatman opened his mouth to speak, but Gabriel had said the words with such authority that he gave up in mid-breath. Kit saw the other boatman grin. The ferryman then sank into a sulky silence and Kit, too embarrassed to catch his eye, looked out at the view. A chill wind was blowing from the southwest, rippling the surface of the river and bringing with it the howls, roars and abattoir stink from the bear-baiting pit on

Bankside. Tilt boats and wherries plied back and forth, the boatmen calling and cursing as they went.

Rooftops clambered up the hill from Fish Wharf to Old St Paul, whose hulking tower loomed over the whole city. The massive walls of Baynard's Castle rose out of the river, green and damp, and the filthy Fleet River branched away as they floated on past the City boundary.

Now, as they rowed on, instead of wharfside warehouses, grand palaces came into view: Arundel House, Somerset House, the Savoy Palace and Durham House, each with its own private jetty and river gate.

They stood like lordly courtiers, showing their best face to the river. Durham House, standing on a bend in the Thames, had one of the best; its roofline bristled with chimneys, its towers and leaded turrets, topped with glittering weather vanes. Kit thought of the house's owner, Raleigh, and of White, and wondered again what went on behind those huge white walls.

The boat headed towards Westminster, the ancient church looming over the river. Water lapped against the green struts of the wooden jetty next to the Star Chamber, where a group of soldiers stood in a furtive huddle. Suddenly a great peal of laughter erupted from them and they parted, shaking their heads, pointing to one another and laughing again. As Kit's boat approached, they fell silent, assuming a not entirely convincing air of officiousness. Kit smiled.

There were people milling about on the Lambeth

Stairs on the opposite side of the river, waiting to cross at the horse ferry: dourly dressed clerics and their servants, on business from Lambeth Palace, two men holding horses returning from hawking. Mist hung over the Lambeth marshes like a shroud.

The land around the river turned quickly to open pasture and woodland, and reeds grew under the pollarded willows along the banks. Swans sailed through the grey waters like miniature galleons.

'Ah,' said Gabriel. 'Here we are.'

The boatmen dropped their oars and grabbed the jetty. The one at the back of the boat hopped out with practised agility, a hemp rope in his hands; he tied the boat to a mooring post, then went to the prow to hold it steady for Kit and Gabriel to jump out.

'Should we wait, sir?' asked the boatman on the jetty.

'Aye,' said Gabriel. 'We should not be long.'

Kit took heart in that 'we'. He had begun to wonder if he was coming back at all! Gabriel gave the ferrymen a handful of coins and led Kit along a pathway towards high walls and the house beyond.

'Do you really know Sir Francis Drake?' Kit asked.

'Our paths have crossed,' said Gabriel. Kit waited for more, but Gabriel left it at that, walking towards a gateway.

'Who calls this day?' said the guard at the gate.

'A true servant of the Crown,' said Gabriel.

'God save Queen Elizabeth,' said the guard.

'God save her!' said Gabriel.

This conversation was spoken in the mechanical voices of fairground actors and Kit realized that it must be a password of some kind; Gabriel had obviously passed the test because the gate swung open.

'Good day, Master Gabriel,' said the guard, and Kit smiled at the pointlessness of the previous staged greeting, when Gabriel was obviously known here. A similar charade occurred at the door to the house before they were shown into a hall and then through to a large study with windows overlooking the garden.

'The master will be with you shortly,' said the servant as he backed out of the room, leaving Kit and Gabriel alone, standing on a large Persian rug. The walls were hung with tapestries and paintings and there were tall cabinets filled with books. Kit noticed a door with a panel that was intricately pierced with a pattern of small holes. He thought he detected the slightest of movements behind it.

A framed print then caught his eye and he leaned forward to peer at it. It showed a great city where a scene of mayhem was taking place: a mob was running through the street, hacking with swords, firing into the crowds with muskets; people were being thrown from upstairs windows and clubbed to death with whatever was at hand; a soldier dangled a child over a river. Kit looked round as a door opened.

As their host walked into the room, the temperature seemed to drop. He was tall and, like Gabriel, dressed completely in black with no trace of decoration save for a white lace ruff at his neck and more lace at his sleeve cuffs. On his head was a black skullcap. He had a neatly trimmed moustache and beard and his skin was sallow. His eyes were heavy-lidded but as piercing as an eagle's and his long face wore an expression of mild contempt. When he smiled, Kit had the impression it was not an expression he employed very often. He recognized him straight away from Hampton Court: the man the Queen called her 'Moor' – Sir Francis Walsingham.

'Master Milton, is it not?'

'Yes, sir,' said Kit nervously.

'I see you were looking at the print,' said the man. 'Do you know what it represents?'

'No, sir.'

'Do you have no idea?'

'No, sir.'

'It shows the events of the twenty-fourth of August fifteen seventy-two,' Walsingham said. 'The city is Paris. It is the massacre of St Bartholomew's Day.'

Kit looked back at the picture. He had heard of the massacre, of course; everyone in the world had heard of the St Bartholomew's Day Massacre.

'It started as an attack on the Huguenots – do you know what a Huguenot is, boy?'

'French, sir?' said Kit. 'French Protestant?'

'Indeed,' said Walsingham. 'They were falsely accused of plotting a rebellion and attacked in their homes. But Catholics are like wild beasts, boy; once they had tasted blood they could not have enough and they became frenzied, attacking any Protestant they could find. Their bloodlust spread out from Paris like a plague, moving through the whole of France. Thousands of Protestants were killed that day, boy: men, women, children . . . even babies still clinging to their mother's breasts. It is a constant reminder of what Catholics are capable of. It is a constant reminder of the threat we face.' He said the word 'Catholics' as if a bone was caught in his throat. 'I was there,' he continued. 'In Paris. I saw it with my own eyes. It is a day I shall never forget.' He seemed lost in his own thoughts for a moment, but then turned to Gabriel and smiled. 'Gabriel, it is good to see you.'

'And you, sir,' said Gabriel.

'You are nervous, boy,' Walsingham said, turning to Kit again. 'Do not be. You are quite safe here at Barn Elms. Had I wanted to harm you I would not have chosen my own house as the venue.'

Bringing up the subject of the best place to harm someone did not make Kit feel any more comfortable.

'You are part of John White's household now,' their host continued. 'Is he a kind master?'

'Kind enough,' said Kit.

Walsingham nodded and looked away. 'And has he many visitors?' he asked.

'Visitors?'

'Yes,' said Walsingham. 'Visitors. Does he have many visitors? It is a simple enough question.' He turned his back on Kit and Kit looked at Gabriel, who stared impassively back at him.

'Why are you asking?' said Kit.

Walsingham turned slowly back and walked towards Kit, his fingers interlaced at his chest. 'Can it be that this thief feels a loyalty to Master White?' he queried with a smile.

Kit frowned at the mocking tone. 'Master White has been good to me,' he muttered.

Walsingham nodded and leaned closer, dropping his voice to a whisper. 'At one word from me, you will be arrested as a thief,' he said gently, holding Kit's ear between his finger and thumb. 'I will see that you are fairly punished for your crimes and have a hole burned through this ear with a white-hot poker. You will smell your own burning flesh and then, while the pain is still raw, I will bring you back here and ask you the very same question again.' He pulled his face away from Kit's and let go of his ear, rocked his head on his neck as if his shoulders ached and then looked at Kit with bored, half-closed eyes. 'Now,' he said. 'I shall ask you once again. Does Master White have many visitors?'

'Some,' said Kit, his throat so dry he could hardly recognize his own voice. 'Master Harriot from Durham House comes quite often. Sir Christopher Hatton has been with Master Wylam. A foreign man who knows metals called . . . called . . . Ganz – yes, Ganz. Another foreigner called Fernandez who is a sea-faring man, Master White says.'

Walsingham smiled. 'You do not like Master Fernandez?'

'No, sir,' said Kit.

Walsingham smiled. 'Neither do I. Anyone else?'

'No, sir, not apart from his daughter and her husband.'

'There now,' Walsingham said. 'That was not so difficult, was it?'

'No, sir,' said Kit unconvincingly.

Walsingham let out a deep breath as if he had been holding it for the length of the interview. 'Very well,' he said. 'I may want to talk to you again.'

Kit's eyes were stung by salt and he realized he was sweating. But there was relief also. So this was about White and not about him.

'Good day, sir. Come on,' said Gabriel, nodding towards the door. Kit needed no further encouragement, but as they were about to leave, their host called for them to stop.

'Can you read?' he asked Kit.

'No, sir,' he replied.

Walsingham took a sheet of paper and hurriedly wrote a message. He smiled at Kit while the ink dried and then folded the letter and handed it to him.

'Gabriel will take you back to London. I want you to take this to a man at the sign of the Green Man in Thames Street. Can you do that?'

Kit nodded and stuffed the letter into his jerkin, then Gabriel ushered him out.

Gabriel barely spoke on the journey back to London, and Kit was in no mood to talk in any case. He could not decide what bothered him most – that he was being asked to spy or that he was living in the household of someone who was attracting the attention of the Queen's agents.

'Say nothing of this meeting,' said Gabriel when they had walked clear of the river. 'You may think we will not know, but we shall.'

'Yes, sir,' said Kit. 'I mean no, sir.'

Gabriel smiled and then peered at Kit as if seeing him for the first time. 'Do I know you, boy?'

'No, sir,' said Kit a little nervously. 'I can't see how you could.'

Gabriel looked at Kit for an uncomfortably long time before smiling unpleasantly. He then bid Kit farewell and walked away, leaving him standing in almost the same place where he had grabbed him earlier in the day. It gave him the sensation that the whole experience had been a dream, though he knew that it was not.

With Gabriel gone and back on home turf, Kit began to feel a little stronger. Anger began to replace fear; anger at being plucked off the street and threatened; anger at being made to play the spy on a master who had been kind to him. It was then that he remembered the letter.

He took the folded paper from his jerkin and smiled at the lack of seal. He wanted to know a little more before he went delivering messages. The man in Thames Street would never know that Kit had read it first. He opened it slowly and read the carefully written words it contained:

'*It appears that you can read after all, Master Milton. Let that be the last lie you tell me if you want to keep your life.*'

Kit read the words again and again, his fear growing with each re-reading. For he *was* still lying to Walsingham about one thing: his true identity. Maybe he should have told Walsingham who he really was. He was not at fault for his father's crime, but if Walsingham discovered who he was now, after they had met twice, it would seem as though he had some reason for hiding his identity. Maybe Walsingham would even think that he was a spy himself, gaining access to court through White; a Catholic spy out to avenge his father? Yet now that he realized that this perspective could be put on his presence in the White household, Kit understood that it would be madness to admit who he was. No good could come of it.

'Where is the bag?' asked White as Kit walked in through the door, still dizzy from the shock of Walsingham's interview.

'The bag?' he said, momentarily baffled by the question. 'Oh – aye – the bag . . . It's not ready yet, sir.'

'Not ready?' said White. 'Really! And I sent you all that way. I'm sorry, Kit, but they assured me it would be ready. I shall have something to say about it when I see them.'

'No, sir,' said Kit, more sharply than he had intended. 'Not on my account.'

'As you wish,' said White, looking quizzically at his young servant. 'Is everything well, Kit?'

'Quite well,' said Kit, walking away. 'Everything is quite well, sir.'

Chapter 16

Kit lived in fear of Gabriel's appearance over the following weeks. The black-clad intelligencer would loom without warning from some alley or other and quiz Kit on the comings and goings at White's house. Kit was nothing if not adaptable, however, and in time he grew accustomed to Gabriel's appearances.

Gabriel and Walsingham clearly had no idea who he really was. Kit was just some urchin they could use for their own ends, that was all. Even his revulsion at spying on White faded as Kit came to realize that Gabriel – and presumably Walsingham – seemed more interested in White's visitors than in White himself.

Kit had feared that his master was the subject of Walsingham's interest and there would be some hideous repeat of history, where his life would once again be ruined by the work of Walsingham's intelligencers, but he allowed himself some morsel of comfort by believing that his information could actually exonerate White and free him from any taint of suspicion.

It was December now. As winter took hold of the city, snow fell on London, making the steep streets treacherous. Icicles glinted under the eaves outside the workshop as Kit gazed out of the study window. And Christmas came to the household of John White.

Though the strict and humourless Puritans frowned on the vulgar celebrations surrounding Christmas, White was of a more relaxed persuasion. His wife had always given gifts to her servants and he had carried this on in her memory.

He called all the members of his household together on Christmas Day and placed a small neatly wrapped parcel in front of each of them, blushing slightly as they pulled away the string and paper.

White had given Annie and Mrs Fisher a new pair of gloves each, with their initials sewn into them. Annie was so overcome with gratitude that she leaped up and kissed her master on the cheek, causing him to fluster and blush and making Mrs Fisher slap her on the backside and chuckle despite herself.

To Kit, White gave a cap of dark green velvet, which Kit placed self-consciously on his head, prompting Mrs Fisher to say that he looked as though he were gentry through and through. As Annie giggled, it all became too much for Kit and tears filled his eyes.

White had been invited to spend a day at the Queen's palace at Greenwich as part of her Christmas celebrations. He would rather have stayed at home and continued his work, but though he was sure the Queen would not notice his absence, he felt it was prudent to go. He asked Kit to accompany him and Kit's heart sank. He would have said no if he could have thought of any believable excuse. While he was in White's house, he could forget about Wylam and Raleigh and Walsingham and the whole lot of them, but he knew that they would all be there, buzzing round their beloved Queen. And so, a few days later, Kit found himself sitting in a ferry heading east – away from the City. As they passed the Tower of London, he saw the water lapping at Traitor's Gate and looked away downstream, unable to bear the memories it conjured up; his father had entered there, never to return.

Eventually the Thames swung south, with the flatlands of the Isle of Dogs to its east. At the bottom of a great lazy loop in the river sat Greenwich Palace. It was on the south side of the Thames, but well away from the stench of Southwark and Rotherhithe. Kit and White got off at the jetty and walked up to the gatehouse.

Again, Kit found himself wondering how many of the fine ladies and gentlemen who were milling about had known his parents. How many had danced with them, joked with them? How many had smiled one day and avoided their eyes the next? How many had cursed them as Catholics, as traitors?

Again, Raleigh was there with the American Indians, Harriot hovering in attendance. Raleigh was immaculately and expensively dressed as usual in a pale silvery grey doublet studded with pearls and a black velvet cloak. Kit had the feeling he stood next to the dourly dressed Harriot on purpose, just to make himself look better.

Kit caught tantalizing, distant glimpses of the Queen as she moved among her courtiers, her clothes spun through with gold thread and embroidered with gaily-coloured flowers, glowing like an exotic butterfly. Her orange hair was piled up in small curls above her forehead and hung about with pearls and jewels, which twinkled in the light from the windows.

The Christmas guests were treated to a performance by the Queen's Men, though Kit could see that this did not go down well with the Puritans like Walsingham, who would have banned all such frivolities if they had the chance.

Richard Tarlton, the Queen's jester, leaped about, calling to the audience to shout out any word they chose so that he could work it into a humorous poem. Kit raised an eyebrow. He had seen far funnier acts at the fair – Hugh had been funnier too. But the Queen collapsed into giggles every time, and anyone with any sense joined in.

After the performance Kit wandered about with White. Games of gleek and primero were in progress at the card tables. Kit stared wide-eyed at the pots of money that would pay an honest man's wages for years.

Not that honesty was especially evident among the card players. Kit was much impressed by the standard of cheating taking place, and he was not easily impressed.

He had seen the best coney-catchers in London ply their trade.

Young gentlemen chatted self-consciously to ladies-in-waiting, stopping immediately if the Queen happened to look in their direction, for it was the job of all the men there to appear as if they were courting the Queen, and the job of all ladies-in-waiting to think only of Her Majesty.

White stopped every five minutes to talk to somebody, and Kit grew more and more bored. The combination of the roaring fires and the great number of people made the rooms stuffy and airless. As White listened avidly to a thin man with an extraordinarily bushy beard who was telling him about a new plant he had discovered, Kit yawned so hard his jaw almost dislocated. He was suddenly nudged violently from behind and nearly fell over.

'Hell's teeth!' he said, forgetting where he was for a moment. 'Have a care!'

Kit noticed straight away that the sound bled from the room and that the epicentre of this new silence was right behind him. He squinted and closed his eyes, hardly daring to turn round. Who had he offended? Raleigh? Walsingham? Lord Burghley?

'On your knees, boy,' said a gruff voice nearby, and a hand pressed down on him until he dropped to one knee.

A woman now stood beside him. He could feel the touch of her embroidered dress against his hand and he turned to face her. Her long, pale face was as white as the enormous ruff that encircled her neck, giving it the appearance of a severed head on a wide dish. Kit stared, dumbstruck. A hand clamped itself to his shoulder and shoved him even lower to the floor.

'Come now,' said Elizabeth. 'Do you not know your Queen?'

'Yes. Of course. Sorry. I know you well, Your Majesty,' said Kit, looking up and squinting. 'I was at Tilbury when you was on the *Golden Hind* with Sir Francis Drake after he came back from around the world and he was knighted. Though you were a bit further off, Your Majesty.'

'Ah,' she said, smiling. 'What a day that was. Our Pirate cannot sadly be with us today. No doubt he is planning fresh adventures. Arise, sir, and let us take a look at you.' Kit staggered to his feet. 'Do we know you, boy?' asked Elizabeth, peering at him.

'No, Your Highness,' said Kit nervously. 'I am Master John White's assistant.'

'Ah,' she said. 'Master White is a clever man. You are a lucky lad indeed to have such a master.'

'I am, Your Majesty.'

Elizabeth smiled. 'We were born here, you know,' she said with a wave of her long pale hand.

Kit looked at the Queen, then at the throng of courtiers, and then back to the Queen. 'What? All of you?' he said.

There was a moment's delay as Elizabeth frowned

at Kit, trying to discern whether he was joking at her expense.

Kit felt a shiver run through him at that frown; the same shiver that had run through the spine of many others before him. But the Queen's long face first creased into a smile and then her mouth opened into a laugh; a gentle laugh that was not often heard, but was all the more pleasant for the rarity. After a second's delay, the court joined in.

'Your *Queen* was born here,' said Elizabeth. 'So, for that matter, was Queen Mary, our sister, rest her soul.' The mention of Bloody Mary sent a shiver through many of those present who could still smell the bonfires and the burning flesh of Mary's reign. 'Our father, King Henry, was born here.'

Those who could remember Henry VIII and his violent tempers did so with mixed feelings, none more so than Elizabeth herself. Henry had signed her mother's death warrant here also.

'Well,' said the Queen. 'We must away, for as you can see, our conversation has interrupted the dancing and there must be dancing. So we shall bid you *adieu*, Master . . .'

'Milton, Your Majesty. Kit Milton.'

The Queen smiled. 'We shall bid you *adieu*, Master Milton.'

White, who had sidled nearer and nearer to try and head off any problems, gave Kit a quick kick in the side of the leg and Kit took the hint, dropping to one knee again. The Queen tilted her head slightly and moved away towards her throne at the other end of the hall.

Kit stayed down until White whispered that it was safe to rise, and they walked over to stand by the wall, while the dancers took their places and began to move about the room in time to the music.

'I have never in my entire life had a conversation with Her Majesty,' said White sadly, staring off towards Elizabeth, who was now seated and clapping her hands to the beat. 'I have met her many times, of course, but we have never had an actual conversation.' He shook his head and sighed.

'I think you would be advised to keep a tighter rein on your servants,' said a voice behind them in a thick West Country accent. They turned to see Walter Raleigh looking decidedly peeved. He walked away before White could answer and stood at the centre of a knot of admirers, loudly holding forth. As the dance ended, his voice sounded like a shout in the sudden quiet.

When the music began again, the dancers took to the floor and the Queen began to tap a foot to the tune. Kit walked around the edges of the crowded room. White was standing next to Harriot and Raleigh's voice was still to be heard above the music. Kit could see several of the dancers frowning and muttering under their breaths. Then the Queen's foot stopped tapping and she narrowed her eyes in Raleigh's direction.

Raleigh was just about to speak again when the Queen interrupted, beckoning him over. He stopped immediately, bowing briefly to his listeners, and advanced towards the Queen, bowing so low his hand touched the dance floor.

The Queen bade him rise and stood up herself, leaning towards him, examining his face. The dancers nearby feigned an interest in their movements while trying to see what was about to happen.

'Why, Water,' said Elizabeth, using her pet name for Raleigh; a teasing reference to his accent. 'Do we see a mark upon your face?'

'A mark, Highness?'

'Yes,' said Elizabeth. 'It is a little dirt, nothing more.' She produced a handkerchief and moved towards him as a mother might to a child, but before she could wipe his face he did so himself.

'Thank you, Your Highness,' he said with a bow. 'There is no need.'

Elizabeth peered at him and Raleigh could not move while she did so. 'Yes,' she said finally. 'It seems to be gone.'

'Thank you again, Your Majesty,' he said, moving away backwards until he was in the centre of the room among the dancers. He bowed once more and left the room, the Earl of Leicester smiling wryly. Kit saw a half-smile play across Elizabeth's face as she returned to watching the dance. For a brief moment she looked in Kit's direction, and he could have sworn she winked at him.

Chapter 17

In a far shorter span of time than Kit could ever have imagined, his life with John White had become normal. His time on the streets of London with Hugh increasingly seemed like a dream, as his life with his parents had seemed a dream to him then. Only the thought of Gabriel troubled him but he had not contacted Kit for weeks. The longer he stayed away, the less of a spy and a double-dealer Kit felt.

Ever since having discovered that Kit could read, White had taken it upon himself to develop Kit's education – he claimed it would make him a better assistant if he were to be tutored – and this now continued apace. To Kit's great surprise he found that he had begun to look forward to White's lessons. It was as if his brain were a muscle that had gone to sleep. Now knowledge flooded back in as it awoke. Kit had always known he was crafty; you needed to be crafty to work a con. Now he realized with a growing pride that he also had intelligence.

In fact, his life with White was a constant education. As they walked through the streets, White would point here and there. Every steeple and tower was a prompt for a story, and Kit listened in rapt attention to tales of ancient battles and rebellions, kings and usurpers; of acts of heroism and of darkest treachery.

'I never have said how grateful I am you took me in, sir,' said Kit as they walked through the City one day. 'And I'm grateful for all you've taught me. Not many would have taken a thief into their household.'

White stopped and put a hand on each of Kit's shoulders. 'You work hard, Kit,' he said. 'And I have to say I have grown right fond of you. I like to think you feel likewise.'

'Yes, sir,' said Kit. 'I do.'

'Good. Then we need speak no more about the whys and wherefores of how you came to be in my household.'

Kit nodded and White clapped his hands together.

'Kit,' he began. 'I am required to sail to Plymouth on business and . . .'

'Yes, sir?'

'And I wondered if you would like to accompany me.'

'To Plymouth? The Plymouth where Drake lives? On a ship?'

White laughed. 'Aye. What do you say?'

'Yes, sir,' said Kit excitedly. 'I would. I definitely would.'

'But you must say nothing of this to anyone, Kit,' said White.

'Of course, sir,' said Kit. 'Not a word.'

Hugh was sharing a joke with two other actors when he saw Kit over their shoulders; he strode towards him, grinning. The old friends embraced and Hugh asked how his work was going. Kit told him that his master had decided to take him with him on a trip he had planned and that he had come to say farewell.

'A trip?' said Hugh a little jealously. 'You're to travel out of London?'

'Aye,' said Kit. 'My master has business he must attend to.' He was itching to tell Hugh that he was going to Plymouth, but he had already betrayed White by talking to Gabriel and he had no wish to break any more confidences.

'God, I'd love to travel,' said Hugh. 'Where are you going? Are you going far?'

When Kit said he could not say, Hugh frowned, but Kit insisted that he was bound to secrecy.

'You can tell me if it's near or far,' said Hugh.

'Far. Very far.'

'Norwich,' said Hugh, waving a finger in the air and grinning. 'I bet it's Norwich.'

'Why Norwich?' said Kit with a smile.

'I don't know. I just think it is, and since you're not telling me, then it's as good as any place.'

'Norwich it is, then.'

'Look, I've got to go, Kit,' Hugh said. 'Rehearsals.'

'I've got to go too,' said Kit. 'Good luck with everything, Hugh. And thanks.'

'For what?'

'For everything.'

Hugh smiled and they embraced again.

'Come on, Hugh!' shouted the man from the stage.

'Farewell, Kit,' he said.

'Aye,' said Kit. 'You too.'

Hugh walked across the pit towards the stage. Kit watched him go, feeling a little as he had done when Hugh had left him in the street to go acting. Hugh climbed to the stage and turned, waving and smiling.

'Good luck in Norwich!' he shouted.

As Kit was leaving the theatre, he saw out of the corner of his eye a black figure, more shadow than man, flit across the entrance to a courtyard opposite.

The effect was so horribly reminiscent of his recurring nightmare that Kit wondered if he might be dreaming. He edged towards the doorway and stepped through, peering into the darkening corners. A cat hissed and ran past him to escape.

Kit could see no one, but there were barrels and carts littered about, with many places to hide. A door creaked back and forth on its hinges at the far end as if recently opened, but Kit had the distinct feeling that this impression was intended. Someone was watching him, he was sure of it. It took all his courage to turn his back and walk away.

Chapter 18

The day finally came to set sail, and Kit and White had said their farewells at the house. Although they would not be gone for long, Kit was touched to see how emotional everyone became at their departure. Eleanora and Ananais had come to see them off. Eleanora held back tears as she said goodbye to her father, while Ananais slapped Kit on the back and wished him luck.

Kit was almost squeezed to death by Mrs Fisher, who then proceeded to rub his face between her huge hands as if it were a ball of dough. Annie said a choked farewell on the doorstep, her bottom lip quivering and her eyes sparkling with tears, and then suddenly lunged at Kit and hugged him, causing Ananais to chortle and slap him on the back again.

White had hired a cart to take their things to the river and Kit had just loaded a couple of bags when he was suddenly aware of a woman standing next to him in the dawn's half-light.

'Can I help you?' he asked, taking half a step back.

'Kit!' hissed the woman. 'It's me, you fool.'

Kit stepped back again, screwing up his eyes and peering at the strangely familiar face caked in white make-up. Then a great grin ripped across his face.

'Hugh?' he said.

'Yes,' said Hugh, stepping closer. 'But keep your voice down. I'm risking my life coming here.'

'I'll say you are,' said Kit. 'Dressed like that!'

'Shut up, Kit! Listen. There was a man looking for you. He came to the theatre. He must have followed you and seen us together. He . . .' Hugh looked away and closed his eyes. When he looked at Kit again, he had tears in his eyes.

'You told him who I was, didn't you?' said Kit angrily. 'What happened to "I'll never tell anyone, Kit"?'

'I swear I didn't mean to, Kit,' said Hugh. 'He got me drunk and then he threatened to . . .' He put his face in his hands.

Kit had never seen Hugh so distressed. The anger went out of him and he patted Hugh on the shoulder. 'How did you know where I lived anyway?'

'I bumped into Blind Peter,' said Hugh. 'He said he'd seen you and followed you here.'

Kit shook his head, trying to think. 'This man?' he said. 'Was he lean, short hair and beard, dressed all in black?'

'Aye,' said Hugh. 'You know him?'

'Aye. I know him all right.'

'Kit?' said a voice behind him, making both boys jump.

'Master White,' said Kit. 'I didn't see you there.'

White was staring at Hugh; his appearance was not improved by the light from White's lantern.

'I must go,' said Hugh, backing away before turning and hurrying into the shadows. 'Take care in Norwich.'

'You certainly have some colourful acquaintances,' said White, peering after Hugh. 'Come along. It is time to leave.'

For a moment, Kit could only stop and stare after Hugh, trying to take it in. Trying to absorb the fact that Gabriel, and through him, Walsingham, would now know who he was and that he had withheld information from them. '*Let that be the last lie*' the letter had said.

But what was Gabriel up to? What reason could he have for asking about him in the first place? Did he suspect him of something? Now that he knew that Kit was the son of an executed traitor, would he think that he was a Catholic spy?

'Come on, Kit, we need to go,' said White.

Kit nodded distractedly.

They caught a boat near Billingsgate and headed downriver past the Tower. On the east side of the bridge, the Thames snaked away towards the sea and to a world beyond, which Kit only knew about through the cargoes that spewed out at the quaysides destined for the markets and workhouses of London.

The great river widened and deepened, and the little

ferry boats to the west of the bridge were now replaced
by fishing boats and sail-barges, cargo ships, barks and
galleons, a forest of masts growing up on either side.

They got off at Wapping, climbing onto a rickety jetty
and up a greasy green ladder to the docks, where carts
rolled by laden with sacks and kegs; here even Kit, who
was used to the jabber of the City, had to adjust to the
din of shouting and yelling, the thundering of cartwheels
on cobbles and the mournful groan of rolling barrels.

'This way,' said White, pointing along the waterfront,
and they shoved their way through the mêlée – Kit
groaning under the weight of their bags – until they
stood alongside a large ship.

'So, Kit,' said White with a flourish. 'Here she is
– the beauty that will take us to Plymouth, the *Tiger*; a
gift from Her Majesty to Sir Walter.' (Raleigh was Sir
Walter now, thanks to another gift from the Queen on
Twelfth Night.)

'The Queen's damned sweet on Raleigh, that's for
sure.'

'Be quiet!' said White angrily. 'Never say anything like
that in public again. Do you understand? Do not even
think it!'

'Sorry, sir,' said Kit, shocked at the anger displayed by
the normally mild-mannered White.

'People get killed for less,' said White, calming a little
but still looking around. 'For much less.'

The docks were bustling as the *Tiger* was readied for
her journey to Plymouth. White told Kit it was to

be captained by a kinsman of Raleigh's: Sir Richard Grenville, yet another West Country mariner and adventurer. Kit recognized Simon Fernandez at the captain's side, the navigator's skills clearly in demand on even this short voyage. Kit helped White to take their bags aboard, then his master sent him ashore again to buy them both a jug of beer. As Kit was walking towards the tavern, the voice he was dreading hissed out from a warehouse doorway. He turned to see Gabriel leaning against a wooden post, barely visible in the gloom.

'Kit,' he said again. 'Come . . . here . . .'

Gabriel's voice was coming out in short gasps, as if forming words was causing him pain. Kit thought about running and taking his chances among the crowds, but as he was trying to make his mind up, Gabriel slumped to the floor.

Kit cursed to himself as his feet took him towards the fallen figure rather than towards the *Tiger*. He crouched down beside the intelligencer and saw that his hand clutched his side. Gabriel coughed, and blood bubbled at his lips and trickled down his face.

'I . . . am . . . dead,' he panted. 'But . . . I must . . . speak . . .' His voice was getting fainter.

'Who did this?' asked Kit.

Gabriel shook his head. 'It . . . is . . . a . . . dangerous . . . profession,' he said. 'Did . . . not . . . see.'

'You know who I am, don't you?' said Kit.

Gabriel nodded and reached out to grab Kit's arm as a spasm of pain went through his body. 'I have . . . a

137

confession,' he gasped. 'I . . . arrested . . . your father. That day . . . That day of the masked ball . . .'

Kit shook his arm away angrily, any trace of pity gone.

'It was . . . me who . . . found the letters that incriminated him,' Gabriel continued.

'And this is what you've come to tell me?' said Kit.

Gabriel grabbed his arm again. 'Listen . . . Listen . . . to me. I . . . believe . . . your father . . . was . . . was . . . *innocent*.'

Kit stared at him, wondering at first if he had misheard. 'What?'

'Letters . . . forged.'

'But he confessed,' whispered Kit, turning nervously at the sound of laughing sailors nearby.

Gabriel grinned horribly, his teeth stained with blood. 'I . . . would . . . confess . . . to being . . . Joan of . . . Arc . . . if racked,' he said. 'Confessed to . . . save your . . . mother . . . from . . . rack.'

Kit screwed his eyes shut and clenched his teeth in a silent scream of pain.

'Forgive . . . me,' said Gabriel.

'No!' hissed Kit.

Gabriel slumped back and nodded resignedly.

'How long have you known that he was innocent?' whispered Kit.

'Two . . . years,' said Gabriel, his voice now almost inaudible against the clatter and clamour of the quayside. 'But the . . . man . . . who . . .' His voice

138

trailed away.

'The man who what?' said Kit, shaking him.

'Who put . . . letters there. Must . . . think . . . we still believe . . . your father . . . guilty.'

'Who is it?' said Kit. 'Who did it?'

Gabriel shook his head and coughed, his breath rattling in his throat. 'Do . . . not . . . know . . .'

Kit thumped the wooden post, in a sudden realization. 'The devil!' he hissed. 'There was a man in a devil mask.'

'What's that?' said Gabriel, grabbing at Kit and using all his strength to pull himself off the floor. 'What . . . did you . . . say?'

'I have a nightmare,' said Kit. 'I've had it many times. A memory of that day. I see a man . . .'

'In . . . your parents' . . . bedroom?'

'Aye,' said Kit. 'I was hiding in a linen chest and could see out of the keyhole. He wore a black devil mask.'

Kit could see by Gabriel's wide-eyed expression that something about what he had just said had struck a chord with the dying intelligencer. His eyes flicked back and forth in an expression that was a mixture of incredulity and revelation. He moved his lips, trying to form a word. A name, perhaps.

'What is it?' asked Kit, pulling him forward so that he might hear. '*Who* was it?'

Gabriel's mouth moved silently several times before he finally made a sound. 'Why?' he whispered, then fell back, his eyes open.

Kit stared at the dead man for a few moments before he realized how it would look if someone were to find him with the body; how it would appear to Walsingham if Kit were connected with this death. He prised away Gabriel's fingers, which still gripped his sleeve, stood up and left the warehouse, walking with the thief's practised nonchalance.

Finally, Grenville barked his orders, the mooring ropes were cast off and the *Tiger* set sail. For the first time Kit felt the wind filling the sails and pulling at the rigging like a horse tugging at the reins. He could feel the power of it gripping the whole ship. The timbers seemed to flex and tense like muscles. The ship in dock had been asleep. Now it woke into life.

They headed slowly down the Thames, leaving London far behind them, the reflected sky distorted by their rippling wake. The Thames, which had seemed mighty enough in London, now grew into a giant, pushing north and south into the flatlands of Essex and Kent.

Kit had never been further east than Woolwich, and knew nothing more about the places he saw than the names White gave them as they passed by: Purfleet, Northfleet, Tilbury, Canvey Island and then out into the wide mouth of the Thames, past the Isle of Sheppey and Herne Bay, the open sea stretching ahead of them and south round the headland of Margate, past Ramsgate, Deal and Dover and on into the Narrow Sea.

They sailed along the south coast to Plymouth, making slow headway against the prevailing westerly wind, the sea lanes busy with ships bound for London and the southern ports, France and the Low Countries.

Kit stood at the prow with White, his mind reeling with thoughts of what Gabriel had said before he died. Could it really be true that his father was innocent after all; that he had been executed on a lie, on a trick?

The pain he had always felt at being the son of a traitor was now replaced by a searing sense of injustice. He had needlessly blamed his father for all these years and had shunned all memory of him; now he felt as though he had betrayed him.

Gabriel and Walsingham must have allowed themselves to be duped in their rabid hunt for Catholic plotters and Spanish spies. His hatred for them was now surpassed only by his hatred of the devil-masked villain who had planted those forged letters. And what had Gabriel meant by that last whispered 'Why?' Kit made a silent oath that should he ever discover the identity of that masked man, he would avenge his parents; he would kill him no matter who he was, no matter what the cost.

Chapter 19

Kit and White eventually found themselves ashore in the West Country town of Plymouth. Kit marvelled at the novelty of all he saw and heard, being particularly amused by the strange lilting language of the locals, which he could barely understand as English.

Plymouth was the town to which Drake had returned after his circumnavigation of the globe in the autumn of 1580. Drake was Lord Mayor of Plymouth, but to Kit's sore disappointment the famous sea dog was away planning another of his hell-raising adventures and was not at home, though Kit had insisted that they look at his house. He stood gazing up in awe and, had he not been pulled away by White, would have stayed there for the rest of the morning.

They had only been in Plymouth for a couple of days when White woke Kit early – on the 9th of April, as Kit recalled later – and led him to Plymouth harbour. White carried a lantern, which swayed back and forth as he walked and made their shadows lurch about drunkenly on the walls of the houses they passed.

Kit's eyes were slowly getting accustomed to the gloom as he followed White down the steep winding street, curling away from them towards the quay. They had been staying in a tavern near St Andrew's Church while White was conducting his business: he had explained to Kit that sleeping on a ship was not something anyone should do unless they absolutely had to.

Traders were already moving about at the market cross, setting up stalls and putting out baskets of fish as they were hauled up by cart from the quay. Kit followed White as the streets fell away down towards the harbour. The castle loomed over the quayside, its towers just beginning to stand out against the dark skies to the west.

Even before sunrise, the harbour was a hive of activity. Kit could see lanterns moving this way and that, and silhouetted figures thronged the quay and clambered over the ships moored there. He heard the sound of sailors calling to their fellows mixing with the bleating of sheep, the lowing of cattle, the squawking of ducks and chickens.

A man sidled up to them from the shadows. He held up a bag that was sewn up and tied with a rope. Something inside was leaping about and trying to get out.

'Wind? Buy a fair wind, sir?' said the man. 'You'll wish you had when you find yourself becalmed.'

'If we do,' said a sailor nearby, 'we'll need more than a

rabbit in a bag to move us. Now get off with you!' He kicked out at the cunning-man and he scuttled away into the shadows.

'Kit,' said White as they came to the harbourside, 'I must ask you to make a decision. My business in Plymouth is now concluded, but I need to tell you of my plans and to ask you if you wish to be part of them. Do you see that ship over there?'

Kit followed the line of White's pointing finger and saw a three-masted silhouette. 'Aye, sir,' he said, confused.

'She is called the *Fox*, and is sailing for London in three hours. The captain will know who you are—'

'What do you mean, sir?' asked Kit. 'Do you not want me with you?'

'Aye,' said White. 'But you may not want to be with me. For it is my fate now to be part of a great adventure, Kit. I have told you of the lands in the Americas which it is our right and our duty to colonize. The Queen has given her consent to such a venture and has even given one of her own ships – the *Tiger* – for the fleet.'

'Fleet?' said Kit wide-eyed. 'Americas? You mean you plan to start the colony in Virginia?'

'Aye, lad,' said White, dropping his voice and looking about him. 'If you wish to return to London, then the *Fox* will carry you home, and you would of course be welcome at my house. What is it to be, Kit? London or the New World?'

Kit thought of Gabriel. Walsingham would be sure to

discover he had been murdered. Maybe he would even think Kit was his killer. In any event, there was nothing to lure him back to London and a world of adventure waited for him in the west.

'The New World, sir!' he said.

'Excellent!' said White. 'We have a fleet of five ships crewed by seasoned mariners, a force of men, a band of young gentlemen who thirst for adventure and a party of those – like myself – who possess some useful skill. There will be others you will recognize. Master Harriot is here, as is Master Ganz, whose knowledge of metals and minerals is second to none.' Kit curled his lip and White smiled, slapping him on the back. 'Come on! What say we go aboard?'

Kit followed White up the gangplank and onto the *Tiger*. Once aboard the ship, their main task seemed to be to keep out of the way. The *Tiger* had been relatively empty when they had sailed to Plymouth, but now every square inch of the ship appeared to be in use and every step they took only led them into collision with another set of muttering sailors or cursing artisans trying to load their equipment into the hold.

Eventually they found a place to stand, with their backs pinned up against the forecastle. It was like standing in the street on market day, with animals complaining and men rolling barrels and hurling down sacks as they loaded the ship's hold. Kit was just thinking that there was enough food to feed an army when that army seemed to appear at the top of the gangplank.

Dozens of men thundered aboard the *Tiger*. Breastplates and helmets shimmered dimly and a brawl almost broke out when one of the soldiers ripped a hole in a sail with the point of his halberd. Heavy bundles clanged and clattered noisily as they were dropped on the deck.

Kit could see they carried muskets. He had seen muskets before, but had never seen one fired. He still found it hard to understand how these great hunks of metal worked. They looked too heavy even to lift, let alone aim at anything. In fact, so heavy were they that the soldiers had to carry a stand with them to rest the barrel on when they came to fire them.

A soldier nearby carried a pistol. Again Kit had seen these before in London, but had never actually seen one used. Could they really hurl a metal ball so hard and fast it could kill a man? Kit stared at it, fascinated. There seemed nothing about it to hint at its deadliness; there was no blade or point. It seemed more like a tool than a weapon.

Kit had no fondness for soldiers at the best of times, but there was something particularly sinister about the appearance of these men, some featureless in the gloom, some lit by the glow of shipboard lanterns. It felt as though they were about to sail into battle rather than found a colony.

A low growling took Kit's attention away from the soldiers and their muskets. He peered into the darkness beyond a lantern hanging from the mainmast, but could not make sense of the curious tangle of heads and legs that seemed to be coming towards him until they came into the light.

Three bull mastiffs lumbered into view on thick chains bound to spiked collars, snarling and snapping at anything that moved. They looked like the three-headed dog White had told Kit about which guarded the gates of the Underworld. Kit stepped back out of the way as they passed by on their way to the hold below.

Dawn broke, and as the clouds in the eastern sky soaked up the pink light of the rising sun like bloody swabs on a surgeon's platter, they sailed out of Sutton Harbour, past the fort on Drake's Island, out into the Sound and on to the sea. They were on their way!

Most of the men on board were West Country men, like Sir Richard himself. Plymouth wives and children had come to the quay to bid farewell, and now Kit could see the soldiers and sailors looking out towards the rolling hills and the villages and hamlets of their loved ones.

To the east, the water shimmered in the light and seemed almost metallic, as if the Narrow Sea were formed of molten silver. To the west, the sky was still clinging to night and the sea dissolved into mysterious darkness.

The five ships sailed in a line: the *Tiger*, the *Elizabeth*, the *Dorothy*, the *Lion* and the *Roebuck*. The *Tiger* towed a single-masted pinnace. Kit was just imagining what a sight they must be making for the waking folk of Devon and Cornwall as they passed when he became aware of someone standing next to him. It was the American Wanchese.

'Good day, sir,' said Kit, no longer alarmed at the sight of the foreigner.

Wanchese smiled, seemingly amused at being addressed as sir. 'Look sad,' he said.

Kit had not realized that he looked sad, but recognized now that he did feel downhearted. 'I have never been so far from home,' he answered in explanation.

'Home,' said Wanchese, nodding. 'Yes. Home.' Then instead of looking back towards the retreating coastline of England, Wanchese turned towards the prow, his eyes narrowing as if searching for something on the horizon, his head tilted back slightly as if he were sniffing the air for a familiar scent.

The fleet sailed on, the craggy coast of Cornwall still visible in the growing light of morning. Fishing boats and smaller craft hugged the shore, their sails glowing apricot in the dawn light.

Gulls whirled about the ship as if they were kites being flown from the deck, wobbling in the air, adjusting themselves to the changes in the currents before suddenly falling back to another position and swooping up, turning left and right, crying forlornly and looking hopefully towards the galley and any waste that might be tossed overboard by the ship's cook.

A large ship appeared as if from nowhere, heading east towards the sun. It passed between the *Tiger* and the

land, and Kit could see great rips in the sails as if they
had been mauled by a giant cat.

'They've had some weather,' said a sailor standing
nearby.

'Aye,' said another. 'But at least they had it heading
home.'

It unsettled Kit to hear the mariners sound so
apprehensive. As the last sight of Land's End faded from
view, he felt as if he were falling from a great height. It
seemed to him that they were launching themselves into
some gaping void and his stomach fluttered.

Land's End: the very words unnerved him. Kit knew
that the world was round. He was not one of those who
thought Sir Francis Drake had made his voyage up. He
knew the world was round. The only thing was, just at
that moment, as they sailed towards the far horizon, the
world did not feel round.

White had been speaking to Harriot, but now he
came to stand alongside Kit, and when Grenville strode
past, he stopped him and asked where Raleigh was;
neither he nor Harriot had seen him board the ship and
they had been under the impression he would be sailing
on the Tiger.

'Ah,' said Grenville, looking a little embarrassed. 'I am
afraid that there has been rather a change of plan in that
respect.'

'Sir?' said White.

'I am afraid Sir Walter shall not be accompanying
you.'

'What?' said White. 'But he is the governor. It is his enterprise.'

'I realize that,' said Grenville, frowning. 'But the Queen has forbidden him to go.'

Kit had to stop himself smirking, remembering Elizabeth aiming to wipe Raleigh's face as though he were a child.

'Forbidden? But surely . . . ?'

'Master White!' said Grenville loudly. 'I am to be admiral of the fleet and military commander of the expedition. Master Ralph Lane will be governor of the colony itself. I do not wish to speak of this further. Do I make myself understood?'

'Perfectly,' said White.

'Excellent,' said Grenville, smiling cheerlessly. 'Then if you will excuse me, I have matters to attend to.'

'Raleigh has become a plaything,' said White, almost to himself. 'He pays the price of all his fawning now. If he is not careful, he will become a mere bauble that the Queen picks up to amuse herself with. And she will just as easily throw him away.' He shook his head, then seemed suddenly to realize how critical he had been of his patron and looked about him nervously. He smiled at Kit, his face a little flushed, and walked away, muttering to himself.

Kit stared out to sea. All sight of land was gone. The Narrow Sea had been a wider, mightier Thames in comparison. This was the real thing. This was the wide and monstrous Atlantic Ocean, devourer of ships and mariners' graveyard. It would be many weeks before he saw land again—

A hand came down on his shoulder, making him jump.

'Ahoy there, shipmate!'

He turned to see Henry Wylam grinning at him. 'Master Wylam!' he said. 'It's good to see you, sir! I didn't know you were coming.'

'Nor I, Kit, to be honest,' said Wylam with a forlorn sigh. 'Sir Christopher had a sudden urge that I should go, and you do not argue with Hatton, so here I am, worst luck.'

'Well I'm glad,' said Kit. 'I'm glad you're here.'

Wylam smiled, instantly regaining his usual good humour. 'Aye. Things could be worse. Anything is better than swapping pleasantries at Durham House.'

Kit nodded.

'Has White told you that we are bound for the Americas?'

'Aye,' said Kit with a huge grin.

'I can't say I share your enthusiasm, friend,' Wylam said. 'But then I've been to Ireland and it has to be an improvement on that hell-hole.'

Almost as soon as they lost sight of land, White had begun to turn grey and, just as on their earlier voyage from London to Plymouth, he had gone below, smiling weakly and reminding Kit how he suffered from sea-sickness. Kit, on the other hand, was delighted to find that he suffered no such ill effects and he spent most of the first day on deck, trying his best to keep out of the way of the sailors. He found the world below oppressive, filled as it was with surly soldiers playing dice, telling bawdy jokes and cleaning their muskets.

The artisans whose job it would be to build and maintain the colony were already grumbling about life aboard. They sat about on sacks and barrels, drinking beer and kicking out at the rats that scuttled among them. Sheep bleated mournfully and were answered by the bilious grunts of pigs and strangled squawks of chickens.

As the sun set and lanterns were lit about the ship, Kit realized suddenly how tired he was, and when White announced that he was going to his bed, Kit said that he would do the same.

White had explained to Kit that because Kit was a servant he would have to sleep with the artisans and soldiers rather than with the gentlemen, and so he made for the ladder leading to the lower decks and climbed down into the gloom, the light of a lantern glimmering dimly. He was taken aback by the sight of men sleeping in the air, on hammocks suspended above the cannons, and decided that he would make do with the deck, reluctantly taking a space next to Ganz, the dour mineral man. All the lanterns were extinguished, except for one that cast a morbid glow across the scene.

As the men around Kit began to settle down for the night, an old sailor entertained them all by telling tales of voyages he had taken in his young days and stories he had heard from other mariners in ports around the world. They were tall tales and there were occasional snorts of disbelief – most of them from Ganz – but any interruptions were good-humoured.

'America is a cursed land, if you ask me,' Ganz said. 'No good has ever come to any Englishman who has ever set foot there.'

The talk of curses and storms and shipwrecks did not help Kit fall asleep, any more than did the alien noises that filled the darkness around him: the rhythmic creaking of the ship's timbers, the wheezing, sighing sound of the sea against the hull, the clanking of lanterns as they swung with the roll of the ship, the scuttling of the rats, the snoring of his shipmates.

But eventually he did sleep. He slept and he dreamed. He dreamed he was walking the deck towards Grenville's cabin. But when Kit entered the cabin, he no longer seemed to be aboard a ship. He was in fact back in his parents' house again; back in the old dream.

There were people laughing and joking, dressed in colourful costumes and wearing all kinds of masks; some grotesque, some beautiful. He walked past the painting of St Sebastian, up the stairs and to his parents' room. Again he climbed into the chest to hide. Again he peered through the tiny keyhole. Again the masked man turned to face him with his hideous devil face, made all the more hideous now by the knowledge that behind that mask were hidden the features of the man whose scheming had killed his parents. But now Kit noticed – where he had never noticed before – that the masked man held several folded pieces of paper in his hand; the forged letters that would trick his father to the block.

Then all of a sudden, the sides of the chest rocked and water began to come in; slowly at first, but then spraying and bursting through and flooding the chest. Kit tried to escape but the lid would not budge. The water rose up around him until he was completely submerged and desperately holding his breath; waking panting and coughing as if he had been pulled from the sea.

Chapter 20

'How did you sleep?' asked Wylam the next morning as he walked over to Kit, who was staring out to sea. Kit turned, bleary-eyed. 'Oh dear!' said Wylam, laughing. 'Not so comfortable among the cannons, eh?'

'No, sir,' said Kit, squinting up at Wylam, who stood in front of the sun.

Wylam laughed again and slapped him on the back, but then saw that something was troubling the boy. 'Is there something amiss?' he asked, playing with the large silver ring he wore on his right hand.

'No,' said Kit. 'I just . . . I just need to think.'

Wylam nodded. 'I'll speak to you anon, when you have had time to come back to life.'

He walked away, and a sudden impulse came over Kit to call him back and tell him about Gabriel; to share the truth about his life; but he stopped himself, turning back to the sea and to his thoughts.

The dream had reawakened thoughts of Gabriel. Kit was sure that the intelligencer knew the identity of the masked man, but if he did, that knowledge had died with him. The only other witness to those events seemed to be Kit himself. Though it pained him to admit it, he felt he would never know who the masked man was. He also had to admit that he would rather live with the pain of knowing that his father had died on the basis of a lie than continue to believe that lie to be true. His father was no traitor and his anger – for so long directed at his father – could now be aimed at Walsingham and the masked devil who had tricked him.

Gabriel had made him love his father again, and for that he was thankful. But that love only made the pain of the loss more raw; and so Kit seesawed between these emotions of anger and sadness, love and loss; he barely spoke a word to anyone.

White was still complaining of seasickness and had spent most of the time below deck; Kit fetched him his meals and helped him to wash, but was glad to leave the fustiness of the cabin and come up on deck once his duties were concluded. He needed air. He wanted to feel the wind in his face. He stood on deck as often as he could, leaning on the gunwales and losing himself in the wide ocean.

At first his thoughts were filled with London and with Hugh and with Walsingham, with Hampton Court and Greenwich, and with the Queen. But gradually the ocean washed these thoughts away and Kit could stand as if in a trance, not thinking at all; his mind's horizon as wide and empty as the sea's.

The *Tiger* sailed on, the other ships in their small fleet always within view, all heading south towards the Canary Islands. Whenever there was a break in work or any excuse presented itself, Kit was surprised to see whistles and fiddles, bagpipes and drums being brought out and played. The mariners would dance and prance like children at a May Fair, though their bawdy songs were shocking even to Kit's calloused ears.

The day-to-day life on the *Tiger* was spartan, but no worse than the lives of many city folk, and certainly no worse than Kit had known in his time on the streets. Not that the finer things in life were completely absent for all on board.

Grenville's cabin would have graced many a fine house, and Kit was amazed to see that he dined off silver and gold plates and drank from a silver cup. A trumpeter announced dinner with a piercing blast on a clarion; a straight trumpet whose tortured screech made the entire crew wince.

Kit could not stop looking out to sea, fascinated by the unaccustomed view of wide, open nothingness; the expanse of watery desert unbroken beyond the boundaries of their small fleet. All his memories were of being squeezed between crowds and shadowed by overhanging buildings. Never in his life had he been able to see so far. The horizon had always been hidden from view; now it lay stretched out like the fabled edge of the world that Kit reminded himself, again and again, could not really be there.

The edge of the world might be a myth, but there were plenty of other things preying on Kit's mind. He had heard there were monsters in the sea; great monsters which could devour whole ships or smash them to splinters. There were mermen and mermaids who had the tails of fish and lived beneath the sea. There were beasts so huge that men landed on them, mistaking them for islands, only to have the sleeping monster rear up when they lit a fire on its back. The monster would swallow the party whole and wreck their ship, disappearing into the inky depths from which it had risen. There were monstrous serpents as long as the Thames; murderous sea-dragons that cut through the ocean waves, their massive heads filled with jagged teeth, craning out of the water like swans and moving at a speed no ship could outrun.

Even if a ship did reach land safely, there were all manner of savages to contend with: dog-headed men, men with no heads and their eyes and nose and mouth embedded in their chests. There were cannibals that hunted men like beasts and cooked them alive before feasting on their carcasses.

Kit had seen drawings of these wonders, and there were countless stories of sailors who had survived such encounters and lived to tell the tale. He and Hugh had once gone to see a mermaid they had on display at Bartholomew Fair but they had not been able to afford – or steal – the entrance fee.

Kit had also read grisly accounts of men who had fallen into the hands of the Spanish and languished in stinking dungeons or, worse still, been tortured by the Inquisition. It suddenly struck Kit that for all he had to keep his Catholic upbringing a secret among these men, to the Spanish he would simply be English and would share the same fate as his shipmates.

As he was staring out to sea one morning, these thoughts filling his head, Wylam walked up beside him. He seemed to read his mind.

'It is an awesome place, this world of water,' he said.

'Aye, sir,' said Kit. 'It is.'

Wylam slapped him on the back. 'But how like Argonauts we are,' he said.

'Like what, sir?'

'Argonauts, Kit,' said Wylam. 'It is a story from Ancient Greece. A hero called Jason gathered about him other heroes and sailed into the unknown to capture the fabled Golden Fleece.'

'Any thieves?' asked Kit wryly.

Wylam smiled. 'I suppose in a way they were all thieves,' he said, 'as their mission was to steal the Golden Fleece.'

'Greetings,' said a voice behind them. They turned to see White smiling weakly.

'It's good to see you up and about, sir,' said Kit.

'Did I hear you say something about the Golden Fleece, Master Wylam?'

'Aye, Master White,' said Wylam. 'I was likening our venture to that of the Argonauts, but your lad here does not know the story.'

'Well, we must put that right,' said White. The ship rolled steeply and he took a deep breath. 'But I must lie down again, Kit. I shall tell you the story of the Argonauts another time.'

'I look forward to it, sir,' said Kit, smiling as he watched White stagger away.

Chapter 21

The days passed slowly. White began to appear on deck more and more, looking even paler than usual, wrapped in a blanket and ceaselessly jotting in his notebook. Kit was familiar with his master's skill in drawing, but there was always a knot of gentlemen or soldiers craning to see his work, following his gaze and gasping in amazement when they realized that he was setting down in line what was there in the life in front of them. White feigned annoyance at the distraction but Kit could see he was flattered by the attention.

Kit was at hand to fetch and carry anything his master needed, but there was little real work to do and he was left with plenty of time to watch the sailors go about their work, looking on in awe-struck admiration as they scaled the rigging and went to their tasks as casually as if their feet had been firmly planted on solid ground instead of high up in the air on a rocking ship. He could see Fernandez too, consulting with Grenville and constantly checking his maps or staring at the stars as he plotted their course through this vast ocean. Ganz – the mineral man – was rarely to be seen, preferring to spend his time below decks.

The soldiers also mainly stayed below, their voices joining with the bleats and grunts of the livestock in the hold. Occasionally Kit would hear the grating bark of the mastiffs as they tested their chains, aroused to black temper by something or other.

The gentlemen – including Ralph Lane, the appointed governor once the fleet reached Virginia – strode purposefully but redundantly about the deck, usually getting in the way. They dressed as though they were going to the Curtain Theatre instead of the other side of the Atlantic. Even Wylam looked more suited to Westminster than to a ship, though he had an easy-going charm that few of the other gentleman adventurers possessed. He seemed equally at ease with the sailors and soldiers, Harriot and the other gentlemen, Kit and Grenville.

When the entertainment value of the ship itself was exhausted, there was always the view and, landlubber that he was, Kit found that fascinating. He watched the ocean for hours at a time, hypnotized by the flickering surface.

One day a bird flew into sight, gliding along, low across the waves, disappearing every now and then behind a crest, one wingtip almost touching the water.

'Storm bird.'

Kit turned at the voice. It was Grenville. 'Sir?' he answered, surprised to be spoken to by the captain.

'We're in for some weather,' Grenville said, walking away.

Sure enough, the wind that had been blowing steadily for two days began to gust, making the sails crackle and snap and the rigging creak and whine, as taut as lute strings.

The sailors too strained at the ropes, heaving and straining, the sinews and muscles of their arms mirroring the bloated sails and stretched hemp ropes. They looked like rebellious puppets come to life and pulling at their strings in defiance.

Kit faced the sea, which was beginning to churn and heave, the wave-tops frothing. The gusts began to grow like blasts from a bellows, the sky at the horizon became leaden and dark clouds rose up like black ink bleeding across wet paper. Suddenly he was sent stumbling sideways by a sudden kick of wind that struck him as solidly as if he had been hit by a sack of corn. For the first time, he could see concern on the faces of the mariners. Every so often they would leave off whatever they were doing and look to the sails and to the sky with tight lips and furrowed brows.

Then the storm came.

It bubbled up along the western horizon and hurtled towards the fleet in a solid mass, hitting them like skittles and hurling them hopelessly out of formation. The crew of the *Tiger* swarmed about the deck, answering the order to shorten the sails and wrestling to control the bucking and rearing ship.

The waves grew into a range of watery mountains, stretching away as far as Kit could see. The sky was so black now that the sea seemed to glow in comparison, but it was the sickly, clouded glow of a dead eye, pale green and grey.

Kit stood near the base of the mainmast and watched the sailors in the rigging as they climbed the main channels, each man moving in rhythm, hand and foot up the ratlines, climbing into the black sky like Jacob climbing his ladder to Heaven.

The sails flapped like monstrous birds as the ship listed wildly to starboard and then pitched into a wave that broke with a crash over the beak head at the prow, drenching the forecastle and bringing the *Tiger* to a standstill by almost turning her about.

Kit clung onto ropes and watched as the other ships from the fleet fought with the wind, leaning almost into the frothing waves, wrestling and grappling with the force of it.

The *Tiger* fought too. For all his dark temper, Grenville was a fine sailor and rallied his crew against the storm as if they were going into battle against a Spanish galleon. He struggled to make himself heard above the roar of the winds, but he seemed to be everywhere, holding onto the rigging with one hand and waving and pointing with the other as he urged the men on.

Then the *Tiger*'s pinnace was overwhelmed by the huge waves and sank beneath the boiling waters, its small crew taken with it. Several of the sailors ran to look, pointing at the stricken vessel. One man shouted that the voyage was cursed. He had barely spoken the words when he was knocked headlong onto the deck.

'The next man who talks of curses,' yelled Grenville, 'will be hanging from the bowsprit all the way to the Americas. Now get to work, you bilge rats, unless you want us to join the pinnace at the bottom of the sea!'

The men returned to work without hesitation, and though their actions were sluggish and reluctant at first, soon they were lost in their tasks.

Grenville stood scowling from the stern of the ship, holding a rope with one hand for support and gripping his sword hilt with the other, occasionally looking up at the sky as if he might draw his sword at any moment and do battle with the storm.

There was a crack like a musket being fired and Kit looked up to see a piece of the mainmast falling towards him. He just managed to leap aside as the huge shattered piece of wood smashed through the bulwarks.

At the same moment the ship lurched sideways, a great wave crashing across the deck and knocking Kit off his feet. The ship rocked, the deck tilting at an acute angle and the wave rolled back towards the dark and mountainous sea, flooding through the gaping hole in the bulwarks – carrying Kit as unwilling flotsam.

As he hurtled towards the waves, Kit managed to grab

a rope, and though his palms were skinned by the rough hemp and his shoulders were almost pulled from his sockets, he held on, smacking wetly against the hull like a fish on a line. He looked up. He could see the sailors in the rigging, climbing up the main lines like so many spiders on a web, the masts lurching and staggering like drunken giants. He yelled, but even as he did so he knew the futility of it: his voice was drowned out by the roar of wind and sea.

He began to lose his grip and the salt from the waves that leaped about him stung his bleeding hands. He could not hold on much longer and the thought of falling unnoticed into the black mass of the ocean below filled him with horror. He closed his eyes and bellowed out with rage against his fate, but as he did so he felt the strangest sensation of rising up.

He opened his eyes, blinking against the rain, the spray and his own tears, and saw strong arms pulling the rope upwards and him with it; arms on which black lines coiled and curled. He felt a surge of energy and gripped the rope with new strength despite the pain, scrabbling with his feet until he felt a hand grab him under his arm and haul him onto the deck, away from the side and away from the ravenous sea.

Kit lay panting and sobbing with relief. He looked up and saw Wanchese staring down, his big hands holding onto him lest the sea make another bid to drag him under. Rain fell, driven hard like pellets by the force of the gale.

'Thank you,' whispered Kit almost to himself, then taking a deep breath, he shouted, 'Thank you.'

'Kit! Are you all right?' White had suddenly appeared at their sides, his face a sickly grey.

'Yes, sir,' said Kit over the roar of the ocean. 'Master Wanchese saved me from falling.'

'I saw,' said White. 'I was going to persuade you to come below. You have my thanks, sir.'

Wanchese nodded.

'Quickly, now,' White went on. 'We must all get below and leave the sailors to their struggles. We must put our faith in their skills and in God's benevolence.'

They headed off towards the stern. Waves pounded against the hull and shook the ship from keel to topcastle, making even the simple task of walking a matter for careful concentration and strenuous exertion.

Grenville was standing by his cabin door as a wave crashed over them. He grabbed White's sleeve as they passed.

'Do you see, Master White!' he yelled into the wind. 'Do you see how these dogs run for me now? And do you know why?'

White was caught between his desire to escape the storm and his efforts to come up with a suitably complimentary reply.

While he dithered, Kit answered for him. 'Because they're more frightened of you than of the storm, sir!' he shouted.

Grenville roared with laughter. 'Good lad!' he said.

167

'That's it! That's it! We'll make a sea dog of you yet!'

'I don't think so, sir,' said Kit as another wave spilled over the deck. 'Give me dry land any day.'

'We'll see, we'll see,' said Grenville. 'Sometimes the brine gets in your blood and you are hooked like a fish.' As if to illustrate this point, a huge wave crashed over the side, soaking them all once again.

'I'm more bothered about joining the fish,' said Kit, water dripping from his face.

Grenville laughed again. 'Don't worry, lad,' he said. 'The storm is blowing itself out. You'll see.'

Sure enough, the storm passed during the night and the seas slowed their frantic breathing, the waves rocking back and forth hypnotically once more. It was as if a monster had been roused and now, exhausted, had settled back down beneath the waves to sleep again.

White emerged shakily from below deck and stood with Kit, looking forlornly out to sea. Though the change in weather was welcome, the view was not, for there were no other ships in sight. The *Tiger* was alone in the wide sea, not knowing if the others had survived the storm or not.

'Don't look so worried, Master White,' said a voice behind them. It was Grenville. 'All the ships have sound captains and they will turn up soon enough. Storms are part of the price of this voyage. We will see the others presently. I am certain they will make our rendezvous.'

'How can you be so sure, sir?' said White.

'I would not say I am sure,' said Grenville, looking

out to sea. 'But you get a nose for these things when you have sailed as often as I have.' He slapped White on the back, making him cough slightly, and walked along the deck to curse an unfortunate sailor as the son of an ass and send a bucket skittering across the deck with the toe of his boot.

'Is it my imagination,' said White, 'or did Sir Richard enjoy that storm?'

Kit smiled. It certainly seemed so as Grenville clapped his hands and disappeared into his cabin, singing a jolly song about Neptune.

Chapter 22

Kit stood watching the sailors go about their duties, fascinated as always. This day their duties entailed trying to mend some of the damage wrought by the storm. Carpenters tried to make good the rail through which Kit had fallen, and everywhere on the *Tiger* there was the sound of sawing and hammering and the calls of sailors working in the rigging or singing as they repaired the ropes and swabbed the decks.

The only sign left of the storm was the range of charcoal clouds on the eastern horizon. The sea was a shimmering pale grey and a fair wind filled the sails. It seemed almost impossible that only hours before Kit had feared for his life.

The storm had driven White back below decks. Kit looked for Wanchese and found him standing staring at the horizon. Though the other American Indian, Manteo, was now dressed as an Englishman, Wanchese was stripped to the waist, gradually returning to his native dress.

As Kit approached him, he noticed strange marks on his body – armlets and bracelets painted into his skin in dotted lines. Then he saw that there was a tattoo of four vertical arrows across his left shoulder blade, each one smaller as the arrows moved to the right. Wanchese turned to face him and nodded with the half-smile that now seemed like a wide grin.

'You saved my life,' said Kit. 'I wanted to thank you properly.'

'You thank me last night,' said Wanchese. 'It is enough.'

It did not feel nearly enough to Kit, but he could think of nothing to say that would ever be enough. He simply smiled and nodded and held out his hand.

Wanchese frowned quizzically and then took it, nodding again. 'Good,' he said.

'Yes,' said Kit, feeling a little awkward as Wanchese had not let go of his hand. He prised his fingers away. 'Master Wanchese, sir?' he asked. 'Those marks on your back? What do they mean?'

Wanchese looked baffled for a moment, not realizing what Kit was referring to. Kit picked up a marlinspike and scratched an arrow shape into the deck and then pointed to Wanchese again.

'Yes,' he said. 'Know now. This is mark of my village. Boys get this mark when they are men. I had forgot . . .' He closed his eyes as if trying to picture something. 'It is long time since I saw. Cannot see own mark.'

Kit nodded, wondering what it must be like to have

this indelible mark on your skin – a stain you could never wash off, a mark you could not see yourself but which told others instantly of your history.

'I dream of my country,' said Wanchese. 'In my dreams I am there. I am hunting again. The deer are many in the woods.' He turned to Kit. 'Do you dream, English boy?'

'Yes,' said Kit. 'I dream. But my dreams aren't happy like yours.'

Later that day, prayers were said on deck for the ill-fated crew of the pinnace. For the first time, looking at the grim-faced men around him, Kit began to understand a little of what made the mariners so different. They lived as near to death as living men could, kept afloat by luck and skill and the sea's blessing.

But though luck had blessed the *Tiger*, there was no sign of any of the other ships in her wake – she sailed on alone. Kit found himself restlessly searching for any sight of the rest of the fleet. There was something unnerving about being the only vessel in sight. But instead of a ship, the sailor in the topcastle sighted land.

'The Canaries,' said White as he walked up beside Kit. 'Perhaps we shall meet the others of our fleet there.'

But there was no sign of the other English ships at either Forteventura or Lancerota. The *Tiger* readied itself for the next stage of the journey, re-supplying and repairing the storm damage before setting off into the wide Atlantic, bound for the West Indies.

Then one day, about a fortnight after they had left England, a sinister gloom seemed to descend on the world about them: a dramatic reflection of Kit's mood. Instead of the day continuing to get brighter, the twilight of dawn returned as noon approached, as if time were moving backwards and the night were about to be replayed.

Low clouds covered the sky, but it was a thin mantle and could not in itself account for the unearthly light. The sea shimmered weirdly, not as it did with the clean low light of morning, or the deep glow of evening, but with a sunken and melancholy iridescence.

The sailors began to murmur and cast wary glances to heaven as they went about their work. Kit could feel their apprehension as keenly as he felt the sea wind. Then, as the men stood on the deck at their prayers, someone shouted and pointed to the mainsail.

Kit looked up and with everyone else was astounded by what he saw. The disc of the sun, its glow dampened by both cloud and sail, was visible through the canvas and there was a huge piece missing, as if a monstrous bite had been taken out of it. Kit gasped and looked towards John White, who observed the sun with a benign, untroubled smile, shaking his head gently in the way he always did when fascinated by something.

The normal activity of the ship had been replaced by a weird stillness as the crew stood about in groups, gathering behind the sails to look warily up at the sun. Manteo and Wanchese mumbled to each other.

'What the devil—?' hissed Grenville.

'No cause for alarm,' said Harriot, who was standing nearby. ''Tis but an eclipse. If you remember, sir, I did predict the event.' He raised his arms and called to the men. ''Tis but an eclipse! Fear not!'

'It's an evil omen,' muttered Grenville. 'Whatever name you give it.'

'That is nonsense, Sir Richard—' began Harriot, but Grenville turned and glared at him, leaning so far forward that Kit thought for a moment that the captain was going to bite Harriot's nose.

'Nonsense?' he hissed. 'You dare to say *nonsense* to me? Raleigh might think I need a wizard, but don't think that will save you if I feel the urge to throw you to the fishes.'

Harriot made no reply and Grenville turned to his crew, raising his voice back to its normal volume.

'Well, what do you think you are all staring at?' he bellowed. 'We are on the Queen's business, you weevils. Get back to work!'

There was a moment's pause and then the whole ship burst into life again, with sailors moving this way and that, calling to each other from the rigging. Kit turned to White for reassurance and took comfort from the calm smile on his master's face.

'It is as Master Harriot says, Kit,' said White. 'It is a glimpse into the workings of the universe, nothing more – whatever the wise women and fairground soothsayers would have you believe. The moon has simply moved into a position whereby it obscures a part of our view of the face of the sun. Nothing more than an oft-repeated celestial movement.'

Kit nodded but was far from convinced.

'Come on,' said White. 'We'll be in the West Indies before you know it.'

'The West Indies?' said Kit. 'I thought we were headed north. Aren't the Spanish in the West Indies?'

'The prevailing winds are wont to blow from the west,' said White. 'We need to head south in a wide arc before heading north once more. And we need supplies.'

Kit nodded, still thinking of the Spanish.

'Fear not, lad. They say the islands of the West Indies are like a kind of Paradise,' said White. 'There are clear waters with fish of every size and colour, and birds with feathers like rainbows fly over beaches of sand as white as salt. We shall see things that few Englishmen have ever seen, Kit, and I shall be there to paint them.' He clapped his hands on both of Kit's shoulders. 'And you shall be there to help me.'

'Aye, sir,' said Kit. 'I will!'

Part Two

Chapter 23

Kit stood on the deck of the *Tiger* and looked ashore at a view that could not have been less like the Paradise White had described on their arrival a month earlier. The bare and blackened trunks of trees standing out on the dawn horizon looked more like the barred gates of Hell, the breeze bringing dying embers back to life to throb bright red among the shadows. A lot had happened in thirty days.

The *Tiger* had weaved her way through a cluster of tiny islands, picking up what meagre supplies they could purchase, then sailed on to Puerto Rico to a pre-arranged rendezvous point at a place called Guayanilla, where they expected to meet the rest of the fleet.

They had indeed sailed under clear skies on a deep lapis blue sea, but though they had seen all manner of wonderful lizards, turtles, birds and fish, one of those fish – a large and hungry shark – had taken the lower leg off one of the gentleman explorers, who had then had the bitten stump sealed with molten pitch.

And having survived the storm, the men of the *Tiger* had now had to deal with the very different challenge of a Caribbean May. Many of the crew were familiar with such climes from other transatlantic expeditions and voyages to the coast of Africa, but though London had known some hot summers during Kit's short life, nothing could have prepared him for the heat of the tropics.

The sailors all had skin like leather, burned by the sun, beaten by winds and lashed with salt water until it looked like hide that had been worked on by the tanneries in Rotherhithe, but Kit's pale London skin burned quickly and painfully, sizzling like a sausage, and the aptly named White fared even worse. For the first time on the voyage, he had some colour in his flesh to replace the grey pallor of his sea-sickness, but it was hardly an improvement. His face now looked as though he had been slapped several times by an angry fishwife. It gave him a slightly comical appearance which was at odds with his pained expression.

By now, the food they had loaded in England – or taken aboard from the smaller islands – had begun to rot in the heat. The hold smelled like a butcher's drain, and the stench drifted up to pollute the whole ship. The cheese was rancid and the bread had grown a coat of blue fur. The whole food store was a seething mass of creeping and crawling, wriggling and scuttling.

Cockroaches ran from the approaching lanterns and

flies filled the stale air, searching for an escape route through the hatches above. Stowaway rats ran among the open bags of grain, their tails disappearing from sight like huge scaly worms.

The ship's carpenters had constructed a new pinnace to replace the one that had been lost in the storm, and they had dug defensive earthworks at Guayanilla while they waited for the *Lion*, the *Dorothy* and the others, unloading a forge and cannons that they had brought on the ship for protection. But their activity had only aroused the interest of the Spanish. Not even a ravenous shark could fill Kit with the kind of fear he felt whenever he thought of the Spanish. Like every English boy, he had been brought up on tales of their taste for torture. Kit had never seen Spaniards before, and the sight of a troop of armed horsemen on the horizon filled him with terror.

A tense stand-off ensued, and when one of their missing fleet — the *Elizabeth* — appeared, to great cheers from the fort, Grenville decided that it would be safer to haul anchor and sail on, burning the nearby woods in a show of senseless bravado against the Spanish.

As the two ships set sail once more — the *Tiger* leading the way, piloted by Fernandez — Kit assumed, as others did, that they were now finally heading for Virginia, but Grenville shocked everyone by announcing that they were making instead for Isabella Bay on Hispaniola.

'But there is a Spanish garrison there!' said Ralph Lane, the man appointed by Raleigh to govern the colony when Grenville sailed back to England. 'You cannot be serious, Sir Richard.'

'They will have supplies,' said Grenville calmly. 'The supplies we desperately need, gentlemen. The stores are ruined. There are Spaniards there, of course. There are Spaniards all over these islands, and French pirates too. But we are two ships and we have arms and men. Do not tell me you are afraid?' No one answered, and with that he walked away.

'The only thing I am afraid of is what madness we will be led into next,' said Lane quietly, and several of the gentlemen muttered and nodded in agreement.

As the *Tiger* sailed into Isabella Bay on the 1st of June, with the *Elizabeth* close behind, Kit could see groups of men rushing about nervously on the quayside of the nearby Puerto de Plata. A trumpet sounded and armed Spanish soldiers appeared, hastily putting on their armour as they ran. Kit could hear the clangs of pikes being dropped and helmets clashing against breastplates as they gathered themselves along the harbour wall, obviously prepared for action should it be necessary.

Grenville sent men ashore to negotiate for the supplies they needed and ordered everyone to be on the alert. Their own military were visible too, arms at the ready to show that the ships were defended. Time seemed to stand still while they waited for their men to return. Kit had a dread that he could see was shared by most of the crew, but to everyone's great relief the English boat began its way back to the *Tiger* after about twenty minutes, a Spaniard whose smile was visible from a hundred yards away sitting in the prow with their men.

'Captain Renfigo de Angulo,' he said in good English as he climbed aboard. 'Governor of Hispaniola.' Grenville bowed and opened his mouth to speak but Angulo interrupted him. 'No, no. You, sir, need no introduction. We have all heard of the famous "Green Field".'

Grenville could scarcely contain his pride at being so well known among the enemy and his cheeks reddened like those of a little boy who has been complimented on his manners.

'Welcome, English,' said Angulo. He looked at Lane's soldiers with their weapons tightly held and their grim faces shadowed beneath helmets. 'No, no,' he said. 'There is no need for such as these. We are not savages. Come. You shall be our guests.'

Chapter 24

Captain Angulo turned out to be a generous host. Tables were brought out onto the beach with leafy branches fixed over them for shade, then a huge banquet was prepared for Spanish and English alike. Kit walked over with Wylam to see what the Spaniards had prepared for them.

At first Kit picked warily at the food, sniffing suspiciously at the strange smells and odd foreign ingredients, but it did not take much encouragement from Wylam for him to join him in eating heartily.

'Tuck in,' he said to Kit. 'You won't eat this well for a long time. I am going to see what else is going on.'

The food was delicious and a decided improvement on weevil-ridden biscuits. Kit picked up a piece of spiced chicken and walked about among the crowd, fascinated by the strangeness of being guests of men he had always thought of as scarcely human. There was something dreamlike about being here among them. He had assumed that Grenville hated the Spanish, and yet here he was, happily eating and drinking with men he would have shot at under different circumstances. Was hate something you could put on and take off, like a hat? Kit shook his head, unable to understand it.

He noticed Wylam was now standing over by one of the food tables. He walked towards him, and as he approached, he saw that Wylam was talking to Captain Angulo, and not in English. As Kit drew closer, Angulo spotted him and nodded his head.

Wylam turned and smiled at Kit, twisting his silver ring on his finger – a habit of his that Kit had noticed before. 'I was telling Captain Angulo about the storm, Kit,' he said.

'I didn't know you spoke Spanish so well,' said Kit.

'You pick up a little here and there,' Wylam said. 'Captain Angulo is very patient to let me practise.' Angulo shrugged and smiled and said that Wylam was too modest, then asked Kit's name and repeated it once or twice, seemingly enjoying the sound.

'Keet,' he said, nodding. 'Si. Keet. Keet.'

Kit laughed. Angulo apologized and went over to invite Sir Richard to join him at his table under the awning.

Grenville readily agreed and the two men walked to their seats. Black slaves darted about in attendance, and then stood off at a distance, watching from the shadows. As soon as Grenville and Angulo were seated, they began an animated conversation, with much laughter and banging of the table. Not everyone was amused.

'Look at them!' sneered Lane as Angulo poured wine into Grenville's cup. 'We have not seen the *Dorothy* or the *Roebuck* or the *Lion* since the storm. More than likely they have been taken by Spanish ships and even now our comrades sit in stinking dungeons somewhere while Grenville sits filling his guts with that Spanish oaf.' He stomped off.

Wylam looked at Kit and rolled his eyes. Kit chuckled.

'I fear that Master Lane would have us all hanged for fraternizing with the enemy,' said Wylam. Kit nodded. Just at that moment, they were interrupted by a sudden surge forward in the crowd and they followed along behind to see what was going on.

A group of Spaniards were shouting and calling to one of their number to come forward. He put up his hands and shook his head, but his comrades pulled him on, making him spill his wine onto the sand at his feet.

He laughed and shrugged his shoulders as someone handed him a guitar, then sat on a stool and suddenly strummed. The sound grabbed the attention of most present and they turned to face him. A space cleared around him and he strummed again, then lifted his head to sing – the sound he made was like the crying of a lover at his beloved's graveside or the call of a father for his lost child, and it caught hold of every man there. The sound hung in the air and hovered over the sea.

When he finished, even Lane was moved to applaud, but there was a feeling among the English that they should respond, so they called a young sailor forward. After taking a long drink of wine, the sailor began a lilting song about a woman who waits for her lover to return from the sea, not knowing that his ship has gone down with all hands.

The Spanish were as warm in their applause as the English had been in theirs. Those who spoke no English were as moved as those who had understood a little of the meaning, for the tune was so melancholy and the sailor's voice so brittle and clear. The song seemed to skim along the sea and shimmer in the waves.

The mood was sombre now as the thoughts of all those there – Spanish and English – turned to home and to the families, friends and loved ones they had left behind.

Another of the English sailors came forward, urging his friends to come with him. He had a small flute and began to play a jaunty tune. Another sailor with a drum joined in and two others began to dance, kicking up sand as they did so.

The Spaniard with the guitar began to play along and the Spanish clapped and cheered the dancing sailors. Everyone was eager to chase away their homesick thoughts and soon the whole company was one merry throng. The English and Spanish exchanged dance steps, and even Kit was persuaded to join in, collapsing in a giggling heap at the end.

Angulo, who had long since discarded his lace collar, suddenly got to his feet and banged his glass down on the table so hard that on the third occasion it smashed. He put his finger to his lips and shushed loudly.

'Do you know what we must have?' he called out.

'No,' answered Grenville. 'What is that?'

'A bullfight!' said Angulo.

A loud cheer went round the men and a chant of 'Bullfight! Bullfight!' was started up. Kit turned to Wylam, who was grinning back at him, his hands at the side of his head with the index fingers raised as mock horns.

Two days later, the English and Spanish gathered on the beach again. The magic of the night of songs and dancing had been broken and the two nationalities, whilst still reasonably relaxed, now stood apart from each other again.

Three bulls had been chosen and an area marked on the sand; a large round arena was constructed with a fence enclosing it and soldiers standing at intervals with pikes. The bulls were let out one at a time.

The first two bulls did not put on much of a show, looking dazed and startled by the cheering crowds. Unlike in England, where the bulls were attacked by dogs, here the Spanish rode against them on horseback, spearing them with javelins until they could be finished off by sword.

Kit had been to the bull-pit many times. He was no more squeamish or sentimental than any other boy of his age; and yet – and yet he had never really enjoyed bull-baiting. He saw the excited faces of his friends in London reflected in the faces of the crowd around him on the beach, but he did not share their eagerness.

In London, more and more, he had found himself rooting for the bull or the bear. There was something about seeing such great beasts brought low by dogs that seemed wrong and sad. Kit thought of the mastiffs on the *Tiger* and shuddered.

So when the third bull, having been struck several times by a javelin, lowered his head and charged, hurling the horse to the sand and leaving the rider groaning and clutching his gashed leg, Kit cheered with genuine relish. And when the bull, thrusting his horns at anyone who dared come near, turned to crash headlong through the crowd, Kit whistled and yelled like an apprentice at a hanging.

The bull ran into the waves and turned, standing in the foam at the water's edge, looking back at them with what seemed to Kit like contempt. The bull snorted and shook his head. Then he bellowed, stretching out his powerful neck.

Angulo grabbed a musket and walked forward. The bull stood still, the water washing round his hooves and splashing up against his legs. He snorted as Angulo approached and tilted his horned head, but still he did not move.

Angulo walked steadily towards him, stopping when he was only feet away. He raised the musket to his shoulder and there was a tremendous silence. Kit felt as though time was standing still for those few seconds. Nothing seemed to stir but the slowly lapping sea. Then Angulo fired. The bull quivered and fell with a mighty splash into the sea.

A huge cheer went round the Spanish and Angulo turned to accept the applause, holding the musket above his head triumphantly.

Kit watched the sea wash over the fallen bull, whose body now was unrecognizable as the proud beast he had been; it seemed more like a black rock on the shore, the sea giving it a polished sheen, blood colouring the foam at the water's edge.

The provisions Grenville had paid for were brought to the quayside to be loaded aboard the waiting ships. Kit watched as the livestock were herded noisily into the hold along with, much to Lane's annoyance, sacks of ginger and sugar, and even some pearls to sell on their return to England.

Kit stood beside White and could sense his nervousness. Had the Spanish been toying with them, delaying them long enough for a fleet to arrive and blast their ships out of the water?

'It was a pleasure to do business with you,' Angulo said.

'Likewise, Captain,' said Grenville. He held his hand out for Angulo to shake, but the Spaniard embraced him like a brother, kissing him on both cheeks. Grenville blushed and glanced sideways at Lane, who stood scowling.

'But tell me, Green Field,' said Angulo. 'These provisions you need?'

'Yes?' said Grenville.

Kit could see that Lane and White had both stopped in their tracks. Even the animals being loaded seemed to have fallen silent.

'Between friends,' said Angulo, 'these things are not for a voyage.'

Grenville smiled but did not reply.

'You have too much,' continued Angulo. 'Also you have masons and men who know metals and you have those savages. Tell me truthfully, you plan a colony, do you not?'

'Truthfully?' said Grenville after a moment. 'Yes.'

Lane's eyes nearly popped out of his head.

'I knew it!' shouted Angulo.

'Sir Richard!' shouted Lane. 'Have you taken leave of your senses?'

'Where?' asked Angulo.

'Newfoundland,' said Grenville.

Lane, who had been walking towards Grenville, stopped in his tracks.

Angulo nodded. 'I thought it might be,' he said. 'You think there is gold there, do you not?'

'You are well informed, sir,' said Grenville.

Angulo smiled. 'Do not feel bad, *señor*,' he said. 'You are but a small country and we are mighty. Go in search of your gold. We have already more than we will ever need.'

'Farewell, then,' Grenville said to Angulo.

'Farewell, Green Field,' said Angulo. 'We part as friends, yes. But if we meet another time it might be as enemies.'

Grenville nodded. 'Let us hope then that we do not meet again,' he said.

'*Sí*,' said Angulo.

Grenville and Angulo embraced again and the English rowed out to their ships at anchor in the harbour. Kit could see that every man on board the *Tiger* was casting wary glances over towards the horizon, checking for the Spanish fleet they all thought might be about to appear. But no ships came and the English sailed away from Hispaniola, bound for Virginia.

Chapter 25

The *Tiger*, the *Elizabeth* and the replacement pinnace they had built in Puerto Rico all sailed north hoping that the other ships of the fleet had survived the storm and avoided the Spanish and would meet them off the coast of Virginia. It was very hot, and steam rose from the bone-white decks. Kit peered into the distance, White standing alongside.

They sailed on for several days, the land clearly visible all the time. Kit could see features now: long swathes of sand, inlets to rivers, huge areas of woodland. Once or twice he saw smoke rising up from the trees and turned to watch Wanchese and Manteo peering into the forest. They were about to enter *their* world now.

Fernandez told White that they would soon be approaching Virginia. He pointed to the map White held. 'Here we are,' the navigator said with an unpleasant grin. 'Cape Fear.'

Kit looked out towards the land, staring into the distance at the wild expanse of woodland on the horizon.

His mind rocked between curiosity and foreboding. They were here at last; but what was 'here'? He glanced at Manteo and Wanchese, who stood some way away, also looking landward. He had grown accustomed to these Indians, but a whole land peopled by such men? Kit could not quite imagine it, even now.

'Let's hope we fare better than the blessed Huguenots,' said a sailor standing nearby.

Kit's ears pricked up at the mention of Huguenots, instantly reminded of his visit to Walsingham and the print of the St Bartholomew's Day Massacre.

The sailor saw the look on Kit's face and pointed inland. 'You know they had a colony there?' he said. 'On the coast of Florida – the Spanish-held lands we've just passed? They tried to do what you're doing. I served on a ship with a Frenchie who survived.'

'Survived?'

'Aye,' said the sailor. 'Twenty years ago it was. They founded a colony – Fort Caroline – to give the corsairs, the French pirates, a base against the Spaniards and to shake a fist at the damned Catholics.'

Kit gulped a little at the man's fervour. 'What happened?' he asked.

'The Spaniards did for them, didn't they?' said the sailor, as if no other outcome had ever been likely. 'Surprised them like. They slaughtered over four score of the poor swine: men, women and children. I know they were only Frenchies, but even so . . .' The sailor spat in disgust. 'And that ain't all,' he continued. 'The

Huguenots had been trying to get supply ships to the fort, and they got shipwrecked on the way in a storm. The Spaniards hunted them down and butchered them. Two hundred of them surrendered, but they tied their hands behind their backs and slit their throats like pigs.' The sailor traced a filthy finger across Kit's neck. 'They won't never take me alive, those bastards. I swear—'

'Dawkins!' shouted a sailor in the rigging. 'Are you going to do some work, or what?'

'All right!' he shouted. 'I'm coming.' He turned to Kit. 'I wish you well, son,' he said. 'But I'm glad I'll be sailing on after you are all landed and settled.'

Kit stared after him, his mind whirling.

'I am sure he was only trying to frighten you, Kit,' said White.

'Well he's done a good job then,' said Kit.

Suddenly the whole ship lurched, knocking Kit to the deck. With his ear to the boards, he heard a terrible scraping and screeching and the ship tilted madly. He slid sideways, grabbing at a rope to stop himself. He hauled himself to his feet and lurched drunkenly about the deck.

'Cape Fear seems to be living up to its name!' shouted White.

Sailors in the rigging fought to prevent themselves falling to the deck and shouts went up all over the ship as it became clear that the worst had happened: the *Tiger* had run aground.

Kit staggered to the gunwales and looked over the

side. Through the silt churned up by the *Tiger*'s impact, he could see a sandbar stretching across the inlet. Now the *Tiger* was stuck.

To make matters worse, the captain of the *Elizabeth* had realized too late what was happening and he too had struck the sandbar and become trapped.

Grenville immediately blamed Fernandez. 'The Queen shall hear of this!' he yelled, staggering slightly against the tilt of the deck.

'I cannot know every grain of sand, Sir Richard,' pleaded Fernandez. 'Every storm makes a new inlet and every tide shifts these sandbanks.' The pilot looked in genuine fear for his life as he confronted the purple-faced Grenville, who was now holding his sword hilt with white knuckles.

A huge wave smashed against the side of the ship and she lurched wildly towards the shore, her masts dipping so they were nearly level with the horizon before coming up again.

'She'll break up if we don't shift her, sir,' shouted a sailor nearby.

'Keep to your tasks, men!' shouted Grenville, turning away from Fernandez. 'This is a strong ship and we're on God's work. The tide's coming in and it'll carry us off for sure. Have faith. God save the Queen!'

'Aye!' cried the men. 'God save the Queen!'

The high tide came, and with it came relief for the captain and crew of the *Elizabeth*. Cheers rang out from her decks and rigging as the ship drifted loose from the grip of the shoals. Even the crew of the *Tiger* cheered, though their ship, further up the beach and deeper of draught, remained held.

High tide came twinned with strong winds and surging seas; waves crashed into the *Tiger*'s hull, causing her to shake and rock. Kit could see by the expression on Grenville's face that this was a mixed blessing, as the hull was now being lifted up and dropped again and again on the sandbank below.

The timbers began to growl and whine as they strained under the weight, squeezing and squashing them, crunching them into the sand. The wood squealed like an injured beast and then splintered and cracked as the ship was rocked by wave after wave.

'She's holed, Captain!' a sailor cried.

'Damn and blast it all!' shouted Grenville, running to one of the main hatches to hear the yells of men below as they desperately climbed to higher decks for fear of being trapped. In the holds below, the livestock began to panic, their squeals adding to the awful cacophony.

There was an eerie moment when all around, including Kit, looked to Grenville for their order and none came. There were a few seconds when there was a kind of stillness and then Grenville snapped into action.

The soldiers and sailors, gentlemen and artisans were all, to a man, marshalled into teams on the beach. Ropes were tied to the *Tiger*'s prow and thrown across, then each team took up a rope and each man got the best grip he could.

Everyone took their place. Kit stood near the back of one group, White in another. Kit was amazed to see that even Harriot was there, as were Wanchese and Manteo. Even Grenville now took up the strain, and as he shouted 'Heave!' so did every one of them.

Kit pulled, but at first the *Tiger* did not budge an inch, and the only movement seemed to be in the skin on Kit's palms as the thick hemp ropes bit into his hands just as they had done when he had fallen in the storm. Then all at once, the ship lurched forward slightly and Kit almost fell backwards into the sand.

'Heave!' shouted Grenville again.

The men took up the strain, and again the ship lurched forward, making them all readjust their feet as they moved back and hauled again. Again and again they hauled on the ropes, and after what seemed like hours, there was a shout from one of the crew that the *Tiger* was now above the high-water mark. A great cheer went round the men as they slumped exhausted to the ground.

But Grenville did not let the men rest. Some he organized to unload the surviving livestock and foodstuffs from the *Tiger* so that they could do an inventory of the damage; others he sent inland in search of timber to repair the broken hull.

Another party of men were sent south along the dunes to search for other inlets where they might be able to anchor more safely, while the remaining men attached ropes to the *Tiger*'s mainmast and hauled at her again, this time pulling her over onto one side so that the damage could be inspected and mended.

Kit looked at the broken hull and felt sick. He had risen to the excitement of this new adventure and of the prospect of being part of a new American colony, but suddenly the thought of being left here, stranded, castaway on this wild and savage shore, filled him with dread.

It was one thing to imagine himself walking among the neat and newly built houses of an English settlement; it was quite another to be left here on some godforsaken sandbank.

''Tis but a scratch,' said an old sailor nearby, seeing the look on Kit's face.

'A scratch?' said Kit. 'There's a ruddy great hole in the bottom.'

'Nothing a good ship's carpenter won't be able to put right.'

'Are you sure?' said Kit.

'Ought to be,' said the man. 'Me being the aforesaid carpenter and all. We carry a bit of spare timber on board for such things and there's plenty in those woods if we need more. And we carry pitch for sealing. We'll have her mended in no time. It'll give us a chance to scrape her down and get rid of all this weed she's grown since Plymouth. I'd best get on. Don't want her lying belly-up in this sun for too long or the timbers'll shrink.' He shook his head. 'This climate ain't natural for ships. T'ain't natural at all.'

★ ★ ★

A few days later, the men who had been sent south returned with thirty colonists. The crew of the *Lion* had dumped them on the shore and set sail again, leaving them stranded. Whilst there was relief at the reunion, Grenville was furious and ranted about what he would do to the *Lion*'s captain the next time he clapped eyes on him.

Kit walked down towards the shoreline, amazed as he began to fully realize that he was standing off the coast of Virginia, one of the few Englishmen ever to do so.

White strolled over and stood next to Kit as he stared out to sea. 'It is a strange sensation, is it not,' he said, 'to be out of sight of one's own country?'

Kit nodded, his mind racing past images of Hugh, Annie, Mrs Fisher and then on to Walsingham, Raleigh and the dying Gabriel. 'Yes,' he said. 'It is hard to think it's even there.'

'All the same,' said White with a smile, 'it is there, never worry.'

Kit nodded and looked away to the east again, wondering why England was any concern of his anyway. There was nothing there that he missed greatly apart from Hugh, and Hugh had his own life now. However bitter he felt about what happened to his parents, that life was gone. He should have been happy to have an ocean between himself and Walsingham, and yet he felt melancholy all the same.

'Come along, young friend,' said White, putting his arm round Kit's shoulder. 'Grenville is holding one of his meetings and we don't want to miss anything, do we?'

Kit nodded as if in a trance, and followed White back towards the *Tiger*, where a group of gentlemen were clustered around Grenville, Lane and Harriot.

Grenville was clearly in a foul temper. He explained first that the damage to the *Tiger* was superficial and there was a collective sigh of relief. No sooner had they registered their relief, however, than he went on to tell them that most of the supplies had been ruined by sea water flooding in when the hull had been broken.

The biscuits, the rice, the corn – almost all their foodstuffs had been spoiled. The seeds they were to plant in Virginia were likewise ruined, as was much of the beer and cider. Even some of the livestock had been lost. Grenville became angry and jabbed an accusing finger at Fernandez, blaming him for the damage, while Fernandez in turn scowled murderously.

Grenville decided that a reconnaissance mission was needed to explore the local area and that he himself would lead it. White was to accompany him, and therefore – much to his excitement – so would Kit. White and Harriot were to record as much information as they could and explore the local area and make contact with the natives. Manteo and Wanchese would be guides.

'Fifty or so armed men will accompany us,' said Grenville.

'Is that really necessary, Sir Richard?' interrupted White. 'Does it not give the wrong impression?'

'On the contrary, my friend,' said Grenville. 'It gives exactly the correct impression.'

Chapter 26

The expedition was split into four small boats, including the newly built pinnace. Kit was to travel with White in the lead boat, which to Kit's uncomfortable surprise as he saw it being unloaded from the *Tiger* and pushed into the water was a very familiar craft – a Thames tilt boat, just like the one he and Gabriel had travelled to Barnes in all those months ago.

He dutifully carried White's bags to the waiting boats. One clinked as he walked, and Kit could recognize the sound of pigment jars knocking together, but there was another that seemed mysteriously light and he could not resist having a peek inside. He saw to his astonishment that it was full of puppets and dolls, dressed in the clothes of ladies and gentlemen of the court.

White walked over to the boats and smiled at his assistant's confusion. 'Do not worry,' he said. 'I have not taken leave of my senses. They are presents for the savages. They have been known to take a great pleasure in such trifles.'

Kit smiled weakly. He could not imagine Manteo or Wanchese taking any pleasure in such things.

The boats were being loaded with supplies for what might be a long trip, and the sight of so many muskets being carried aboard made Kit fear that Grenville and Lane were preparing for an all-out assault on the natives. Manteo stood nearby and watched the proceedings with his usual expressionless face until he realized Kit was watching him, then he smiled and nodded.

Kit sat with White's bags at the back of the tilt boat, away from the oarsmen. Wanchese climbed aboard and sat opposite him. Kit had expected the Indian to show some excitement now that he was approaching his native land, but instead of looking eager, Wanchese looked tense and troubled and this made Kit feel even more uneasy.

At the prow sat Harriot and Manteo, with Grenville sitting shadowed beneath the awning. The boats passed easily over the shoals that had hindered the *Tiger* and moved out into a huge lagoon that stretched for miles in every direction, reed beds and marshes at its edges. A flock of waterfowl took flight as they rowed away from the shore.

Behind the tilt boat there were two smaller boats – and the pinnace. The pinnace, from which Wylam waved to Kit, was filled with soldiers and weighed down with muskets, baggage and provisions. The mastiffs stood at the prow, sniffing the air.

The sounds the English made – the grate of armour

against wood, the clunk of musket butts – seemed alien to this place and echoed across the water. Strange birds shouted a warning of their approach. At least, Kit *hoped* they were birds.

The tilt boat cut through the rippling waters of the lagoon and Manteo pointed and guided the helmsman towards a particular part of the mainland far across the other side. The lagoon seemed so wide that it felt to Kit as if they would never reach the other side.

In fact it took most of the day to cross the lagoon and the rowers slumped in exhaustion as the tilt boat came to rest on the muddy banks among the reed beds of the mainland. Kit grabbed White's bags and jumped ashore.

When he had stepped off the *Tiger*, he had felt a strange sense of treading onto another realm. Now he felt it even more keenly. He looked back towards the inlet and realized that that shore had been a false shore – not on the mainland at all. He looked down at his feet and felt strangely dizzy, as if he had been spinning about. Now he was finally here. He was in the New World.

The other boats pulled up alongside them and everywhere groups of heavily armed men clattered onto the banks, looking nervously about them, and not wanting to turn their backs on the woods that fringed the shoreline. Kit began to sense what it must feel like to be a deer.

'Quiet!' hissed Grenville. 'Every savage for a thousand leagues must have heard us.' He turned to Manteo. 'Do you know the way?' Manteo nodded. 'Then lead on.'

Manteo moved off but Grenville grabbed his arm. The Indian stopped, looking at Grenville's hand on his arm as he might have done a fly that had landed there.

'Mark you well,' said Grenville. 'If you play false with us in any degree, I shall cut out your heathen heart.' Grenville let go of his arm.

'Follow,' said Manteo, and started off through the woods.

'Well, Kit,' said Wylam, walking up beside him with his usual cheerful smile. 'Here we go.'

Kit peered into the forest that quickly encircled them. The path they followed was soft with moss and last year's leaves and fallen pine needles. Dead trees lay where they fell and sometimes hung drunkenly, propped up by neighbouring branches, warts of fungus along their flaking bark.

Kit had barely ever left the City of London, but even if he had, it would not have prepared him for such a landscape. This was not the carefully managed woodland of England, with its charcoal burners and hurdle makers, its coppices and glades. This was wildwood filled with the chatter and squawk of unknown animals and birds, the air alive with the flit and buzz of strange insects.

All the time that they walked, Kit found himself flinching at every twig snap and hunching himself over, anticipating the thud of an arrow. There might be savages hidden everywhere in these woods and they would never know it.

Presently the party reached a clearing and Manteo stopped at the wood's edge. White walked ahead to join Grenville and Lane at the front and Kit followed, edging nervously past the queue of soldiers. When they got to where Grenville was standing, Kit could see that there was a vertical wooden structure ahead of them, like the wall of a fort.

'No harm will come if no harm is given,' Manteo was saying gravely.

'You have our word that no man here will strike the first blow,' said Grenville. 'Upon my honour.'

'Good,' said Manteo.

'But you also have my word,' said Grenville, peering into the depths of the forest, 'that we shall certainly strike the last if trouble starts.'

Manteo and Grenville stared at each other until the Indian half closed his eyes and looked away up the trail. Kit followed his gaze but could see nothing but a vast army of trees.

'Come,' Manteo said, and he walked towards the palisade that lay ahead of them.

'What is this place?' asked Kit, turning to Wanchese.

'Pomeioc,' said Wanchese without turning.

Kit craned his head round the men in front of him to see where they were going. A track led across the clearing to a curving wall of huge wooden spikes, made from trees stripped of their branches and sharpened at the tops. Smoke was rising up from the other side.

As they got closer, Kit could see through the gaps that

there were houses of some sort inside, and a fire from which smoke rose in a twisting grey column.

'Should we send someone ahead to warn them of our arrival?' asked White. 'We do not want to startle them.'

'They know we are here,' said Manteo. 'They have been following us for the last hour.'

Kit looked back into the woods and thought he saw someone but it might have been a deer. There was movement, this time to his right, but again, when he looked, he saw no one there.

A bird cried out with a rasping call like a magpie as they approached the entrance to the palisade, and Manteo signalled for them to wait. Grenville told the bulk of the men to stay outside and be on their guard while he and Manteo, Lane, Harriot and White walked towards the entrance. Kit stayed put until White waved for him to follow.

Kit looked about him, amazed. He had become used to the sight of Manteo and Wanchese over the last months, but for the most part he had seen them in clothes that had been fashioned to make them fit into London life, or at least to stand out less.

Now it was Kit and the other Europeans who were foreign, who stood out, surrounded by Indians in their own land; naked children running into the arms of their bare-breasted mothers, who wore fringed aprons made of animal skins that hung down to their knees at the front, but hid nothing behind.

Kit blushed at their bare breasts and backsides and found it hard not to stare at the tattoos that covered their arms and legs and even their faces. The tattoos were made of dotted lines and circled their arms and legs like bracelets. Kit turned to White, who was already furiously scribbling in a notebook, his tongue flicking in and out as always as he drew the native huts and encircling palisade.

Kit saw that the young Indian men wore the same fringed aprons as the women. The elders of the village wore cloaks of animal skin that were thrown over one shoulder, leaving the other arm bare. Kit could see that unlike Wanchese's four arrows, the men here had a criss-cross pattern on their shoulder blades.

Their hair was shaved at the sides to form a crest on top, which grew longer at the back and was bound up into a knot behind their heads. Some had feathers tied into their hair, behind their ears and on the crest. There was a strange echo between the Indians and some of the English soldiers, with the crested hair of one and the crested helmets of the other.

None of the Indian men wore a beard, as was the fashion among most of the English. They stood proudly, arms folded, watching the Englishmen with the same fierce intensity that Kit might have expected from the guards at Hampton Court.

Manteo walked across to greet a group of men, and one of them stepped forward. He and Manteo talked, occasionally turning to look at the party of Englishmen with expressionless faces. Kit had the distinct impression that things were not going well.

He suddenly noticed that there was a girl of about eight years old standing near them. She flinched as he turned to look at her and backed off a little. Her mother, who was standing some twenty yards away, called to her, but the girl did not move. Kit smiled at her, then remembered the dolls. He searched through the bags at his feet until he found the right one. He took out a doll and held it out to her. Her eyes widened, and after a moment's hesitation she overcame her fear and snatched the doll away from him, running back to her mother.

The girl's mother took the doll and poked and prodded at its strange clothes, turning it upside down to look under the skirts, laughing heartily as she did so. Other women came over to see it too as the girl hopped about trying to get the doll back.

When the girl's mother gave her back the doll, the girl ran over to the Indian Manteo was talking to and showed it to him. The Indian took it and he and his fellows all broke out into uncontrollable laughter, pointing at the doll and then at Kit and the others, with Manteo joining in. Kit realized he had never once seen Manteo laugh and it was not an altogether pleasant sight.

'Well done, lad,' said White. 'I think the little girl is the chief's daughter. Come on.'

White walked about the village, taking notes and drawing all the time. Kit followed close behind, trying to take everything in. A village dog growled and snapped at his heels. Kit kicked out at it and the dog whimpered and ran for cover, making some nearby children hoot with laughter.

The children of the village seemed to have taken a shine to Kit and formed a motley band, walking and toddling a few steps behind him; stopping when he stopped and walking on as soon as he moved off again. One of them sniffed at White – like a dog might sniff another dog – and Kit laughed out loud, making White turn round and the Indian child scuttle away shrieking.

Kit strolled round the village, smiling at anyone he met and allowing an old woman to tentatively touch his face and his hair with her long delicate fingers. She turned to a younger woman, encouraging her to do the same, but she was either too frightened or too embarrassed to do so and Kit moved on, grinning, soaking up the wonderful strangeness of it all. All fear had drained away.

White then clapped him on the shoulders and told him it was time they moved on; they needed to see as much of the area as possible. Kit nodded, reluctant to leave this place, but eager to see others. The elders of the village exchanged nods and farewells with Grenville, Lane and Harriot; Harriot even tried out some of his Algonquian – to much appreciative nodding.

Chapter 27

The English walked back to the boats, the village children running along behind them and the dogs barking a farewell. Kit waved enthusiastically and the children waved back, some of them following them all the way to the water's edge.

They set off south and then rowed west, the woods perfectly reflected in the mirror-like surface. Finally, they turned up a river inlet, mooring at the muddy shore.

Again Manteo led the way, and again they came to a fortified village; this village, Manteo said, was called Aquasgococ. Kit did not feel anything like the dread he had felt at approaching Pomeioc. Instead of hiding behind the soldiers at his side, he looked about him as they drew near, but his wariness returned as soon as they entered the village.

Kit immediately felt something was different here. He had a thief's heightened sense of danger, and it was telling him that all was not well. In Pomeioc the natives had seemed curious and nervous; here they seemed suspicious and hostile. Manteo walked ahead to meet the elders of the village. Harriot went with him while both Lane and Grenville held back, assessing the situation.

'Ready with those muskets,' hissed Grenville to his soldiers. 'I can smell trouble here.'

Sure enough, one of the men with Manteo and Harriot pointed angrily in the direction of Kit and the others. Then he leaned forward, staring into Harriot's face, examining him, *sniffing* at him.

'Frazier,' said Grenville.

'Sir,' said the musketeer standing nearby, a smoking taper around his neck ready to light his musket fuse.

'Can you hit the savage from here?'

'I can, sir,' the soldier replied. 'But I might hit our savage or Mr Harriot.'

'We will have to take that risk,' said Grenville, nonchalantly. 'Load your weapon.'

'You cannot risk hitting our friends,' said White.

'That savage may be a friend of yours,' said Grenville. 'but he's no friend of mine.'

Before the musket was fired, however, Harriot and Manteo returned and told Grenville that there was nothing to fear, but that the elders of the village did not want to meet them. Grenville raised an eyebrow, clearly offended that these people did not want to know him. Kit and White exchanged a worried glance; Grenville was not a man to snub.

At that moment Kit heard a noise to his left and saw

an Indian hunting party returning along the trail. There was an awkward silence as the dozen or so Indians approached the soldiers at the entrance to their village. The evidence of their ability to use their bows was there for all to see, as two of them carried a dead buck deer tied to a pole.

Kit watched the Indians intently, fearfully at first, but then in fascination, noticing that on their backs they bore a single arrow as their village mark. Two of the Indians started rummaging about in the bags that the party had dumped by the trail. Wanchese chased them away, grabbing one of the men and pushing him off. The soldiers were about to draw their swords when Lane stopped them, telling them to be calm, but Kit could feel the tension in the air like the heaviness before a thunderstorm.

As some of the Indians carried their game into the village, two or three others came over after they spotted the men carrying muskets; they stared and pointed at the strange new weapons, curiosity overcoming their fear. Kit turned to Lane, who in turn looked at Grenville.

'Let them look if they want to,' said Grenville. 'But keep good hold.'

The most inquisitive of the Indians reached out and touched the barrel of one of the muskets and recoiled, clearly surprised by the coldness of the alien metal. He tried again and ran his hand down the barrel, encouraging his friends to do the same.

'Fire it for them!' said Grenville. 'Let them see what they are dealing with.'

'Is that wise?' said White.

'Fire it!' repeated Grenville.

The musketeer loaded his musket with powder carried in small pouches on his bandolier, while the Indians watched, grinning, oblivious to the purpose of the man's actions. Then the musketeer stuck his prop into the ground, hoisted the musket onto the crook, lit the fuse and fired the gun.

The noise was devastating. Kit shook his head to shake off the roar, and the Indians who had been standing close by fell to the ground in fear, their hands over their ears, their terrified eyes staring at the musketeer, who was surrounded by a plume of smoke.

The Indians got to their feet, yelling and chattering in fear, and ran into the village.

Grenville laughed and slapped Harriot on the back, making him cough and take a step forward. 'Perhaps that will make them a little more hospitable next time, eh, wizard?'

'I am not a—' began Harriot, but Grenville was already marching away.

Kit followed, but first he looked back towards the Indians cowering in the stockade and wondered at how quickly things had changed.

The party took to their boats again, but stopped to rest further downstream. Kit asked if he could look at the drawings White had been doing in Pomeioc and marvelled at the amount of work White had managed to do in such a short space of time.

'These are just quick notes to refresh my memory,' said White. 'Later I will draw more detailed pictures to show Sir Walter and Her Majesty when we return.'

'Thieving savages!' shouted Grenville suddenly, making Kit almost drop White's notebook in the river.

'What is it, sir?' asked one of Grenville's men.

'My cup. My silver drinking cup. You know the one. Those damned savages have stolen it.' Kit could see the colour rising in Grenville's face as his temper boiled. He thought back to the incident with the Indians and the bags, but White spoke before he had a chance to say anything.

'Are you sure it has not been lost on the journey?' he queried.

Grenville turned on White with such violence that Kit took two steps back, fearing he might be caught up in his rage. 'Of course I'm sure!' he shouted. 'Do you take me for a fool? You saw those Indians rooting round in our baggage.' He turned to the soldiers who were resting nearby and told them to get to their feet; they had to teach the Indians a lesson.

To Kit's amazement, White challenged Grenville, stating that Raleigh had laid down strict guidelines for their conduct.

Before Grenville could answer, Lane stepped forward. 'Master White is right,' he said. 'It is only a silver cup, Sir Richard. I am sure you can "find" another.'

Lane's stress on the word 'find' brought a sharp look from Grenville, but he seemed to let the matter drop and walked away.

However, Kit noticed that Grenville was still muttering half an hour later when the party was ready to leave. Wylam went across to talk to him and Kit saw the two men locked in discussion for a minute or two, until Wylam walked back. When he saw Kit looking at him, he smiled weakly and shook his head sadly. Kit then saw that Grenville was taking a couple of his men to one side. He could not hear what was said, but the soldiers grinned and nodded and then went across to their companions by the boats.

When it came time to leave, these soldiers did not follow as they had done but headed back upstream in one of the boats. Kit, sitting in the tilt boat, saw them disappear round the headland and he turned to see Wanchese looking in that same direction with tightly furrowed brows.

The other boats stopped again and they prepared for another trek to a third village. As Kit gathered up White's bags, he saw smoke rising up above the trees to the east. When he turned back to the party, Wanchese was standing beside him.

'What is it?' asked Kit.

'Bad,' said Wanchese, peering hawk-like into the distance.

Before the party set off, the soldiers returned and moored their boat with the others. Kit saw Grenville patting one of them on the back and they were laughing as they loaded the boats.

White came back for more bags and saw Kit staring at the smoke. 'What is that smoke?' he asked.

'I think it is the village we came through,' said Kit.

'I tried to talk Grenville out of it,' said Wylam, fiddling as usual with his silver ring. 'I could see what he was planning.'

'But the cup—' Kit began, confused. Something about this wasn't right, he was sure.

White looked at the laughing soldiers, then over to the smoke, and then back at the soldiers. Kit had hardly ever seen White angry; now his face had turned red with rage as he marched across to Grenville.

'Sir Richard!' hissed White. 'You have endangered the expedition over the theft of a silver cup!'

'Watch your tone, mapmaker! Do not seek to lecture me about my duties! I am in command here!' shouted Grenville. 'If the theft had gone unpunished, they would have thought us weak. Men are men the world over, and men respect force and nothing else.'

'You credit them with being men then?' said White.

Grenville took a deep breath. 'You are troubling yourself over nothing, Master White. My men tell me they ran away like children,' he said. 'We burned their crops and their shacks but no one was harmed.'

'You have burned their houses and destroyed their food. Is that not harm?' said White. 'Master Lane, I assume that Sir Walter shall hear of this.'

'When you are dealing with people like these,' said Grenville, 'you need to be hard, Master White. They had the same trouble in Ireland and used the same cure. Sir Walter could teach these savages a thing or two himself. He might look like a court prancer, but he was fearsome in Ireland, you know; fearsome.'

'Aye,' said Wylam grimly. 'That he was.'

'You were there?' asked Lane.

'I was,' said Wylam, though Kit had the impression he wished he had not mentioned it.

'Some of my men are Irish themselves,' said Lane. 'Come over to our side. They are good fighters, Master Wylam, I'll tell you that. Nugent there, for instance, is worth ten English soldiers and that's the truth.'

Kit looked at the man called Nugent. He had noticed him aboard the *Tiger*; noticed him and avoided him. He had watched him arm wrestle one of the sailors for a wager. Not only had he won easily, but the sailor had barely been able to use his arm for a week.

'How those Catholics would like to get revenge for Smerwick,' said Lane.

'Aye,' said Wylam between gritted teeth.

'What is Smerwick?' whispered Kit to White.

Wylam overheard him. 'A force of Italians and Spaniards flying the Pope's flag landed in Ireland back in the winter of fifteen eighty, Kit,' he said. 'They landed at Smerwick – St Mary's Wick – on the south-east coast and occupied the earthworks of an ancient fort.'

'What happened then?'

'English ships blocked their exit by sea, and English troops their escape by land. Without any chance of supplies, they were forced to surrender.' Wylam paused before continuing. 'They begged for mercy, of course, but they weren't going to get any. First the English soldiers took two Jesuit priests to the local blacksmith, where they had their arms and legs smashed with hammers. Then they were hanged and quartered.' He saw the horrified look play across Kit's face. 'Then there were local women who had visited the camp. Some pleaded the belly – saying they were with child – but they were all hanged anyway. Six hundred Catholic soldiers were put to the sword.'

'May God have mercy on their souls,' said White, but it was not clear if he referred to the butchered or the butchers.

'And do you know who was there that day in the thick of it?' asked Lane of no one in particular. 'Why, our friend the Governor of Virginia, Sir Walter Raleigh himself – though he was just plain Captain Raleigh then, of course.'

'If we have had enough discussion,' said Grenville finally, 'we need to keep moving. Where to now, Manteo? What is the name of this next village we are to visit?'

'Secota,' said Manteo.

'Is it far?'

'Not far,' said Wanchese. 'But different.'

'How so?' asked White.

'The men of Secota are warriors,' said Wanchese.

Grenville gave the Indian a hard look. 'I want the men ready,' he said to a nearby soldier. 'We may have to face an attack. I don't want us taking any chances.'

Kit looked at White and saw the concern on his face, while Wylam was staring out over the river, lost in his own thoughts.

Chapter 28

After Wanchese's words about the men of Secota, Kit was expecting this village to be the most heavily fortified yet, and all his earlier sense of trepidation had returned. But he was surprised to find that there was no palisade or fortifications at all, and the houses were scattered about alongside fields of crops – like an English village.

But the similarity to England ended there. The houses were made of poles stuck into the ground, had curved rather than pitched roofs, and instead of thatch or tiles, they had overlapping rush mats to keep the weather out. Windows, such as they were, were simply holes in the walls and the entrances were doorless openings.

Manteo and Harriot went ahead of the group to speak to the elders, who were looking at the band of heavily armed Englishmen with understandable suspicion. The village dogs barked at the English mastiffs and the mastiffs barked back, tugging at their leads, the hairs standing up on their backs. Kit could feel the tension in the men beside him as they gripped their muskets and sword hilts, ready for the attack.

But Manteo and Harriot came back to tell them that the villagers welcomed them to Secota. They had arrived on a special feast day to celebrate the ripening of the corn and the Indians asked if they might offer the Englishmen some food and entertainment.

'We will accept their offer,' said Grenville. 'But keep your guard. This may be a trick.'

'It is not trick,' said Manteo.

'We shall see,' replied Grenville, gripping his hilt. 'We shall see.'

Kit walked alongside White and Harriot as they took in all there was to see of Secota. There were houses built along a kind of main street, with fields of crops alongside. Pumpkins were ripening by the main thoroughfare and White pointed to some plants growing at the edge of the village.

'*Uppowoc*,' said one of their guides.

White took a leaf and sniffed it, rolling it between his thumb and forefinger.

'What is it, sir?' Kit asked.

'Tobacco, Kit. The Indians set great store by it as a medicine for all manner of ills.'

Many of the sailors smoked tobacco on the *Tiger* but Kit thought it a bizarre thing to do; to swallow smoke. They continued past a field of tall crops. White asked Manteo what it was.

'*Pagatowr*,' he answered.

223

White pulled one of the stems and bent it towards them so that they could see the grains growing in a long tightly packed clump.

'It is like the maize that grows in the West Indies,' said Harriot, leaning forward to inspect it. Their guide fired off a burst of Algonquian and Harriot nodded. 'It seems to be their corn,' he continued. 'They boil it in broths and grind it to make bread. The festival today is to celebrate its ripening.'

'Wonderful!' said White. 'It will be a kind of harvest festival.'

Kit wandered off the path and stood between the rows. The corn was six or seven feet high, and after only a few yards, Kit could see nothing but green in all directions, save for the ragged window of sky directly above him. A light breeze rustled the yellowing leaves and made the heavy cobs sway.

Suddenly Kit became aware of a whispering above the rustling, then a stifled giggle. He peered into the corn, but every time he looked, the sound seemed to come from somewhere else. Then he caught sight of something: feet running past the next row of corn. He lunged through the stalks, but there was nothing there. He looked each way down the empty row and the giggling started up again. He turned quickly and this time he saw figures flicker past between the corn stalks; but again, when he tried to follow, they seemed to disappear. More giggling.

Kit could feel his face flushing red. He knew he was

being made fun of, and it felt no better in America than
it had in London. He changed tactics, standing still and
waiting. Sure enough, he heard a rustle louder than that
made by the breeze and, if he strained his ears, he could
hear the sound of laughter being stifled.

He spun round as quickly as he could and parted the
corn as if it were a curtain – to find himself face to face
with a beautiful girl about his own age. She was naked
except for a buckskin apron round her waist and a string
of beads around her neck.

She gazed back at him like a startled deer, until her
friends also appeared; they dragged her back and they all
ran away screaming. They, like her, were naked. Before
Kit could gather himself, they had disappeared into the
corn once more. But as Kit stood there, stock-still, he
could hear the sound of breathing behind him.

The corn swayed in the breeze. Kit spun round once
again and pulled it aside. This time it was not a young girl's
face on the other side, but a man's: a strange man with
piercing eyes. Kit recoiled and staggered backwards.

The Indian stepped forward. He wore nothing but
an otter pelt hanging from a belt at his waist and a
large tasselled bag strapped to his side. His head was
shaved except for a crest like the other Indians, but as he
stepped forward, Kit saw with some horror that he had
a dead bird fixed to the side of his head, its black wings
outstretched, its dried and shrivelled head lolling down,
the beak half open.

As Kit watched, wide-eyed, the strange figure lowered

his head and raised his arms, making claws of his fingers. He began to shake his head and mutter to himself, and his feet began a rhythmic shuffling, hopping from one foot to the other. Then all at once he brought his hands together in a clap in front of Kit's face and Kit stumbled backwards, falling over in the dusty earth. When he looked up, the figure was gone.

Kit got to his feet, gingerly parted the corn and looked through. The row was empty. Then the laughter started: not the playful giggling of girls this time, but a weird and strangled laughter, more like a jay or a magpie than a human.

Kit ran. He had no idea where he was going or in which direction the village lay; he just had an uncontrollable desire to be out of that field of corn. And as night was falling, he had no wish to be trapped there in the dark.

Then, suddenly, he was out. He crashed through the last barrier of corn stalks and found himself among the houses of Secota once more. He turned at the sound of footsteps to see Wylam walking towards him.

'Master Milton,' he said, as if he were walking down the Strand. 'You look as though you've seen a ghost.'

'Not a ghost exactly,' said Kit, looking back towards the cornfield with a shudder. 'It was nothing.'

Wylam looked at the building next to them. 'What is this place, Kit?' he asked casually, tapping the bark walls with his knuckles. 'Any idea?'

Kit shook his head, still thinking about the cornfield,

but he followed Wylam into the light of the fire that was burning on the ground within the hut. Kit could now see that there was a raised section inside, a tall platform resting on stilts made of tree trunks. There was a strange smell.

'Maybe it's a food store,' said Kit, grabbing a log from the fire to use as a torch. Climbing a rickety ladder and peering into the gloom, he could just make out what looked like long sacks lying on the platform.

'What's up there, Kit?' whispered Wylam.

'Can't quite see.' Kit lowered his makeshift torch and held it in front of him towards the sacks. To his horror, he now saw that the sacks were not sacks at all but the shrivelled remains of human bodies lying in a line, hollow-eyed, their skin like dried leaves. 'Dead bodies,' he gasped. 'Lots of them.' Shocked, he looked along the rows of corpses until he noticed with a start that there was an upright figure to one side, sitting on a small bench. The figure did not move and Kit realized with relief that it was a painted statue.

Wylam grabbed another torch and climbed the ladder to see for himself. 'Sweet Jesus,' he said as he came down again. 'Come on, Kit, let's get out of this place. This whole country gives me the shivers. Why did Hatton send me on this expedition? The sooner I'm back in London the better!'

They stood at the base of the ladder with their backs to the platform, looking out of the hut towards the rest of the village. Then Kit became aware of a noise behind him; he turned, holding his torch in front of him. Shuffling towards him along the ground, shielding his eyes from the light, was a wizened old man. Kit dropped his torch in surprise, and the old man scuttled back beneath the platform. Wylam held out his torch and peered after him; Kit could see the man's eyes glinting in the light.

'He is the watcher over the dead,' said a voice from the doorway. Manteo. 'It is a great honour.'

'Is it now?' said Wylam, screwing up his face. 'We shall have to take your word for that. Come on, Kit. I can smell food. Perhaps the savages are cooking Harriot.'

'Master Wylam,' said Kit. 'You know the cup – Grenville's cup that was stolen . . . ?'

'Aye?'

'I've been thinking,' Kit said seriously. 'I knew something wasn't right when Sir Richard first spoke of it. But I am sure I am right. The cup – it wasn't stolen by the Indians. The Indians were never near that bag.'

Wylam frowned. 'Are you sure?'

'Yes,' said Kit. 'But how could I say anything when Sir Richard was in such a temper . . . ?'

Wylam shook his head and sucked in the air between his teeth. 'The theft played into Sir Richard's hands,' he said. 'He was happy for an excuse to show his strength. But the cup is still missing, Kit. That means there is still a thief among us – and there is nothing I like less than a thief.' Kit flinched a little at these words and Wylam smiled, patting him on the arm. 'But come, Kit; what's done is done. There is no sense in worrying about such things. Thieves have a way of giving themselves away in such a small company. We shall be on our guard from now on, eh?'

Kit nodded, and the two of them turned to follow the sound of drums. A crowd was forming, both of natives and of their comrades. In a clearing stood a circle of huge wooden posts -tree trunks split in half and set into the ground. At the top of each was carved a human face looking inward. It did not seem to be quite the harvest festival White had envisaged. As the night fell, a fire was lit within the circle and its flames glimmered in the gathering darkness.

Then three girls walked into the centre of the circle and put their arms round each other, facing inward like the carved posts. Then members of the village took their places next to the posts. They held small branches and sprigs and were wearing feathers in their hair; some carried gourds or arrows.

Then the music started, though it was unlike any music Kit had ever heard. Drummers beat on hollowed logs and clashed sticks together in a startling rhythm, while others took up a chanting – singing and shouting.

The men and women by the posts began to dance. Kit had seen dancing at court and he had seen country dancing at the May Fair, but this was not like either. At first he saw mocking grins appear on the faces of the soldiers, but these soon disappeared as they too fell under the spell.

The dancers moved around the circle as maypole dancers would, but here the dancers seemed lost in the dance. They kept the rhythm but they moved independently of one another, spinning, hopping, bowing, skipping, throwing up dust with their feet and flailing their arms, shaking the gourd rattles and rustling the sprigs of leaves.

Firelight played across the glistening, naked flesh of the dancers, across sinewy arms and legs and bared breasts and buttocks. It threw crazy shadows across the ground and made mysterious silhouettes of those who wandered between Kit and the flames.

At the centre of the circle the girls bowed their heads and rotated slowly, one way and then the next. Occasionally they would lift their heads and look up to the night sky. As the girls lowered their heads into a bow once more, Kit saw that one of them was the girl from the cornfield, her eyes twinkling.

As the original dancers exhausted themselves, others came to take their places, waiting their turns at the edge of the circle, crouched on their haunches before bouncing forward and rising gradually to their full height, whooping and chanting and hurling themselves into the dance.

The movement of the flames as they flickered in the breeze was echoed in the carved faces on the wooden posts; the shadows in their features shrank and stretched as if the faces tensed and relaxed. Sparks floated off into the night sky to join the stars.

The dance did not seem to have any set time or agreed set of movements. Each dancer seemed to dance until they were too exhausted or too intoxicated with the rhythm to continue, and their places were taken by others.

Gradually, the beat of the drums slowed and the dancers' movements became slower or more fitful, and what had been a giddy flight of energy was now a heartbeat and a lullaby, soothing the dancers and the onlookers alike. Kit found himself blinking and shaking his head as if to try and clear his mind of a dream. Then it was all over. The spell was broken. The dancers walked away; the music ended.

White came over to talk to Kit, telling him that he had been taking notes about the village when the music had started, then left off what he was doing to watch. He showed Kit the drawings he had done of the dancers, bemoaning how hard it had been to draw them as they leaped and flailed about. His drawing showed the dancers as they had never been; frozen in wild gestures. Kit could see how White had changed and corrected as the dancers had moved in front of him, and as he looked at the drawings, the dancers almost began to move again, animated by his imagination.

The smell of cooking food floated through the air. Kit could see another fire to which the Indians were bringing fish and vegetables in wicker baskets. Over the fire, they had built a kind of wooden griddle from horizontal branches supported on four posts, and once again White was scribbling in his notebook.

The Indians laid the fish on top of the branches to cook with any extra ones skewered on sticks which were then rammed into the ground, leaning in towards the fire so that these fish, too, were gently cooked. Kit noticed they had cut great slashes in the flanks of the fish to make sure they cooked right through.

Nearby there was another fire with a huge pot sitting on top of it. Kit wafted the smoke away to look inside and could see a kind of broth with huge cobs of yellow corn floating in it, along with vegetables and pieces of fish. It smelled delicious and he wandered over to where the Indians had laid mats with huge wooden bowls and platters. Bowls of bread were placed ready. A woman motioned for him to sit and Kit nodded and sat down.

A voice sounded next to his ear and he turned round: the girl from the cornfield. She smiled at him and looked down, closing her eyes against his gaze. When she looked at him again, he saw the firelight flickering in her eyes and he smiled back. She picked up some bread and offered it to him.

He thanked her and took it, biting a piece off. 'It's good,' he said with a nod.

She giggled at the sound of his voice, as if not ready for the idea of him talking. Then she began to speak, her voice soft and yet strong. He had heard the language now many times, but only in the harsh tones of Manteo and Wanchese or Harriot. On her lips it sounded sweet. Kit patted his chest.

'Kit,' he said. 'Me. I'm Kit. My name is Kit.'

'K–I–T,' she repeated, patting her own chest.

Kit laughed. 'No,' he said. 'I'm Kit. You are . . . ?' He shrugged to show that he did not know. She shook her head and laughed. 'It doesn't matter,' he said, smiling. She smiled back and spoke some more, and he simply listened, enjoying the sound without caring what she said.

'Enjoying the view?' said a voice behind him.

Kit turned away from the girl and saw Grenville standing there. 'No . . . I . . .' he said, suddenly embarrassed by the proximity of the girl and her scanty dress.

Grenville laughed. 'Look as much as you like, boy,' he said. 'She is comely enough for an ape. But keep your hands off.' He walked away.

Kit grew hot with rage and embarrassment, and when he turned back to the Indian girl, she backed away from the fierce expression he now wore. He sighed and smiled. 'Sorry,' he said. 'Though I know you don't know what he said or even what I'm saying now. Sorry all the same.'

Chapter 29

They spent the night in Secota, sleeping around the fire with the village children staring at them from doorways until they grew tired and were led away to their beds. The mastiffs and the village dogs reached a compromise after an hour of barking and growling and settled down to a chorus of whimpering before falling asleep.

In the morning, the Indians offered to feed them again, but Grenville told Harriot to thank the elders but say that they must be on their way. The elders nodded and bade them farewell, but Kit noticed that the young men of the village stood apart, eyeing the English warily and staying close to their bows, just as the English soldiers gripped their sword hilts.

As they were leaving, the girl from the cornfield appeared at a longhouse and stood in the doorway. She smiled at Kit and raised her hand tentatively. Kit smiled and waved back, but an arm grabbed the girl and pulled her back inside.

Then Kit saw the strange man with the bird on his head standing by the entrance to the settlement; he shook a turtle-shell rattle at them as they approached, mumbling rapidly to himself.

'What is he?' asked Kit nervously as he and White walked towards him.

'Manteo tells me that the people here set great store by what he says,' said White.

'Is he a priest then?'

'No. They do have priests, but this man is something else. They say he can call down spirits and see things that other men cannot. They say he has great powers to cure the sick.'

'You mean . . . he is a wizard . . . ?' said Kit, turning round to have another look.

'Of sorts,' said White with a half-smile. He patted his notebook. 'Fascinating, is it not? I have done a rather marvellous drawing of him, even though I say so myself.'

As Kit and White neared the medicine man, he stepped swiftly into Kit's path, reached out with both hands and touched the sides of Kit's face, closing his eyes and humming to himself. His eyes flicked open suddenly and he spoke.

Wanchese stepped forward to translate. 'He says you must open your eyes.'

'Open my eyes?' said Kit nervously, his face still being held. 'What does that mean?'

Wanchese shrugged. 'Only you will know.'

The medicine man let go of Kit's face and danced away, squawking. Kit screwed up his face and looked at Wylam, who was shaking his head and chuckling to himself.

'Fascinating,' said White. 'Quite fascinating.'

Once more, the English boats set off across the lagoon, and once more Kit sat in the tilt boat with John White. This time, though, the view ahead was of the reed beds and the wall of sandbanks and dunes that barred the lagoon from the sea.

The boats rowed out into the open water. A wind was blowing in off the Atlantic, and despite the shelter of the sandbanks, it made rowing hard work. They finally staggered ashore to be greeted by those who had stayed behind to keep watch on the ships and work on the *Tiger*.

'Now that's a sight to warm a mariner's heart,' said Grenville as they climbed the brow of the dunes.

When Kit caught up with him, he saw that the *Tiger* no longer lay drunkenly on the beach; it floated free offshore, seaworthy once more, at anchor with the *Elizabeth* and joined by the other missing ships of their little fleet: the *Dorothy* and the *Roebuck*.

No sooner had they reached the camp than Grenville called another meeting. He told them that there was no time to lose in heading north for safer anchorage. While the ships stayed moored offshore, they were liable to fall victim to the next storm that blew up.

NEW WORLD

They would travel north as they had planned, and renew the links with the natives Raleigh's men had met the previous year. Simon Fernandez was given the task of guiding them to the inlet he had named for himself the year before – Port Ferdinando – where they would unload all their equipment and provisions and build a proper settlement; the first English colony in the Americas.

Chapter 30

So the little fleet set sail again, travelling north, hugging the coast and the strange bar of sand dunes that seemed to stretch for miles in either direction. When they were level with the inlet of Port Ferdinando, they anchored offshore and Grenville announced that the first thing they must do was find the local chieftain the English had made contact with the previous year, when they had first met Wanchese and Manteo: Granganimeo. He was the brother of the local *weroance* – the big chief of the tribe – and it was this chieftain who had invited them to return.

Some of the men who had visited the year before were sent with a shore party to invite him aboard, and in due course the men returned, accompanied by a flotilla of dugout canoes. The number of men startled the English soldiers, and they immediately began picking up their weapons, but those who had been ashore reassured them that all was well.

The chieftain was seated in the first canoe; he

climbed eagerly aboard the *Tiger* and Kit pushed forward to get a better view as the Indian stepped onto the deck. He was tall and dressed only in a kind of buckskin skirt, with several copper loops through each ear. His hair was shaved at the sides, and what remained stood in a crest on the crown of his head. Tattoos coiled around his arms and legs.

However formidable his appearance, the chieftain was clearly friendly and told the English that they were welcome and that he had found a site for them to build on. The *weroance* himself, Wingina, could not come in person as he had recently been wounded, but he would visit them as soon as he could.

There was relief among the English settlers and an eagerness to go ashore and get on with the business of their venture.

The next day, Kit clambered down the side of the *Tiger* and into a boat with White, along with Wanchese and Wylam. Getting into the boat from the side of the bigger ship was not as easy as it had looked, the boat rising and falling every few seconds as the incoming waves lapped against the ship's hull and making stepping aboard like mounting a bucking horse.

The boats rowed towards the land, through an inlet in the dunes and into the lagoon. Behind the sandy bars of the Outer Banks were salt marshes and reed beds as before, the vast expanse of the lagoon itself all around them and the swathe of forest beyond.

They approached what Kit realized must be an island.

Indian children stood among the trees and stared at them in a kind of wonder, and Kit stared back. The only noise was the splash of the paddles and the creak of the oars.

'What do they call this place?' asked White as they landed on the island.

'Roanoke,' said Wanchese.

Kit remembered the word from White's map. 'Rowan-oak,' he said, trying the word out for size. 'It's a good name.'

'I was born here,' said Wanchese, dropping to one knee and picking up a handful of dirt. 'It is my home.' He stared away towards the native village at the other end of the island. 'It *was* my home.'

As the men gathered on the shore, Lane walked across to White, rubbing his hands together. He could hardly suppress his excitement at taking this first step towards finally assuming control of the colony.

The chieftain and a group of elders from the nearby village appeared, long buckskin cloaks over their shoulders like Roman senators. They greeted the colonists warmly, took them to a small clearing and pointed to the ground, showing them where they could build.

Harriot thanked them in Algonquian and they stared at him, intrigued by this white man who could speak their tongue. One of the elders came up to him and stared at his lips suspiciously. Harriot pursed his lips. The elders chuckled and pointed. Harriot sniffed and asked

Manteo to thank them, which he did, and the elders left, still chuckling. It was only then that Kit noticed the young men of the village standing in the shadows, armed with bows. As the elders walked away, they too turned and followed them.

'We need to start clearing the ground and working the soil,' said White, 'if we intend to feed ourselves.'

Manteo nodded. 'They will help,' he said, gesturing towards the retreating Indians. 'They will not have food to spare, but they know this land and how best to use it.'

White smiled. 'Do you hear that, Kit?' he said. 'Do you see? We can live as brothers, can we not?'

The huge task of unloading all the provisions and baggage from the ships now began in earnest. There was no way that Grenville was going to attempt to bring the ships into the shallow lagoon again, so they were anchored well offshore and the supplies ferried to the island in the boats and the pinnace. It took days, but eventually everything was transferred and the building of the colony could start.

As soon as everything was ashore, Grenville called one of his meetings. White put his arm on Kit's shoulder and they walked up the beach to where the gentlemen stood in a huddle around Ralph Lane, the governor of the colony.

'The first thing we need to do, gentlemen,' said Lane, 'is to build a fort to defend our settlement against possible attack, both by the locals and by Spaniards once they become aware of our presence. We have had some practice in Puerto Rico, so you should have few problems here. We are nicely hidden here by the sand dunes on the shore, but even so . . .'

Using the tools and equipment brought from the ships, soldiers and artisans began clearing the area of brambles and shrubs. Kit was helping White to check some of his belongings that had been carried ashore from the *Tiger* when a commotion developed among the men.

'What on earth is going on?' said White as he and Kit watched the men clearing the area shout and jump and scratch.

One man backed towards them, scratching and cursing. When he turned, Kit was shocked to see that the man's eyes and lips were swollen and red and his hands and arms were covered in blotches.

Kit backed away, fearing some kind of disease, but White was peering past the stricken man to the others who were pointing to the ground. Kit followed him as he walked towards them.

'It's this weed, sir,' said one of the men. 'It has some kind of sting in it; some kind of poison.'

White bent down and examined the trailing vine-like weed. 'Fascinating,' he said.

'What the devil's going on?' asked Lane, walking up behind them.

'The men have found some kind of poisonous weed, Master Lane,' said White.

'What's the meaning of this?' Lane yelled at Manteo. 'Is this your idea of a joke?'

Manteo walked over and looked at the weed and then at Lane. 'I do not understand,' he said.

'Why did you not tell us this was poisonous?' Lane bellowed.

Manteo leaned down and picked up a handful of the weed and rubbed it between his hands. 'Not poisonous to me,' he said. He threw the weed to Wanchese, who did the same before dropping it on the ground. Both Indians walked away and Kit was sure he saw a trace of a smile on Manteo's normally implacable face.

'Fascinating,' said White again.

Wylam chuckled and Kit leaned forward to examine the weed, as nervously as if it might jump up and seize him by the throat. Before Lane could think of anything to say, a group of young men from the village, armed with longbows, appeared at the edge of the clearing.

The village elders had not appeared threatening in any way, but these men were different. It was as if a pride of lions had entered the camp. They walked fearlessly into the midst of the colonists, tall and lean, muscular and sharp-eyed.

Manteo and Wanchese went to greet them, and they looked them up and down suspiciously, fingering their English clothes; sniffing them, mocking their hair, which had grown long on the voyage across the sea. Kit saw the sad expression on Wanchese's face and was relieved when two further Indians approached and greeted him warmly, punching him and slapping him enthusiastically. Wanchese and his two friends then walked away, talking, down towards the lagoon, and when they had satisfied their curiosity and demonstrated their fearlessness, the other Indians left too. As they turned to walk away, Kit saw the same four-arrow mark on their shoulder blades that Wanchese bore.

Kit found Wanchese later, sitting on a log. He looked up as Kit approached and smiled weakly. Kit was carrying the bow White had given him in London and Wanchese asked to look at it.

'Fine bow,' he said appreciatively. 'You can use it?'

'A little,' said Kit.

'Then we shall hunt together, English boy,' said Wanchese with a grin.

'I'd like that,' said Kit.

But then Wanchese looked away towards his village. 'Everything change now,' he said quietly.

The construction of the fort got underway as men were set to work felling trees, digging ditches and building banks of heaped sand topped with wooden ramparts. The soldiers were put to work digging and building, their breastplates and helmets piled up neatly under the remaining trees. Their brawn was put to use with axe and hammer, and even though the blows only rained down on wood and iron, Kit found himself wincing with every strike and did not like to be around the soldiers long.

Carpenters and thatchers, masons and hurdle-makers moved about overseeing the construction of living quarters. As well as shelter for the colonists, Ralph Lane saw to it that a small church was built, along with a barn and a storehouse. There was a guarded armoury to keep what was left of the powder dry and weapons safe, and a jail to house any of the soldiers who broke the rules laid down by Raleigh before they left London.

Joachim Ganz, whom Kit had barely seen on the voyage, built himself a little brick furnace to test any ores he might find, and White had the men build him a kind of study, with a covered area at the front to allow him to work outside with some protection from the elements.

When these first buildings were finished, Lane walked about the settlement clapping his hands and declaring the work to be excellent, clearly delighted that he now had a settlement over which to rule. He read Raleigh's Code of Conduct which Sir Walter had issued in London. The rules decreed that no soldier or colonist should strike or misuse an Indian or enter his house without permission, and that no Indian should be forced to work against his will.

'Do you see, Kit?' said White when Lane had left with his bodyguard. 'We will show these people that we are different from the Spanish. We will not enslave or abuse them as the Catholics do. We will show them mercy and respect as true Christians should and they will come to love us for it.'

On the 5th of August, Grenville ordered the *Elizabeth*

to sail back to England and take the great news to Queen Elizabeth that an English colony had at last been planted on American soil; the colonists stood on the dunes of the Outer Banks, waving and cheering as the ship sailed away.

The gentleman adventurers seemed to linger longest on the beach, each perhaps wondering if it had not been better to sail home when they had the chance. Kit stood with White, Lane and Grenville as the party dispersed and headed a little forlornly back to the island.

'These gentlemen try my patience!' said Lane, watching them shuffle back towards the boats and Roanoke. 'They are as vain as actors and have never put their hands to harder work than preening. Some of them are only just out of Oxford! If I had any choice in the matter I'd send every last one of them back to England with you, Sir Richard.'

'No thank you,' said Grenville with a smile. 'You are quite welcome to keep them. Personally I shall be glad to leave this place. Give me England over any land in the world, and give me the sea over England. I know where I am with the sea.'

'No, no,' said Lane. 'I would rather be here than in London. A man can breathe here.'

White nodded approvingly as Lane walked away, humming to himself. 'I agree with Master Lane,' he said. 'There is something wonderful about this place.'

'Do not be fooled by Ralph Lane, Master White. Lane believes there is gold here,' said Grenville with a smirk. 'But there is no gold in this latrine, I'll wager. That's where the gold is, my friends,' he said, pointing out to sea. 'Out there in the holds of Spanish galleons. I shall mine more gold on my return trip than Lane ever will in this place.' With that Grenville followed after Lane.

'When will they understand?' said White, shaking his head.

'Understand what, sir?' Kit asked.

'That this *is* the gold,' he said, taking in the whole landscape with a sweep of his hand. 'The treasure is not hidden in the land. The land itself *is* the treasure.'

Kit nodded. There was something about this place; something that had seeped into his heart and taken hold. He sometimes missed Hugh, and the familiarity of London, but England seemed spoiled to him now. Maybe this place was his chance for a good, true life, not the sham life he had back in London; maybe it was his chance to be something, to *mean* something.

Chapter 31

Wanchese had agreed to take Kit hunting and they walked down to the lagoon to row to the mainland. Two Indians were making a canoe as they reached the shore. They had the trunk of a huge tree propped up on branches and were burning away the inside, scraping off the charred wood with shells.

Seeing the process of manufacture, Kit was a little dubious about getting into a canoe with Wanchese, but it floated beautifully and was as responsive to Wanchese's paddling as an English punt; it was fast too, cutting through the water like an arrow.

They moored the canoe and Wanchese signalled for Kit to follow him, away from the tracks worn by men and beasts and into the dense woodland.

Kit noticed that Wanchese and his kind did not wear their quivers over their shoulders like English archers, but rather around their waists, the wicker container almost horizontal, resting on their hips. He tried to follow Wanchese's footsteps exactly, so as not to break any twigs underfoot. Kit had plenty of experience of creeping about as a thief, but this was new terrain for him. He was filled with pride when Wanchese turned and smiled, nodding in praise at Kit's stealth. Then, suddenly, Wanchese stopped, putting his hand in a signal that Kit did not know, but assumed meant 'Wait' or 'Listen'. He motioned for Kit to come a little closer and then pointed ahead.

At first Kit could see nothing in the dappled shade. Then an ear flicked to ward off a bothersome fly, and he could see two deer grazing in a small clearing. Wanchese took an arrow from his quiver and passed it to Kit, without ever taking his eyes off the deer. Kit took aim, and pulled back the bowstring, worried that his thumping heart would frighten the deer away. Wanchese took aim alongside him, as still as a statue.

Just as they were about to let fly, there was a huge bang to their right and the deer leaped away and ran off into the woods, zigzagging out of sight. Wanchese looked towards the sound of the musket shot with contempt in his eyes.

'English,' he said and the word seemed like a curse on his lips. Kit noticed that Wanchese still had an arrow ready to shoot, trained now on the English soldiers, and it took him some time to lower it.

Laughter and shouting followed the blast and seemed to be coming closer. Wanchese tapped him on the shoulder and Kit shrugged, seeing they had no option but to go. All the game for miles around would have bolted at that shot.

They set off back towards their canoe, Kit leading the way this time. Annoyed with his fellow colonists for ruining his first chance to hunt, he studied the ground at his feet sulkily as he walked. A noise ahead made him look up.

Running towards him at great speed was a huge black bear, panicked by the musket shot. Kit froze as the animal bounded towards him, certain that his last moment on earth had arrived, then Wanchese jumped in front of him and yelled, waving his arms about like a madman. The bear skidded to a halt and stood on its hind legs, roaring.

Kit came back to life, air rushing into his lungs and he yelled along with Wanchese, waving and jumping until the bear dropped its shoulder and leaped away from them, climbing up into a nearby tree.

The soldiers who had fired the musket now came thundering through the woods and saw the bear. A musketeer stood his prop in the soft earth, primed his musket and took aim, blasting a shot at the cowering bear, which dropped heavily, lifeless, to the forest floor. The soldiers whooped and danced about, clapping each other on the back, and two of them took out huge knives and advanced on the corpse.

Kit turned away and he and Wanchese walked back to the canoes. Wanchese did not speak and Kit did not try to make him. He was angry with the soldiers, angry with his own kind, but he was not sure why. After all, he had been about to kill a deer, and if Wanchese had led them to a bear, he would have joined him in the killing of that animal too.

No, it was not the killing but the killers he objected to. They did not belong here with their musket shots and swords, with their helmets and breastplates. They did not belong in this world without metal; this world of wood and shell and fur and flesh.

Kit and Wanchese returned to the settlement, rowing across to Roanoke Island in silence. As they approached the colony, White called out to them from among the trees. He had a strung bow and a quiver of arrows.

'How went the hunting?'

'There was none,' said Kit. 'Those oafs ruined it.' He gestured towards where the soldiers were noisily paddling their way across the water. White frowned, nodding, and Wanchese spat contemptuously.

'What was that, you dog?' said a soldier standing nearby. Without warning he strode towards Wanchese and dealt him a cracking blow on the side of the head with the butt of his musket.

'No!' shouted Kit as Wanchese dropped to the floor, but another soldier joined the first, grabbing Kit and shoving him out of the way.

The first soldier lifted Wanchese up and pinned him against a tree while another soldier walked across and thumped the Indian in the stomach.

'I must protest!' shouted White, but the soldiers ignored him.

'This'll teach you to spit at an Englishman,' said the second soldier, thumping Wanchese again.

'Leave him be!' yelled Kit. The soldiers turned to see Kit aiming an arrow at them.

'Fire away then, boy,' said the first soldier. 'You're just as likely to— *Jesus!*' The arrow thudded into the tree behind them, nicking the soldier's ear as it did so. White stared open-mouthed.

'*Leave him be!*' yelled Kit again.

The soldiers let go of Wanchese and he dropped to the ground holding his stomach. Kit was wondering what exactly to do next when he felt something cold and metallic jab against his neck. It was a pistol.

'Lower the bow, boy, and quickly.' Kit dropped the bow. It was Lane with four of his men. 'You two,' the governor said to the soldiers. 'Get back to your posts before I have both of you flogged.'

'Aye, sir,' said the soldiers, walking away. The one whose ear Kit had nicked glared at him as he did so.

Kit rushed to help Wanchese, who was struggling to his feet, his cheekbone swollen and bleeding from the rifle butt.

'But, Lane, those soldiers attacked this man!' said White. 'Surely they have broken Sir Walter's Code of Conduct.'

Lane closed his eyes as if listening to White took every last ounce of patience he had. 'Sir Walter is not here, Master White,' he said. 'How is the savage?'

'Nothing broken, I think,' said Kit.

Lane nodded. He walked across and looked Wanchese up and down, then leaned close, dropping his voice. 'I don't trust you, savage,' he said. 'I want you out of this colony. Do you understand?'

Wanchese stared at Lane for a long time and then nodded.

'Good.' Lane turned to Kit. 'If you ever raise arms against an Englishman in my sight again, I will kill you myself. Do I make myself understood?'

'Yes, sir,' said Kit.

'You need to decide whose side you're on, boy,' said Lane. 'Good day, Master White.'

Chapter 32

Grenville still called regular meetings of the gentleman adventurers, though even to Kit it was obvious that they no longer held him in awe as they had aboard ship. Ralph Lane took centre stage now. Some gentlemen – White included – saw Grenville as dangerously impetuous and looked forward to his departure and to Lane's governance.

At one of these meetings, Grenville told the gathering that Harriot had some strange news they might find amusing. Harriot laced his fingers together as if about to begin a sermon, and told the assembled gentlemen that he had learned that the Indians believed that the English were supernatural beings; everywhere they had travelled, death had followed in their wake, a terrible sickness spreading through the surrounding land.

Kit listened more intently than usual. Harriot said that many Indians had fallen sick and their medicine men had no cure. The smiling chieftain who had come aboard the *Tiger* when they first arrived was dead. Kit

254

thought of the little girl he had given the doll to, and the beautiful girl in the cornfields of Secota, and he felt a tightness grip his chest.

Harriot explained that the Indians believed that the English were visiting a punishment upon them because the Indians had incurred their displeasure in some way. Several faces turned to Manteo, but he looked on, as expressionless as ever.

'Where would they get such an idea?' wondered Grenville, shaking his head in disbelief.

'It matters not,' said Harriot. 'That they believe we are enchanted beings can only work to our advantage. They are superstitious souls.' Kit saw him sneak a glance at Grenville, remembering his outburst on the *Tiger*.

Grenville saw it too. 'And how are we supposed to be killing them?' he asked crossly.

'They believe we are shooting them with our guns,' said Harriot. 'They think we are shooting them with pestilence.'

Grenville laughed and remarked that they would save on ammunition in any case. 'These people are like children,' he said. Kit glanced across at Manteo, whose face as usual betrayed no emotion, despite Grenville's mocking tone.

'These people have their own beliefs, Sir Richard,' said Harriot. 'Ours must seem very strange to them.'

Grenville snorted. 'You think yourself a god then, Master Harriot?' he asked wearily.

Harriot half closed his eyes and sighed. He took a deep breath and continued. 'These people hold their ancestors in the highest esteem and worship their memory. They think we might be the dead come back to live among them.'

'So they believe us to be ghosts then?' said Grenville with a grin.

'Spirits, more like,' said Harriot with a sour pursing of his lips. 'They say the illness harms us not, but kills them. They say there are no women among us.'

'Apart from you, eh, Harriot,' said Grenville, slapping the table and laughing loudly.

Then Kit noticed that, one by one, all the men of the colony were stopping work and staring off to the north. His view was obscured by part of the palisade and he walked round to see what they were looking at.

Walking towards them across the clearing was a large group of Indians. A flock of birds took flight as they approached, flying in a wide arc over their heads and fluttering noisily away towards the mainland. The Indians at the front of the party were young men, armed with bows.

Grenville walked across to Manteo. 'What's this?' he hissed.

Kit could now see that in the middle of the front line of young men was an older man who had something metallic hanging around his neck, swinging back and forth and glinting in the sun as he moved.

'It is Wingina,' said Manteo. 'Chief of this land.'

'Is it now?' said Lane. 'So this is the great man? I can't say he looks very impressive.'

'He has killed many men,' said Manteo. 'And not with muskets,' he added dismissively.

Wingina strode forward. Lane was right to say he was not physically intimidating. He was not especially tall. He was not especially muscular. He had no weapons at all. The only thing that marked him out from the others was a huge square of copper plate hanging around his neck.

But although Wingina may not have been muscle-bound, his body was lithe and taut like that of a hunting dog or a cheetah. This was not the wasted body of a hungry man, but the toned body of a hunter and fighter. A lion's tail hung between his legs, almost reaching the floor, and for a moment Kit thought it was actually part of the Indian's body. Seconds later, he had realized his foolishness and seen that the tail came from a skin wrapped around his waist. There was something awe-inspiring about this man standing before them, weaponless, dressed in the skin of a mountain lion he had killed.

Wingina looked at them with the same haughty contempt that Kit had seen on the faces at the court of Queen Elizabeth, and he watched them with as much royal disdain as Elizabeth herself showed. For the first time, Kit felt like an intruder in someone else's land. They had been invited here by Wingina's brother, Granganimeo, but Kit had the feeling that Wingina wanted them to be reminded that they were here only because he allowed it. He so obviously ruled here, it seemed an act of rudeness not to bow.

The soldiers watched the Indians suspiciously and the Indians looked back like a mirror. White followed them all, scribbling away as usual. Wingina searched every corner of the fort and cocked his head like a bird, his fierce eyes trying to make sense of these newcomers and their strange ways.

With White, Kit followed the Indian chief, watching his every move. Now and again, Wingina would turn to one of his followers and speak in a clear deep voice, and a discussion would break out for a minute or two while Lane stood impatiently nearby with a fixed smile.

As the tour came to an end, Lane asked Manteo to pass on the thanks of England and of Queen Elizabeth for welcoming them to these shores. He said that Wingina was welcome to visit the fort whenever he liked.

Kit could see Wingina smile wryly at this invitation to tread his own land, to walk on the ground his people had walked for season after season. The chief turned and led his men back to his village at the other end of the island. As Kit watched them leave, he became aware of someone standing next to him and turned to find it was Wanchese.

'I must go,' said Wanchese sadly. 'I cannot stay here.' He glanced at Lane. 'I must be with my people.'

Kit nodded sadly. 'You'll come back, though?'

'Yes,' said Wanchese. 'I will come back. We will be friends still?'

'Always.'

They embraced and Wanchese walked away,

following the other Indians back to their village. As he got to the edge of the colony, Manteo grabbed his arm. He spoke for some time with Wanchese staring impassively, then Wanchese shrugged his hand away and walked on. Manteo hung his head and then came back towards Kit, his face taut with silent anger.

Chapter 33

The hot summer days brought clouds of mosquitoes rising up greedily from the lagoon to feast on the colonists, and the mosquitoes in turn brought swallows swooping after them, gliding across the water, inches from the surface. The swallows roosted in the trees around the camp and twittered as the sun rose.

The warm nights were full of the rhythmic chirping of cicadas, a noise that some in the colony found irritating beyond endurance, but which Kit found strangely soothing – unlike the frogs that croaked incessantly to each other among the moonlit reed beds.

Kit had seen little in the way of wildlife during his life in London – save for scavengers like kites, rats and ravens – and he was fascinated by the animal life around him. Wanchese had been his guide over those first few weeks, naming beasts and giving warnings when necessary – as in the case of the foul-smelling skunk or the turtles in the lagoon, which could rip a man's toe off.

But now Wanchese was gone and the animals Kit

feared the most were inside the colony. He had a dread of the mastiffs the soldiers had brought; he felt that they sensed his fear of them and they seemed to watch him wherever he went. If he came near them, they growled and showed their teeth, and when they were let loose, he felt his heart would stop beating from fear that they would attack him.

One day he stood with his back pinned to the wall of the jailhouse as the three dogs wandered about the colony, sniffing and barking. One stopped and looked at him, then walked slowly forward, growling. A soldier whistled and the dog turned away in an instant and ran off.

Wylam wandered over to stand next to Kit. 'You fear the dogs?' he asked.

'Me?' said Kit. 'No. Not really.' He saw Wylam's sceptical look. 'Yes. Yes. They terrify me. They hate me. I can feel it.'

'No they don't,' said Wylam. 'They think you hate them.'

'They're right. I do.'

Wylam laughed. Another mastiff trotted up and stood nearby, sniffing the air. 'We are going to make friends with this dog,' said Wylam.

'We are?' said Kit with a worried frown.

'But we must not let him know that we want to make friends, or he will be suspicious.' The mastiff looked towards Kit quizzically, cocking his head. 'We are just going to get on with something and ignore him,' said Wylam.

'With what?' said Kit.

'Anything,' said Wylam, picking up a stone and showing it to Kit. 'Take no notice of him. He will either walk away or come and see what we are doing.' Kit fervently hoped the dog would walk away. 'Good, he's coming over. Keep calm, Kit.' Kit heard the mastiff padding nearer and nearer until he could hear him breathing just behind him.

'Take the stone, Kit,' said Wylam. 'Have a good look at it. He wants to know what you're up to.' The huge head of the mastiff edged forward, sniffing at Kit's hand and the stone it contained. 'Speak up, Kit. Talk. Put the devil at ease.'

'What should I say?'

'It doesn't matter,' said Wylam with a laugh. 'It's not what you say, it's how you say it.' The mastiff sniffed at Kit's clothes and nuzzled his leg. 'Soon you will be eliminated from his list of things that might be a threat. You have been accepted.'

Another mastiff wandered up and joined the first in sniffing Kit's clothes; then they both looked at the stone and began to whimper.

'I think they want you to play,' said Wylam.

'Play?' said Kit doubtfully.

'Throw the stone.'

Kit lifted the stone over his head and both animals tensed, their faces suddenly alert, their ears cocked, their eyes bright. Before the stone left Kit's hand, the mastiffs were bounding away, looking back over their shoulders, jockeying for position, squabbling over the rights to the stone when they found it. They were still fighting over the stone when a whistle sent them bounding away through the colony and out of sight.

Kit shook his head in amazement. 'Thank you, sir.'

Wylam slapped him on the back. 'The trick with animals is not to try too hard,' he said. 'Make them feel at ease, that's the trick.' He smiled his broad smile, twirling his silver ring back and forth. 'The same goes for people.'

On the 24th of August, St Bartholomew's Day, 1585, Grenville's men made their final preparations to leave the colony under Lane's command. Farewells were said among those who had forged friendships during the last few months, and Kit stood on the shore and watched as the sails of the last of the English ships faded from view.

Though he had wanted to stay, he had a moment of panic as they began to disappear completely. Now the colony was truly on its own. Kit thought of the Huguenots at Fort Caroline. Would they fare any better if the Spanish attacked? And suddenly he was overwhelmed by thoughts of what had happened to him in just over a year. For the first time he felt a touch of nostalgia for his old life with Hugh; not for the life itself, which had in its own way been as fraught with dangers as his life in Virginia, but for the familiarity of it.

Summer was waning now. The swallows began to leave for warmer climes, and the trees were filled with roosting bats. The eggs the diamondback terrapins had laid in May now hatched, and herons loped about, jutting their long stabbing beaks greedily among the needle rushes. Orange and black butterflies flitted about, feeding on the myriad yellow flowers that covered the bushes all about.

Winds began to stiffen and blow for days, shaking the mighty cedars and making them roar in an echo of the ocean beyond the dunes. The wind made strange music among the dried grasses and rushes, whistling and moaning as if a wraith were haunting the lagoon. Birds hopped about at the base of the trees, looking for berries the wind had shaken free, preparing themselves for the hardships of winter.

One morning Kit was standing with White, gazing out across the lagoon – as choppy as the ocean, scattered with white breakers – when Lane wandered over to them and told White that he wanted him and Harriot to explore and map the area to the north of the lagoon: it was important that they know something of that country and make contact with the people there.

White readily agreed. 'I am filled with curiosity about this land, sir,' he said. 'A curiosity shared by my young assistant here.'

Lane stared at Kit as if he had never seen him before and was unnerved by his presence, then laughed, clapping his hands together. 'Excellent, excellent,' he said and walked off.

Kit and White exchanged quizzical glances as a huge

flock of geese honked by overhead, heading for the lagoon.

'Well, at any rate,' said White, 'now that Sir Richard is gone, it seems as though we are to see something of this country; and without a troop of bloodthirsty oafs with us this time. There will be no burning of villages on this trip. We can mend some fences, Kit. We can be a force for good. What do you say? We should be away for several months, you know.'

'Yes indeed, sir.'

Kit was eager to go. The island had begun to feel very small. They had come to colonize Virginia, but they were huddled together on a tiny part of a tiny island with an increasingly bored and volatile garrison of soldiers. He would be happy to get away.

Chapter 34

The expedition set off in two boats: Kit, White and Ganz shared one with two soldiers to man the oars, and Harriot and Manteo took the other with two more soldiers. They headed north from Roanoke Island and up a narrow fork in the lagoon, then out into the ocean through another gap in the long sand wall of the coast, before heading back inland and into the wide bay beside the village of Apasus. This bay was named Chesapeake Bay after another village nearby.

As they travelled, Harriot – and sometimes Kit – took measurements of the land around them using the cross-staff, the astrolabe and the compass, and White took notes and made sketches of features in the landscape, detailing every inlet and headland and gauging their latitude. When Kit had first arrived, he had seen what appeared to him to be almost empty forest along the shoreline, but now his eyes had grown accustomed to this world and he had learned to see and recognize even the shyest of animals – even to name them. So too had he learned to see the Indians, who were so adept at standing in the dappled shadows, practically invisible.

They camped at the northern reaches of the lagoon. The days were shortening and the winds brought a chill on their breath. Everywhere birds and animals could be seen stocking up on berries and nuts to see them through the cold months to come. Bears were preparing for the winter's sleep, and one eyed them warily from the bank as they rowed past, sniffing the air and moaning plaintively.

Kit watched as Ganz crouched beside the river and stared into the water with the rigid concentration of a heron. Occasionally he would slowly reach out and plunge his hand into the cold water, bring out a pebble, hold it up to the light and then toss it back into the river. After a few minutes he stood up and shook his head, muttering to himself in his own language. He noticed Kit watching and nodded to the river with his head.

'This country,' he said. 'There is no value here. I would find more gold in the sewers of Prague than here.' He spat at the ground in disgust and walked further along, muttering. Some way off he stopped, his attention caught by something on the ground in front of him. He stooped, picked up a small stone, cursed and tossed it as far as he could throw it before continuing to grumble to himself.

Kit walked over to White, who was sitting on a large

rock. 'He's not very happy, is he?' he said. 'And there's something about him I don't really like.'

'Minerals men are a strange lot,' said White. 'As I discovered on my first voyages to the Americas.'

'You never did tell me what happened,' said Kit.

White smiled, and after a sigh told Kit that the first time he had travelled to America, the expedition had returned with an Eskimo and a piece of black rock they had believed to be an ore. The German minerals men said it was gold, and had built a huge furnace down at Deptford ready to process it.

'Gold!' said White with a shake of his head. 'They always want gold.'

He then went on to explain that he had sailed with another expedition the following summer. The promise of gold had produced £1,000 worth of backing from the Queen. Kit whistled at the amount. White told him they had taken 250 men with them, and another 150 Cornish miners.

'And did they find gold?'

White frowned, clearly disappointed that Kit should be quite so fascinated by this aspect of the trip. 'Well,' he said, 'we came back with twelve hundred tons of the black rock we had found the year before.'

Kit whistled with amazement. 'Twelve hundred tons!' he said, though he had no real idea how much that was. 'How much gold did they get out of that?'

'None,' said White with a smile. 'The ore was fool's gold. The German experts had lied. Gold!' He shook his head. 'It is always about gold.'

'And what do you expect?' said Ganz, walking up beside them. 'This is what everyone wants to hear. If I find gold, then they will use me again. If I do not, I will be sent away like unwanted baggage.' He sat down, pulling out his notebook and beginning to scribble down his observations. 'Such is the life of a mineral man.'

White apologized and said he needed to stretch his legs, something he always said when he needed to relieve himself. He went over to a small clump of trees nearby. Ganz and Kit could hear him singing an old song in a thin voice to frighten away any bears who might be lurking nearby.

'Where do you come from, Master Ganz, if you don't mind me asking?' said Kit as White rejoined them.

'From Prague,' Ganz replied. 'In Bohemia. Have you been to Bohemia, Master White?'

'No,' said White. 'Sadly not.'

'You?' he asked Kit.

'Me? I don't even know where Bohemia is.'

Ganz sighed loudly, returning to his notebooks.

'That writing,' said Kit, looking over his shoulder and feeling emboldened by White's comforting presence. 'Is that Bohemia-nish?'

White chuckled.

Ganz did not join him. 'It is Hebrew,' he said.

'Hebrew?' Kit queried.

'The language of the Jews,' said Ganz.

'The language of the Jews?'

'That is correct. I am a Jew. Does that offend you?'

'Me?' said Kit. 'No. I've never had anything to do with Jews, sir. There aren't any Jews in London.'

Ganz laughed, stopped, looked at Kit as a parent might look at a foolish infant, and then laughed again.

'What?' said Kit. 'What's so funny?'

'Nothing,' said Ganz. 'You make me laugh, that is all.'

Kit scowled. 'What are you saying; that there *are* Jews in England?'

Ganz smiled and shrugged. 'There are not,' he said. 'And yet there are.'

Kit frowned, regretting that he had begun the conversation. He got up to leave, but Ganz put his hand on his arm and nodded towards the ground.

'Forgive me,' he said. 'I wish I were across the sea and it makes me bad company.'

Kit wondered if Ganz was ever 'good' company, but he sat back down. 'I didn't mean any offence,' he said.

'No,' said Ganz. 'It is just that we have to be careful, we Jews. We have to be on our guard always. It can mean the difference between life and death for us.'

Kit thought of his parents and nodded. He knew how religious beliefs could lead to suspicion and death. 'What did you mean just now,' he asked, 'when you said there were no Jews in England, but there were?'

Ganz looked at him and smiled. 'I mean that there are no Jews who turn a Jewish face to the world,' he said. 'But rest assured there are Jews in England. There are Jews everywhere. That is our fate: to be everywhere – and everywhere despised.' He looked about him. 'One day there will be Jews even here.' He screwed up his face and shook his head sorrowfully. 'Such is our fate.'

Chapter 35

The small band of explorers moved north, rowing along the shore. Winter began to bite, snow blowing from the north and east and water freezing in the creeks. They had brought thick fur sailors' hats with them, but the cold still bored into Kit's bones.

They headed away from the Secotan lands in the south and up into the country of the Weapemeoc. As they went, they made varied expeditions inland and met with the local Indians, sharing their fires and trading goods, swapping dolls for warmer clothing. White traded drawings for fur-lined mittens for them all. Soon they were almost indistinguishable from the natives, wrapped in hide blankets and wearing buckskin boots.

They learned not to force themselves on the Indians, but to wait until they were invited. If there was any sign that they were anything but friendly, they would move on. But wherever they were given shelter, they were treated with great courtesy as welcome guests.

They rowed on to the village of Skicoak, which was

built on an inlet on Chesapeake Bay. They were invited to sit near the fire with the elders and Manteo translated their stories of England, while the Indians – smeared with ochre and bear oil to ward off evil and the cold – told tales of hard winters, great hunts and old wars.

Uppowoc pipes were passed around. Many of the men smoked a pipe about the colony now, and *uppowoc* pipes had been handed round at villages they had visited, but White had always avoided it until now. He smiled, nodded and inhaled deeply, collapsing in a fit of coughing, his face bright red and tears rolling down his face.

The Indians laughed heartily at the choking white man, and they were joined by Ganz and Kit; Kit finding it especially amusing. When White had recovered, he frowned and passed the pipe to Kit, but Manteo said he was too young.

'Man's business,' he said, much to Kit's relief.

Only Harriot remained, and at first he pursed his lips and refused, but when it was clear that his refusal would cause offence, he had no choice. He puckered up several times, willing himself to take the pipe in his mouth. To Kit's surprise he inhaled deeply and smiled benignly, smoke coming out of his nose.

The Indians nodded appreciatively. Harriot nodded back, rose to his feet, took a few steps away and vomited copiously. Even White joined in the ensuing laughter, while Harriot walked off as if nothing had happened.

As hard as the travelling was, Kit felt keenly alive

in those woods and creeks and coastal reaches, as if London had been merely a half-life. He was happy, too, to be away from the other colonists. The soldiers who accompanied them seemed less threatening in a small group and kept themselves to themselves.

Kit grew to like Ganz, who he realized had a dark sense of humour that it took a little while to appreciate, but was all the better for the effort, and while he did not develop an affection for Harriot or Manteo, at least they did not frighten him any more.

The travellers sat together when they camped away from Indian villages, sitting around the fire talking about the events of the day, reliving adventures and telling old stories as if they were Indians themselves. On one such evening, the subject of Lane came up, with much mirth at his expense, and Kit broached something that had bothered him for some time.

'What I don't understand is,' he said, 'why do Nugent, and the other Irishmen Lane has, fight for him? The English are trying to take over their land, aren't they? And why would they leave their homeland and work for a man like Raleigh? He was at Smerwick after all, wasn't he? And from what I hear, he was fearsome hard on the Irish wherever he went. They ought to hate him.'

'But Nugent and the other Irishmen among our number are Protestants, Kit,' said White. 'That makes a difference, does it not?'

'But what kind of person would help foreigners against their own countrymen?' said Kit, not realizing until he had said the words that this was exactly what some English Catholics were guilty of.

White cast a nervous glance at Manteo. 'Well,' he said, searching for an answer, 'perhaps they see the greater good for their fellows?'

Ganz snorted and Manteo looked away.

'Pah,' said Ganz. 'Why does a wolf become a dog?' Kit shrugged and Ganz leaned towards him to continue. 'Hunger,' he said. 'It is always about hunger.'

Winter brought raging seas and the Atlantic hurled itself at the coast, churning up the waters of Chesapeake Bay. When the wind ceased its roaring, terrible choking fogs descended, so thick that to float in them was like floating in the clouds and all navigation was impossible.

They explored the sea coast a little, walking out onto the beach, collecting shells and watching dolphins leaping in the surf. Oyster-catchers probed the sands with their vermilion beaks, and black, lizard-like cormorants flew low along the waves.

White said the prayers on Christmas Day while Manteo and Ganz stood at the sea's edge.

After the service Ganz wandered back to them and White frowned at him. 'It is a shame that you take the side of the heathen on such a holy day,' he said.

'A holy day for you,' said Ganz. 'Not for me. Everyone is a heathen to Christians, Master White; everyone who does not share your opinion. Christians do not agree with anyone else in the world – only they can be right. Yet if you can get two Christians to agree with each other about anything, it will only be to agree on what punishment they intend to mete out to another Christian for not following their exact path. Pah!'

Kit laughed but stopped almost immediately when he saw White's frown.

'It is not an opinion,' said White gently. 'It is the truth. It is the word of God made manifest through his son, our Lord Jesus Christ.'

Ganz shrugged. 'What need does God have of a son?' he said. 'He is God.'

Harriot chuckled, but even Kit was shocked by such open blasphemy. By the time White had recovered enough to think of a response, the mineral man was yards away.

'God created the world and everyone in it,' said White matter-of-factly. 'They are God's creatures whether they know it or not, and they must be brought to the truth of Christ, Our Lord.'

Kit looked at Manteo, who was warming his hands on the fire, and realized that, even after all this time, he had no idea what he and his people believed. Questioning, he asked Manteo to tell them about his religion. At first the Indian squinted at Kit, suspecting that he was being made fun of, but seeing that the boy was serious, and encouraged by Harriot, Manteo spoke up, his voice gradually taking on an almost sermon-like tone.

His people, the Indian explained, venerated their ancestors. Kit remembered the lines of dried bodies at

Secota and nodded. It did not seem quite so extraordinary now; nothing seemed so extraordinary now. Then Manteo spoke of a world of spirits – spirits of the woods, of the trees and rocks, the rivers and brooks; of the sun and sky. He spoke of how these spirits might come to a man and guide him through dreams and visions.

'Do you have a spirit guide?' asked Kit.

'Eagle,' answered Manteo. 'You?'

Harriot explained that the English did not have spirit guides, but Manteo ignored him, staring at Kit.

'I'm not sure,' said Kit.

Manteo spoke about the way of the Algonquian warrior. The listeners grew more solemn as he told them how they would smoke *uppowoc* pipes before a battle; how they would prepare a feast and consult the medicine man to call down spirits to aid them in their fight. When he had finished summoning up this vision of bloodlust, there was an awkward silence and Harriot tried to lighten the mood by asking Manteo what his people believed about the world's creation as they had no Bible and no Adam and Eve. He asked him how his people thought the world began.

'We believe that the sea was made first and that all life came from the sea . . .' began Manteo.

White sighed, his patience exhausted. 'Listen to that, Master Harriot! We are fish!' he said.

Manteo looked up at him but said nothing further; he simply returned to warming his hands by the fire.

Chapter 36

The expedition headed south in the spring. The cold waters of the lagoon and the surrounding creeks were gradually warming up, and blue-grey herons and snow-white egrets waded among the marsh grass, hunting for frogs and little fish.

Diamondback terrapins swam about with their heads poking out of the water, looking warily this way and that as rain began to fall, gently at first and then steadily, beating down on the cedars and myrtles and the surface of the water, making a continual and deafening roar.

Harriot made a note of every plant and animal they saw, asking Manteo for the Algonquian name and giving the English equivalent if there was one. Kit marvelled at his insatiable curiosity. It was as if he would not rest until he knew *everything*; until every last living thing was observed and itemized.

Kit and White huddled on the boat under a canvas canopy erected to protect White's notebooks and drawings from the worst of the weather, but the shower passed as suddenly as it had begun and a rainbow appeared above the dunes of the Outer Banks. An osprey hunted along the edge of the salt marsh.

As soon as they jumped ashore at Roanoke, Kit could see immediately that the colony had not fared well in their absence. The houses bore the scars of the winter storms and one was being re-thatched as they arrived. But it was more than that.

The faces of the colonists seemed downcast and exhausted, though they brightened when they saw the boats approaching. A shout went up and the settlers gathered on the shore to welcome them.

'Good to see you back, Kit,' said Wylam, putting his arm round Kit's shoulder.

'It's good to be back,' said Kit, though as soon as the words escaped he knew it was not really true.

The colony was a centre of familiarity in this strange land; the place where England existed in miniature. But looking round at the dishevelled and sullen gentlemen and the hard-faced soldiers, he was not sure he would not have felt more relaxed in an Indian village.

After talking to a group of Indians who had come to the camp to barter, Manteo quickly discovered that relations with the natives had deteriorated while they had been gone. The soldiers had scared away all the game for miles around with their muskets, and boredom and resentment had made them casually cruel to the local people. It soon became clear where the blame lay.

White, Manteo, Ganz, Harriot and Kit found Lane

standing in shallow water at the lagoon's edge, a spear in his hand. They called out and he put his fingers to his lips without turning round, staring at the water ahead of him and suddenly hurling his spear.

One of the mastiffs trotted up to Kit and nuzzled his hand. Kit dropped to his haunches and patted the dog on his flanks. The mastiff wagged his tail and looked wearily at Lane.

'Hell's teeth!' Lane hissed at the approaching group. 'Do you see? Do you see now how you put me off? Who is it?'

'Master White, sir,' said White. 'Master Harriot and I have returned from our expedition. We have come to brief you on our findings.'

Lane stared at them, going from face to face; from White to Kit, from Kit to Ganz, from Ganz to Harriot, looking utterly lost until he shook himself and cried, 'White, White. Yes, of course. Good to have you back.' He splashed his way to the shore with the carefree swagger of a child, and jabbed the multi-barbed point of his spear to within an inch of White's nose. 'See that, Master White?' he said. 'It's the barbed tail of a strange crab they have here that is encased in a kind of helmet. Ingenious, is it not?'

'Very,' said White, gently turning the spear point aside with his index finger.

'I have become rather adept at spear-fishing while you have been gone,' said Lane.

'Have you, sir?'

Kit heard the concern in White's voice and could understand it. Lane seemed oddly animated, gesticulating wildly with his spear as he spoke, making Kit and the others lean back and dodge to avoid being poked by the barbed point.

'Sir,' began White, 'I must advise you that the Indians are losing patience with us.' He paused. 'And who can blame them? They accepted us as guests in their country and we have ill-used their generosity.'

Lane laughed. 'Dear me, Master White,' he said, 'I think these months among the savages have turned your head.'

'Look about you, sir,' said White. 'You have barely enough food to see us through to the end of the winter and God knows if we will ever see Sir Richard again. If we do not get supplies from England soon, we could starve! We need these savages more than they need us.'

Lane sighed and put his hand on White's shoulder. 'Master White,' he said. 'Calm yourself. I want this colony to thrive as much as you. More so, for I am charged with its safety and its success.'

Kit recognized the red-rimmed wildness in Lane's eyes. The streets of London had their share of mad-eyed prophets and crazed old soldiers. Kit had learned through painful experience to see the signs and avoid them. It could mean the difference between staying alive and ending up in the gutter. He listened as Lane told White that he had a plan to lead a further expedition inland. When asked when they would need to be ready to leave, Lane told him that he, White, would not be needed. Lane himself would take a force of men in a search for copper mines Wingina had told him about that lay inland at a place called Chaunis Temoatan.

'We cannot eat copper!' shouted White.

Kit stood staring at White's sudden forcefulness as Lane turned angrily on White, and Kit feared for his safety. There was a kind of deadness in Lane's eyes.

'Listen to me, mapmaker,' said Lane. 'Whether we live or die is of no consequence if we fail to show some profit from our expedition. Great men have pledged money to pay for this undertaking, Master White. Men like Walsingham and Hatton. Men who do not like to be disappointed, if you follow me? Do not forget that the Queen herself has invested in this adventure.' He leaned closer. 'The Queen herself,' he hissed. 'You may draw as many flowers as you like, but Sir Walter and the Queen, they want a return on their investment.'

'But it is only copper,' said White.

Lane grinned at White conspiratorially, then looked suspiciously at Kit. 'These savages use the same word – *wassador* – for all metals,' he said. 'Wingina himself has told me where we will find these copper mines, and we shall see whether this copper does not turn to gold as we follow his directions and travel inland.'

White opened his mouth to speak but could see it was of no use. Grenville had been right; Lane *did* think he was going to find gold here. Lane then clapped his fingertips together excitedly and rose up and down on the balls of his feet, before going to confer with the ever-present Nugent.

Nothing would dissuade Lane from his gold-hunting venture, and some of the gentlemen – bored to the point of recklessness and eager to show some return for the discomfort they had endured – gave him encouragement by agreeing to go with him. Lane had ordered Wylam to accompany him. As the soldiers loaded the expedition boats only a day or so after Kit had arrived back at Roanoke, Wylam said farewell to him at the shore. Manteo, their guide once again on this trip, was standing nearby, staring into the distance.

'You look worried, Master Manteo,' said Wylam. 'Is there something I should know?'

'We go to the land of the Mondoag,' said Manteo ominously. 'It means rattlesnake. You know this snake?' Kit and Wylam shook their heads. 'It is a snake with a tail . . .' Manteo shook his hand and made a rattling, hissing noise with his mouth. 'It is killer.' He made a snake's head with his fingers and lunged towards them, making Kit jump.

'Who are they?' said Wylam. 'These rattlesnakes of yours?'

'They are not Algonquian people like we Secotan,' said Manteo. 'The Mondoag are Iroquois people – old enemy of Algonquian. They are bad men. Dangerous men.'

'Well then,' said Wylam, flashing his customary smile at Kit, 'I am rather wishing I had not asked.' He slapped a hand on Manteo's shoulder. 'Come on, friend,' he said. 'We'll show those rattlesnakes, eh? Farewell, Kit!'

Kit watched Lane and his men row away, the three mastiffs standing proudly in the prow, sniffing the air. He could hear the rhythmic slap of the oars fade away, to be replaced by the chattering and twittering of the woods. And suddenly he saw the medicine man watching the departing men, standing among the trees as still as a statue before vanishing into the woods like smoke.

Chapter 37

They had been in Virginia a year now. The ditches they had dug were thick with weeds, and creepers had begun to climb the wooden stockade. Like the fabric of the colony, the men too were being slowly taken over by the land as broken straps and belts were replaced by native ones and broken shoes gave way to buckskin moccasins.

But Kit could see that the Indians' curiosity had gone and their eagerness to trade had dwindled away. There was less and less that the English had that the Indians wanted; and that which they so desperately desired – English steel and English muskets – they knew now they could never have except by force.

Kit noticed that Wingina was constantly eyeing the English weapons with transparent avarice. He continued to visit the colony and seemed more at ease now that Lane had gone. He was fascinated by the English church services – he seemed to particularly enjoy the hymn singing – and White took this as a sign that the Indians might one day come to Christ, but Kit was not so sure.

The Indians certainly liked to sing, but they had no idea what the words meant. Kit caught Ganz watching one day and saw a look of distaste sour his already grumpy features. When Kit asked him what the matter was, Ganz checked that no one was in earshot before replying.

'Why do Christians want everyone to be Christians?' he whispered. 'I am a Jew. I do not want everyone to be a Jew.'

Kit smiled; he had the distinct feeling that Ganz did not particularly crave company of any kind, Jewish or otherwise.

Ganz shook his head. 'And what is more, it is not enough to be Christian – you have to be the right *kind* of Christian, or . . .' He made a cutting motion across his throat with his finger. 'You know what they would do to a Catholic here? Another Christian like them and yet . . .' He could not find the words for how insane this seemed to him.

As the Indians came and went to the settlement, Kit always searched their faces, looking for Wanchese, but he never appeared. He worried that he had fallen victim to the terrible illness that had swept through the native villages. In the days before Manteo had left with Lane, he had asked him if he could enquire after Wanchese's whereabouts but Manteo had said that he had made his choice; he was an enemy of the colonists now and they should not have anything to do with him. As Manteo had walked away, Kit had noted that his village mark remained hidden under the European clothes he had chosen to wear in the settlement. It was as if he no longer thought of himself as Indian; as if he believed he could shape-shift into an Englishman by wearing English clothes.

Despite Manteo's words, Kit still searched the faces of the natives, and one day – instead of finding Wanchese – he found himself looking into the smiling eyes of the girl from Secota. She looked down at the ground bashfully, then, clearly concentrating very hard, she twisted her mouth into a pained expression and said, 'Kit.'

Kit grinned and nodded.

'Acaunque,' she said, holding her hand to her breast.

'Akka–un–kway,' repeated Kit. She laughed and he was embarrassed to notice that her bare breasts trembled as she did so, but she did not seem to share his awkwardness and so his embarrassment quickly passed.

The Indians she was with were leaving and she nodded towards them, clearly indicating that she must go. Kit touched her gently on the arm as she was about to move away and she turned back to face him, wide-eyed. He did not want her to simply go; he wanted to mark this meeting in some way. Looking down, he pulled a button from his jerkin and held it out to her.

Acaunque took it and smiled sweetly, lifting her necklace over her head and holding it out to him. The necklace was beautifully made of small shells and bones and Kit shook his head, saying it was too much for something so slight as a button. But the girl looked so hurt at his refusal that he changed his mind and took the necklace, smiling and thanking her until she was pulled away by an old woman who clucked her teeth. She looked over her shoulder as she was led away and Kit waved until she was out of sight, then looked down at the necklace in his hands, still warm from her skin.

'Akka-un-kway,' he whispered to himself.

Ganz walked past and raised his hands, mimed a bow and arrow and fired an imaginary shot at Kit. 'Cupid's hunting you, boy,' he said with a grin.

Chapter 38

Whenever the Indians came to the colony after that, Kit would glance up from his work in anticipation of seeing Acaunque's quiet face looking back, and the days on which she appeared seemed more intense somehow; as clear and sharp as a cut diamond.

She would come and stand near him and watch him grinding pigments or stand in fascination as White painted one of his careful studies of the creatures they had seen on their journey, needing to run her fingers across them to convince herself that they existed only as marks on paper.

One day Acaunque was sitting with Kit while she helped Harriot to catalogue some seeds he had collected. Harriot would hold up a seed and she would squint at it and give its name if she recognized it; then he would try and set this down phonetically, the Indians having no written language.

Acaunque was fascinated by the whole process, staring intently at the strange marks Harriot made in response to her speaking. When he was finished, Harriot smiled and thanked her, replacing all the seeds in a wooden box. When he left, Kit and Acaunque turned their attention to White, who was painting nearby.

White was working up one of the drawings he had done in Secota; the drawing of the medicine man. Acaunque squealed in excitement as she recognized the subject, but Kit noticed that this excitement was soon replaced by a look of dread, as she took two steps backwards.

White looked up and saw Acaunque's expression.

'I hope I have not offended her,' said White. 'Perhaps I have committed some sort of sacrilege in their world by portraying such a sorcerer.' But Kit understood Acaunque's concern. It was one he had shared.

'No, sir,' he said with a smile. 'It is because she thinks *you* are a sorcerer.'

It took a little while for Kit to persuade Acaunque to look at any more of White's drawings and paintings, though once she started, her curiosity took over and she could not stop herself. As each new sheet was placed in front of her, she gazed at Kit with a look of wonder.

As Kit looked at White's work once more – at the beautiful pictures of the iguana and flying fish he had painted in the West Indies and paintings of the Indians and their villages here in Virginia – Kit found himself wondering if White was not a wizard after all. Surely it was some kind of magic to copy a man; to capture him in coloured pigments?

Kit happened to look away and saw Harriot standing with a group of native elders. It was obvious from their grave expressions that whatever was being discussed was very serious. White had noticed this meeting also and got to his feet, watching in silence.

The Indians talked to Harriot for some minutes, with Harriot saying little but nodding gravely. When the men had finished, he spoke for some time to them and there was much nodding and patting of shoulders and shaking of hands.

Kit had noticed that the Indians seemed to set a lot of store by these greetings and partings – it was something he liked about them. Normally these formalities were accompanied by smiles; but not this day.

Harriot walked solemnly towards them. He told them that another wave of sickness had moved through the Indian village. Wingina and his father had both been taken ill; although Wingina had recovered, his father had not.

'There is more,' said Harriot, seeing the look of concern on White's face at hearing the news. 'There is word that Lane is dead.'

'Dead?' said White, looking about him nervously. 'What of his men? Are they all dead too?'

'Yes,' said Harriot, shaking his head and almost pushing Kit out of the way. Kit stared away in the direction the boats had gone, remembering Wylam's carefree smile. Harriot kept his voice low and spoke casually so as not to attract attention from others in the colony, looking every now and then at Acaunque. She frowned, understanding the gravity of what was being said from their expressions, though not knowing what the words were. 'They say that some of the men were killed by the Iroquois and the rest starved; now Wingina is apparently telling his people that we are not spirits after all, but ordinary men; men who can be killed.'

'The truth is out then,' said White with a sigh.

'Damn that madman Lane!' said Harriot.

'It was a blasphemy that they believed those lies in the first place,' said White.

'It was a blasphemy that served us well!' snapped Harriot.

'I am sorry, Kit,' said White. 'We will both miss Manteo. And your friend Wylam was among the party, was he not?'

'Yes, sir, he was.' Kit looked forlornly at the water. He felt more numb than sad. It seemed wrong that such a man should have his life thrown away by a man like Lane.

Harriot told them he had learned that the Indians had lost any awe they had felt for the English God when the English God could not even protect his own people from the Mondoag. And Lane's adventure had played straight into Wingina's hands. Wingina had been happy to send Lane and his muskets into the lands of his enemy; they might kill some of the wretched Mondoag before they were eventually killed themselves. Wingina was wary of Lane, but with the governor gone, he no longer felt forced to co-operate with the settlers. He was going to move his people away from the village on Roanoke and take them across the lagoon to his mainland stronghold of Dasamonquepeuc.

'But we cannot survive without their help,' said White. 'We will starve.'

'He knows that well enough,' said Harriot.

White sighed and looked as troubled as Kit had ever seen him. Acaunque squinted into Kit and White's frowning faces, cocking her head, trying to understand what was going on.

'Mondoag,' said Kit.

'Mondoag,' repeated Acaunque grimly, guessing some of Kit's meaning.

Harriot went about the colony to pass on the news. Kit watched the men gather around him in small knots, hanging on every word until Harriot told them of the death of their comrades, and then breaking away with curses and clenched fists. And as one such group passed Kit and Acaunque, fresh from their meeting with Harriot, one of the soldiers spat straight into Acaunque's face.

Kit threw himself on the man, shoving him back, but he was shrugged off and swatted away with the back of his hand. Kit blinked against the sting of the blow and gathered himself again. This time the man knocked Kit to the floor and drew a dagger.

'Indian lover!' he hissed. 'Next time I'll gut you, you little bastard!' And he turned and strode off.

Kit staggered to his feet, still a little groggy, and went

over to Acaunque, who was wiping the spittle from her face and staring after the man who had attacked them. He put out his hand but could not bring himself to touch her. She turned and walked away and Kit watched her go, aching with anger and sadness.

'Maybe it is for the best,' said White.

Kit turned on him. 'For the best?' he said, his voice crackling, caught between tears and fury. 'That she gets spat on?'

'No,' said White calmly. 'That she does not come to the colony so often. There will be some anger at what has happened to Lane and his men.'

'Wylam was my friend!' said Kit. 'But I don't blame her for his death!'

'I know. But not everyone will be so fair-minded. For her sake, Kit. You are putting her in danger.'

Kit frowned at White, hating what he was saying whilst knowing in his heart that it was true.

'Have a little faith, my friend,' White concluded. 'Things are never as bad as they seem.'

Chapter 39

Kit stood at the shore of the lagoon, washing some of White's bottles, brushes and dishes; the pigment traces clouding the clear waters blue, red and ochre. Thick white mist was rising off the water as the sun rose. Kit had accepted the sense of what White had said about Acaunque but that did not mean he liked it. He missed her terribly. Keeping busy was at least some small medicine.

The mainland was visible only as a scene glimpsed through a foggy window. Geese honked by unseen above him. He was about to turn away when he became aware of a faint watery slapping sound.

Suddenly he saw something in the distance, twinkling dimly like a single firefly hovering above the water of the lagoon, and as he watched, strange shapes formed behind it. He strained his eyes to peer into the mist and saw that it seemed to be thickening and darkening at one point and the rhythmic slap, slap, slap grew louder. Then the mist congealed into recognizable forms – two boats full of men.

As the boats loomed out of the mist, Kit wondered in a moment of horror whether these apparitions were Lane and his men or their ghosts, they looked so pale and hollow-eyed. The mist seemed to cling to their ragged bodies like cobwebs, making them look like corpses fresh from the crypt. Manteo sat at the prow of the first boat with Lane beside him. Lane's eyes shone in their sockets.

'You look surprised to see us, lad,' Lane called, standing up as the boat neared the shore.

'We had heard you were all killed, sir,' said Kit. 'Wingina said that—'

Lane jumped into the water and waded onto the sand. 'Ralph Lane takes more killing than that, lad,' he said with a laugh. 'Fear not!' The other boat beached itself beside the first and the men came ashore.

Kit noticed that the dogs were not there. 'Where are the dogs?' he asked.

'We ate 'em,' said one of the soldiers matter-of-factly.

As the soldier stepped aside, Kit saw Wylam standing behind him. Not even he could manage his usual grin. His face seemed drawn and older – harder. *This is what men look like fresh from a fight*, thought Kit; trance-like with fear and bloodlust; drugged as if by hemlock.

'Kit?' said Wylam.

'Yes, sir,' said Kit. 'I am pleased to see you back. We had heard from Wingina that you . . . We heard bad news. Was it very hard?'

Wylam took a deep breath and looked away. 'It was an adventure I'd not like to repeat in a hurry,' he said. 'But I've seen worse. I must eat, Kit. We'll talk later.'

Kit and Wylam followed after the soldiers as Harriot and White approached them from the fort. White had grown in confidence as temporary governor of the colony and it was he who spoke first.

'Master Lane,' he said. 'So you have returned to us at last.'

'Well that's a fine greeting,' said Lane, turning to his men.

'Wingina told us you had all been killed. And you could so easily have killed us all with your ill-thought-out expedition,' said White angrily. 'And for what?'

'Look about you, mapmaker,' said Lane. 'Our stock among the savages has increased tenfold by our safe return with not a single man harmed. Added to which they will now know Wingina to be a double-dealer for telling them we were killed when we were not. Wingina will do as I say.' He patted Kit absent-mindedly on the shoulder as one might a dog or a horse. His hand was damp with sweat and there were still streaks of dirt and blood on the knuckles. At that moment, Kit became aware of a commotion by the boats.

A soldier had grabbed a struggling Indian boy about Kit's age and was dragging him out. The boy snarled and kicked out but Kit could see by his face that he was more afraid than fierce. It was an expression Kit himself had worn many times. White asked Lane who he was.

'We met with a chief among a people called the Choanoac,' said Lane, stopping in his tracks and turning round to face them. 'This boy is his son: Skiko. We took him when we left; he is our prisoner.'

'And why have you brought him here?' said White.

'For our protection.'

'For our protection? And how does it add to our safety to have the son of a powerful chieftain held against his will?'

'I want to know what is going on among these savages,' said Lane. 'I don't trust them. They need to know that I am capable of anything. If they so much as fart near my men, I will have that boy dismembered and put every last piece of him on long poles about the island to show these savages who they are dealing with!'

'I think they already know!' said White.

Kit watched as the soldier brought the boy forward. Skiko stood tall, his chest puffed out, his eyes dark with defiance. When he caught sight of Kit, his expression seemed to darken further, as if this white boy, this invader in front of him, was even more of an insult to him than the men who had stolen him from his village. Kit tried to hold the boy's gaze but found that he was forced to look away.

'Put him in the jail,' said Lane.

'Is that really necessary?' asked White. 'He is but a boy after all and has committed no crime that I am aware of.'

'Put him in the jail,' repeated Lane.

Seeing the way that the soldier shoved the Indian boy towards the jail, Kit was glad Acaunque was not in the settlement. There was danger in the air now; it hovered about them like a thunderstorm waiting to explode.

'I really must protest!' said White.

'Must you?' Lane was already walking away.

'Yes,' said White. 'I—'

'Be still!' shouted Lane suddenly, spinning round to face White. His eyes were red-rimmed and his face pale. He looked like a crazy beggar Kit had once known in Cheapside. 'I am back, and I am the governor here!' he bellowed, turning slowly and looking at everyone standing nearby. 'Governor! You will obey me or suffer the consequences. Is that understood?' No one replied. 'Excellent! Now lock the boy up and keep your wits about you. Those savages did not kill a single one of us! Do you see how invincible it makes us seem? That devil Wingina sent us to our deaths and yet here we are! We have been into the land of the Mondoag – to the land of the rattlesnakes – whose very name strikes fear into these natives, and we have come away unscathed!' Lane was still giddy with the excitement of the escape. He pointed to the Indian boy as he was taken away. 'That boy's father told us that Wingina has been talking against us, trying to forge an alliance of tribes. He means to attack us, mapmaker, be sure of that, but he has not the nerve to try it alone. Well, now we have given those other tribes cause to think again!'

'Or cause to fight us!' said White.

Lane snorted and put his arm round White's shoulder. 'In the summer we will investigate further inland,' he said in a conspiratorial whisper. 'We will find these mines and the pearl fisheries. We will teach these Mondoag a lesson and come back rich!'

Wylam walked up to take a seat next to Kit. He shook his head wearily and sighed. 'This place, Kit,' he said. 'There is nothing here but trouble. The land hereabouts was in turmoil and Lane seemed oblivious to it. The man has lost what little reason he came to this place with. We saw a shortage of food everywhere and the sickness was taking a grip on the whole country.'

'A shortage of food?' said Kit.

'Aye,' said Wylam. 'Think about it. We have had little in the way of rain since we came. I think there has been a drought and there has been a mass of hungry foreigners to boot. They are bound to blame us, Kit. They are superstitious people, these savages. Since we came there has been sickness and drought. If you were them, would you not want us cleared from the land? Only their fear of us keeps us safe, and from what you say, Wingina has done his best to remove that fear. And when their fear of the sickness and starvation becomes greater than their fear of us . . .' He licked his lips. 'Well then, Kit, my boy, things might liven up a little.'

Chapter 40

Wylam was right. Hunger had already begun to grip the colony. Kit had known hunger in his time on the streets and bore it better than some, but he could see that things could not go on as they were. The colonists had eaten all their stores and driven any game from the area with their muskets. The corn the Indians had given them to plant was not yet grown.

The truth of it was that the leaders in the settlement were, in the main, soldiers and gentleman adventurers, when what was sorely needed were farmers and fishermen. The artisans they had brought had built the colony, but they did not have the skills to feed it. Hunger made them ill-tempered. Fights broke out suddenly and were put down viciously by Lane's men. Nugent – the Irishman who was rarely away from Lane's side – strode about the colony striking fear into all those he met.

Lane sent some colonists south to Croatoan – an island in the Outer Banks – to keep watch for any sign of the supply ships they expected Raleigh to send, panicked by the idea that ships might sail past without finding them, and also to lessen the burden at Roanoke. The men at this lookout post would have to fend for themselves, but they all knew that none of the colonists would survive much longer without supplies from England.

But it was not just the colonists who were in danger of starving now. Though the Indians were expert at making the most of their resources, collecting crabs and shellfish and fishing the lagoon and rivers, the colony had become a kind of tumour, greedy and malignant.

Wingina had gone to his mainland village of Dasamonquepeuc, hoping to rid himself of the burden of the English – feeding his own men would be challenge enough in times such as these – but Lane simply sent men there to demand food. Whilst Lane still held Skiko hostage, Wingina had little choice but to agree to their demands if he wished to be seen to protect the boy – something that was vital if he was going to build an alliance against these invaders. He even came to the colony himself, to personally check that Skiko was being properly cared for.

To ease the burden on his own people, he gave the English more land to farm and even sowed corn for them. The Indians also set fish weirs for the colonists and showed them how to use them. Kit sometimes saw Acaunque among the Indians, but since the day the soldier spat at her, she no longer sought him out and he, mindful of what White had said, did not go to her, though it took all his willpower to resist.

One day, as Kit stood looking out across the lagoon, watching the men working, bright sunlight turning the water into sparkling diamonds and the men to hazy silhouettes, he marvelled how from where he stood it was almost impossible to tell Indian from Englishman.

An exasperated groan from Lane made Kit turn his attention back to him and White, who were standing talking nearby, watching the same scene. White had just remarked that at least it was good to see Indian and Englishmen finally working together.

'Mapmaker,' said Lane, shaking his head. 'Why can you not see that these people are as capable of trickery as us? Do you think they have suddenly grown to care for us? Is that why they fish for us?'

White made no reply and Kit saw Lane smile in response.

'They fish for us to bide time, that is all,' said Lane. 'If they could kill us all, they would, in a heartbeat.'

Kit took a deep breath and looked away to the woods.

'You make the mistake, sir, of thinking that everyone thinks as you do,' said White.

'No, sir!' snapped Lane, jabbing a finger towards White. 'It is you who makes the mistake. It is you who believes these people are as children. It is you who thinks we have come to a' – Lane flapped his hands about searching for the words – 'to a kind of Eden.' He threw out his arms to encompass the world about them. 'Open your eyes, Master White. Wingina was recovering from an injury when we first arrived on these shores. He did not sustain those injuries in a fall. He was recovering from battle. Look at the scars on these savages. Look at their weapons. These men are not wood sprites, Master White; they are warriors! The serpent arrived in this Eden a long time before we sailed here.'

White looked away forlornly, not wishing to argue the point. But as Lane smiled and turned to leave, he grabbed at his arm.

'Can we not now return the boy?' he asked gently. 'For the sake of goodwill? As a reward for this cooperation?'

Lane looked at him as though he were a child himself. 'Return the boy?' he said incredulously. 'Return the boy? I do not think so.'

White peered at him. 'But surely . . . ?' he began.

'The boy stays here,' said Lane.

Kit walked over and stood alongside White. Seemingly emboldened by Kit's presence, White adopted a more strident tone.

'Tell me then, Master Lane,' he said. 'If you are so sure of the treacherous nature of these people, why then do you let Wingina visit the colony to look after the boy?'

Lane grinned, raising an eyebrow mischievously.

'Surely,' White continued, 'every time he comes to the colony, he has an opportunity to gauge our strengths and weaknesses.'

'Very good, Master White,' said Lane. 'That is a good point. It is the first sensible question you've asked.' He rubbed his hands together. 'And since you've asked, I shall tell you why I let Wingina in the colony. You are right to say that Wingina will use his visits to spy on us – I would if I were in his shoes. But he will be doing more than that, if I am any judge, sir. He will be plotting a rescue – a surprise attack to free that boy. He will want to impress the Choanoac and get their support.' Lane was staring wildly now, looking from White's face to Kit's, his voice becoming louder and more excited as he went on. 'Because I have allowed him this freedom, he will think us fools and will pass on the secrets of his plan to that boy. And when he does, mapmaker, I will extract that information from the boy right speedily. Indian, Turk or Chinaman, pain is pain in any language.'

Lane looked at them both as if expecting an argument, and when no response came he sniffed, smiled contemptuously and walked away. Kit watched him stride off and knew in that instant what he had to do.

Chapter 41

Kit moved through the colony, walking between the huts and storehouses, skirting the jail in ever-decreasing circles. He felt as though every soldier or gentleman who caught his eye could read his thoughts; see the plan that he had hatched.

Slowly but surely he had convinced himself that he had no choice; that whatever the consequences to himself, he must free Skiko. If he was caught and hanged as a mutineer, then so be it, but he could not simply stand by and let Lane torture and kill this innocent boy.

He thought of his father, wrongly imprisoned and wrongly killed. The threat to this boy was salt to that wound. He could not help his father, but he could help this boy. And he owed it to Acaunque. He needed to show her – to show himself – that all Englishmen were not the same. He thought of Wylam and how he acted like an animal, on instinct; with instant resolve. Kit would be like that.

He walked towards the door of the jail. As usual, the

soldier on duty was whittling away at a piece of wood. He knew Kit by now and smiled as he approached. Kit complimented him on his carving and asked if he could take a look.

'What was that?' he said suddenly, looking away towards a storehouse nearby.

'What?' The soldier stood up and grabbed his musket.

'Don't know,' said Kit. 'Thought I heard something.'

They stood in silence until the soldier said, 'Nah, it's nothing, son. This country makes you jumpy.'

Kit nodded. 'You're probably right,' he said in a voice designed to sound unsure, and carried on looking nervously towards the store.

'I'd better take a look,' said the soldier with a sigh.

As soon as he was out of earshot, Kit lifted the great metal bar that jammed the door and opened it.

'Skiko,' he called softly, peering into the gloom. But there was no response. He looked about him as his eyes became accustomed to the dark and saw that Skiko seemed to be huddled motionless against the wall. He was filled with foreboding and rushed forward to help him, but as he grabbed the blanket, he found it empty. He was momentarily confused before the obvious dawned on him: Skiko had already escaped. Kit grinned with relief, but almost immediately the smile faded. What to do now? He had been willing to aid the boy, but as he had escaped on his own, there was no call for Kit to throw his life away being caught in such an incriminating position. Kit quickly leaped back outside and shut and barred the door. Suddenly there was a great commotion. A trumpet blasted and the guard returned.

'The savage got out!' he reported.

'No,' said Kit, casually. 'Has he?'

'Aye,' said the guard. 'They caught the little bastard trying to get over the stockade. That must be what you heard!'

Kit's heart sank. 'Caught him?' he said, trying not to sound as bitterly disappointed as he was.

'Aye.' The guard spat noisily. 'They're bringing the little devil back. He's for it now.'

Sure enough, Kit saw Nugent dragging Skiko towards the jail. Skiko was kicking him the whole way but Nugent did not even seem to notice. Lane was walking behind them with a group of soldiers, looking even more menacing than usual, with Harriot and Manteo following behind. When they reached the jail, Skiko was shoved in again, followed by a group of soldiers.

'Lock him in the bilboes, Nugent,' Lane shouted, marching into the jail behind them.

Nugent walked forward with the manacles and two soldiers held Skiko down while they forced his legs into the contraption and locked it shut. Skiko struggled, but soon found that the movement only grated his shins and stopped, glowering at his jailers.

Lane paced back and forth in front of the boy and then drew his sword, lunging forward, pointing the blade at Skiko's throat. 'Ask him what Wingina's up to!' he yelled.

Manteo pushed forward and translated. Skiko pressed his lips together tightly and looked up defiantly at Lane.

'Tell him I'll cut his damn head off if he doesn't talk!' shouted Lane.

Manteo translated, but still Skiko said nothing. Lane looked down at the boy and tightened the grip on his sword.

'No!' shouted Kit, rushing forward into the building.

'Shut him up, Nugent!' shouted Lane, simultaneously stepping forward, grabbing Skiko by the knot of hair on his head and pressing the sword blade across his throat.

Nugent slapped Kit across the face and sent him sprawling across the floor.

'Hey!' said Wylam, getting between Nugent and Kit. 'Leave him be!'

Nugent squared up to Wylam, but turned instead as Skiko yelled out.

'What's he saying?' said Lane.

Manteo held up his hand so that he could hear better and he and Skiko had a short conversation, Lane stepping back a little but keeping his sword pointing towards the boy.

Manteo then said that Skiko had told him of a plan to send a force of men to Roanoke. Wingina had joined with Okisko – chief of the Weapemeoc – and had enlisted Mondoag bowmen as mercenaries.

Lane took his sword away from Skiko's throat and sheathed it, smiling grimly. Kit picked himself up and looked at Skiko, who was still scowling defiantly. 'So,' said

Lane. 'Now ask him about this band of men. Manteo?'

White, who had now heard of the boy's capture, came in and immediately saw the red mark on Kit's face; he made as if to speak, but Kit grabbed him and whispered that he was fine. Both turned towards Manteo and Skiko. Manteo was questioning and Skiko was muttering his replies.

'He says that there will be an attack,' said Manteo eventually.

'I knew it!' Lane shouted. 'How many? When?'

As Manteo asked Lane's questions and the boy replied, they began to learn the details. Manteo told them that the plan was to attack at night. The Indians would start a fire and kill Lane as soon as he ran out. Lane smiled at this news, clearly happy that he figured as such a vital part of the plan.

'Tell him that I am very pleased with him,' said Lane. 'And our God is very pleased with him.' White tried to interrupt but Lane repeated the phrase again more loudly. '*And our God is pleased with him!*'

Manteo passed on these words but Skiko made no reply.

'And tell him also,' continued Lane, 'that if he crosses me again, our God will send the invisible death to his home and to his family and wipe them off the face of the earth.'

'Master Lane!' said White. 'This is blasphemy!'

'If you interrupt me once more, mapmaker,' Lane bellowed, 'I will have you hanged for a mutineer. Do

I make myself understood?' White made no reply and Lane turned back to Manteo and Skiko. 'Tell him!'

Manteo passed on the words about the pestilence and the boy's eyes widened in fear and he nodded.

Lane told Manteo to let Skiko know that he was so pleased with him that he would now allow him to return to his people. Kit saw White smile at these words but he could see that there was more to come. Sure enough, Lane said that Skiko was to go to Wingina and inform him that the colonists had received word of the imminent arrival of a fleet of ships from England and that Lane would be going to Croatoan to await its arrival. Manteo looked quizzically at Lane, as did everyone else. Kit glanced at Wylam, who was nodding gently with a barely visible smile.

'Just tell him,' said Lane.

Manteo passed on Lane's words and Skiko nodded.

'Now go,' said Lane. 'Go back to Wingina and tell him what I have said. Nugent, release him from the bilboes.'

Manteo translated once more, and as soon as Nugent had unlocked the manacles, Skiko walked away as bravely as his shaking legs would allow. As he neared the edge of the colony, he turned and looked back, before running away towards the Indian village.

Lane called a meeting and told the assembled men that he had intelligence that the colony was about to be attacked. A murmur ran through the listeners.

White shook his head. 'Do you see now how our behaviour has come home to roost?' he said. 'I cautioned against violence and now look. Violence begets violence!'

Lane looked at the floor. 'Master White's views are well known,' he said with a sigh. 'And no doubt he will still be airing them when the savages are beating upon his skull with their clubs.' Several of the soldiers chuckled. 'What's done is done and we have to deal with it. Wylam, what do you say?'

Wylam looked at White and sighed. 'I am sorry, Master White, but if there is to be a fight, and it seems there is, then our only chance is to hit them before they hit us.'

'But is there no chance for us to talk and settle our dispute?' said White.

'Manteo?' said Wylam. 'You know your people. What say you?'

'If they have set their hearts on blood,' said Manteo, 'then they will have blood. They will already be preparing the war feast.'

Kit felt sick. He had no desire to fight Acaunque's people or see them killed, and yet he was certain that if the Indians attacked, they would kill him as readily as any other Englishman. And he understood what these men were capable of. He knew what they and their kind had done in Ireland. They would kill Acaunque without the faintest pang of guilt.

Just as he had lived between two worlds in London – neither Catholic nor Protestant – here he was caught between Indians and colonists. He would not have seen White or Wylam hurt, but he hated Lane and he understood Wingina's hatred. They were in his land. Kit would have fought and died to save England from the Spanish, but this was not England.

'Very well,' said Lane. 'As you heard, I have sent word that we are to go to Croatoan to meet our fleet. This will give the Indians something to think about for a few days, but when no fleet appears, he will attack anyway, so we need to move. Any thoughts, gentlemen? Wylam?'

'We need surprise if we are to win,' said Wylam. 'The men are in poor shape and the longer a fight goes on, the stronger the enemy will seem.'

'Agreed,' said Lane.

Kit was being haunted by a vision of a screaming Acaunque, of muskets, of blood. Was there a way he could warn her? But it was too late.

'We need to stop any reinforcements from Roanoke reaching Wingina on the mainland,' said Wylam. 'If we capture all the canoes on the island, we can stop any other of the Indians rowing across.'

'Excellent,' said Lane, turning to Nugent. 'Do it.'

Chapter 42

As night began to fall, Nugent sent men to round up all the Indian canoes moored on the island. Kit could feel the tension in the air as the soldiers twitched and flexed, sharpening daggers and swords, priming muskets and putting on breastplates and helmets.

Suddenly there were shouts from the river and then strangled screams and more voices calling one to another in the forest. There were English shouts from the river and then the twittering cries of Indians on Roanoke itself. Men suddenly came running from the darkness into the firelight of the camp.

'They are on to us, sir,' said one of the soldiers as he ran up to Lane. 'Two men tried to escape to the mainland. We beheaded them but we were seen.'

The word 'beheaded' seemed to echo in Kit's mind.

'It seems we have lost the element of surprise,' said Wylam to Kit. 'The Indians from the village are now attacking *us*.'

Lane suddenly grabbed Kit by the scruff of the neck, shoving a bow and quiver in his hands. 'They say you're good with a bow,' he said. 'Stand there and shoot anyone who crosses that ground ahead.'

A hail of arrows pelted down around them, miraculously hitting no one. Then Kit could hear the sound of running feet some distance off in the darkness.

'Come on, you devils!' shouted Lane into the darkness. 'Come on!' Arrows landed to the left and right of him but he didn't flinch.

An Indian warrior ran at Kit, materializing out of the pitch dark like a demon. Kit could see that he had singled him out, that he was running straight at Kit and none other, his wooden war club high above his shoulder, his face contorted in anger. Kit raised his bow and aimed at the Indian's heart but he could not release the arrow.

'Kit!' yelled Wylam. 'Kit! For God's sake, shoot!'

Kit remained frozen and Wylam grabbed a pike and swung it in a great arc, hitting the Indian in the chest and knocking him off his feet, killing him instantly. 'You!' shouted Wylam at a nearby gunner, who stood spellbound by the scene in front of him. 'Fire that damn thing or I shall gut you before the savages get you!'

The gunner snapped out of his trance and fired into the pack of Indians. One of the first of them fell. He had been running so fast that he tumbled head over heels when he dropped.

Other gunners joined the first, and at each volley another Indian fell until the runners stopped and

315

everything became eerily silent apart from the moaning of an Indian lying where he had fallen some twenty yards from the stockade. A soldier walked across and thrust a sword into the fallen man and the moaning ceased.

Kit realized that through the whole encounter he had held his breath, and he released it now with a gasp. As he breathed in once more, fear entered with the air and he began to shake. The soldiers regrouped in the colony and Lane appeared holding a lantern.

'All is not lost,' said the governor. 'We have their canoes. They can neither warn Wingina nor aid him.'

'The Indians on the mainland may have heard the shots,' said White. 'What surprise you hoped to have is gone now.'

'Maybe so,' said Lane. 'But they have heard us hunting many times. Wingina will have no reason to think that everything is not as it was. It is something you will learn, Master White; that when someone believes they have the element of surprise, they become blind and deaf to the notion that they too might be surprised. Believe me, the Indians will stick to their original plan. So we must attack now, while we can!'

'But if we do,' said White, 'they will have the upper hand. They know these woods like they know their own children. Manteo himself told us that they prefer to attack under the cover of night. It would be madness to attack now. It would be madness to attack at all!'

Lane took a step towards White and leaned forward

until their faces were only inches apart. Kit thought that he was about to strike White, but instead he smiled suddenly and clapped his hands on White's shoulders. 'Then what would you have me do, Master Mapmaker?' he said.

'We lay the law down to Wingina,' said White. 'We tell him that we know that he is planning an assault on our colony. We tell him that we have men and weapons enough to destroy him, if he so wishes – aye, and a fleet due to arrive too, if you wish – but it is our desire to live here in peace.'

Lane smiled. 'That's the spirit, Master White,' he said. 'I shall make a fighting man of you yet! Very well; we will go to Wingina and give the old villain a last warning. But it must be soon. This very dawn.'

'Agreed,' said White.

'Good!' said Lane.

Lane and White parted amicably, and Kit could see that his master was trying to contain a satisfied smile. Kit let him walk ahead and wandered down to the shore of the lagoon. A noise made him turn back towards the fort and he saw Lane talking to Nugent. Nugent was nodding. Something about their expressions made him feel suddenly uneasy. Nugent turned to face him and Kit looked away, hoping that he would not hear the Irishman's footsteps coming towards him. When he gained the courage to look back, Nugent and Lane were gone.

Chapter 43

It was agreed that White, Harriot and Manteo would accompany Lane and his soldiers to the parley with Wingina, and that Kit would accompany White. Kit agreed – he had such a need to see that Acaunque was safe – and they rowed across the lagoon to Dasamonquepeuc just as dawn began to melt the shadowed gloom. Kit could see smoke from the village rising up above the trees.

Lane called to an Indian on the shore and, through Manteo, asked him to take a message to Wingina to tell him that they were going to Croatoan to meet their ships, but that first they wished to speak to the chief. The Indian took the message and came back saying that Wingina would see them.

As the men walked, Kit was aware once again of the grating noise they made in the mossy stillness. The natives moved like deer among the trees, but the soldiers from the colony crashed about like a storm. He could hear the terrible clanking of their swords and pikes, muskets and pistols, clattering against breastplates and helmets, all to the beat of boots crashing down the undergrowth as they marched. Birds and beasts fled at their approach and Indians in the woods stopped and stared.

The early morning light gave a dreamlike feel to the scene as they entered Dasamonquepeuc. A large fire blazed in the centre of the village and glowed intensely, the sun still shaded by the surrounding trees. The shadowed world seemed painted in shades of blue, but painted boldly and quickly; the features vague and mysterious, the colours soaking into the crisp air like pigment on wet paper. Birds were singing in the woods.

Wingina stood with a group of men beyond the fire, his features shimmering and melting in the heat haze. The other men seemed as proud and dignified as he did, and Kit thought they must be the elders or maybe even visiting dignitaries from the Choanoac and Weapemeoc.

Kit saw one group standing apart, fiercely clutching their bows. Their heads were completely shaven apart from a top knot tied up in a plume of feathers, and their bodies and faces were stained with nightmarish bands of blue-black stripes and crimson. Wylam had described the Mondoag and their tribal markings to Kit and he realized immediately that these must be the mercenaries Wingina had recruited to help him. They stared at the English soldiers with haughty indifference.

Kit thought about the first time he had entered an Indian village and the fear he had felt. Now, instead, he felt a kind of raw sadness, a sadness that smarted like a burn. But if White could finally find the courage to speak out against Lane, and the English could find some way of working with the Indians, then maybe even at this late hour, all would not yet be lost.

The village dogs had regained their courage now the mastiffs were gone, baring their teeth and barking loudly as Lane strode forward with Manteo, White following with a group of men, and Kit not far behind. When they reached the fire, they stopped and Wingina began to speak.

Kit was standing next to Nugent. He looked around the faces in the village, seeing the tension there as the two sides met. Then, standing near a longhouse with her mother, he saw Acaunque. He wanted to smile, but he could not bring himself to. She looked away and something cold seemed to grip his chest.

Then Kit noticed Nugent fidgeting. He could see him nervously flexing his fingers and took some comfort in thinking that even this hulk of a man was anxious. Then Nugent slipped a finger into the trigger of his pistol. Kit looked from the trigger to Nugent's tongue as it slid along his thin lips, and back to the trigger.

'Christ our victory!' shouted Lane suddenly, and the men about him lifted their muskets and aimed them at Wingina and the group of elders. The look on their faces was one of confusion more than fear. Until the muskets exploded.

Kit was momentarily deafened and the scene around him took on an unearthly quality as Indians ran from their huts, faces contorted in silent screams. More muskets exploded.

Each flash of musket fire illuminated a scene in front of him with nightmarish clarity, the harsh yellow light flashing across the wide eyes, bared teeth and bloody wounds of the attackers as they fell.

This is what Hell must be like, thought Kit: endless pain and torture, figures writhing in the dark with only the flames of their destruction for light. They had turned this place into a kind of Hell.

The sound rolled back into Kit's ears with a terrible roar, like a tidal wave crashing in on him, and he saw White remonstrating with Lane and Lane smiling, his face splashed with blood. The musketeers had already reloaded and Lane ordered them to fire again.

This time Kit put his hands to his ears as the muskets blasted. Wingina and the other Indians shuddered sickeningly as the grapeshot hit them. They fell and lay in a heap of torn clothes and torn flesh.

'What are you doing?' shouted White. 'You will have us all killed!'

'No!' shouted Lane, shoving White away. '*You* would have us all killed! This is what they understand, mapmaker: force! You should have been in Ireland and then you would know. You cannot parley with savages!'

Kit looked around wildly. Where was Acaunque? Was she hurt? Suddenly he saw a movement in the group of wounded Indians. A man squeezed himself out from under one of his dead comrades, crawled free and scrambled to his feet.

Lane saw him too. 'Seize him!' he shouted.

The Englishmen were too startled to grab him quickly and then too weighed down with muskets and pistols to do so effectively.

'It's Wingina, sir!' shouted one of the soldiers. Kit could see now that it was true. Wingina was doused in blood, but clearly little of it was his own because he moved with a speed and grace that belied his years. Lane's soldiers desperately reloaded but they were never going to hit him now.

'Nugent!' shouted Lane. 'Take your best man and get after the bastard. Don't come back without him.'

'Sir!' said Nugent and he signalled to a soldier, who ran with him in pursuit of the fleeing chief.

As the soldiers spread out, firing the huts, women began to emerge, some fleeing from the flames, others overcoming their fear to wail over the bodies of their menfolk lying at the Englishmen's feet. Kit's heart seemed to swell inside him and choke off the air to his lungs.

Where was Acaunque? Skiko peered out from behind one of the huts in the stockade. Kit could see the mixture of grief and anger on his face. Then he saw the bow in his hand.

'No!' he shouted, running over to him as fast as he could. The boy turned just in time to see Kit bearing down on him but by then it was too late. Kit crashed into him, both boys smashing into the side of the hut. Kit held the boy down and snatched his bow. He stood up and looked down at the boy lying in the dust. 'They'll kill you!' he shouted. 'Don't you understand what they are? They'll kill you!' He lifted the bow over his head and smashed it against the corner of the hut with all his might. At the third blow the bow snapped and Kit tossed it away.

'They'll kill you,' he whispered, almost to himself. Skiko looked at him with black resentment, bravely holding back his tears.

Suddenly there was a scream from an old woman near the entrance to the stockade. Everyone turned and Kit saw Nugent and the other soldier stride back into the village. Both men were dishevelled and sweating, hardly recognizable from the pair who had left only minutes before.

But it was Nugent who had induced the scream. The whites of his eyes and the broad flash of his smile shone out of a face that was crimson with blood. His hair was matted with blood, his clothes soaked in it. He looked like a demon standing amid the fires of damnation.

Then he stopped, standing in the light of a burning hut, firelight only adding to the dreadful image. Grinning madly, he raised one arm in the air and held Wingina's severed head by the hair.

White turned away, vomiting. Kit felt his legs buckle slightly beneath him. His eyes flickered back and forth between Nugent's blood-spattered face and Wingina's;

the latter frozen in a look of defiance, the mouth hanging open as if about to speak.

Lane took the head from Nugent and held it up in the air for all to see. Drips of blood caught the light as they fell to earth like crimson pearls. A fearful hush came over the village, save for the crying of the children and the moaning of the wounded. Kit saw Acaunque emerge from a longhouse, but his relief in seeing her safe was almost extinguished by the pain he felt at seeing her terrified expression.

'Translate this,' Lane shouted to Manteo, who stepped forward. 'Your chief is dead!' Manteo echoed Lane's words in Algonquian. 'Wingina is dead. He was slain for treachery and the same fate will befall any who go against us! Spread that word among your people! You are under English rule now! You will obey us or die. God save Queen Elizabeth!'

Kit sank to his knees. The severed head had brought back memories of his father's execution. The burning village, the crying women, all merged into a swirling vortex and Kit began to sob, his lungs heaving against his ribs until his chest ached. Wylam had to pick him up to move him, and half carried him back to the boats. Kit sat as if in a trance as they rowed back, silent among the rowdy soldiers, staring at the back of his hands and at the blackening drops of blood splattered across them.

Chapter 44

Everything had changed since the attack. Kit wandered aimlessly about the colony over the following days, the raucous laughter of Nugent and his gang grating on him, sounding like the cackling of demons to his ears.

Kit had not realized how much, despite the dangers and the difficulties, he had grown to love this place – not the colony, but this land: Virginia, America, Secota – whatever they chose to call it. He had gone from fearing the woods to feeling bonded to them in some way he could never have expressed in words.

Now, all pretence that this was a colony – a settlement – was gone. This was an occupation, pure and simple. This was a military camp, a soldiers' garrison. The only Indian he ever saw now was Manteo; the other natives stood away among the trees, watching and waiting, more cautious now than when the English first arrived.

Kit mourned the loss of his contact with Wanchese and Acaunque, but the more he thought about it, the more he realized that he had been foolish to think it could ever have been otherwise. The people here were just an obstacle to Lane and Raleigh – they would be as happy if they all died. It was the land and its riches they wanted, that was all. Kit felt utterly exhausted.

When White tried to cheer him up one day, praising him for his bravery and loyalty, all of a sudden the events of the past year or so came crashing in on Kit and he burst into great heaving sobs. Eventually he looked up, tears streaming down his face. He was sick to his heart of secrets, of lies; White deserved the truth.

'I'm not brave,' he said. 'And I'm not loyal, neither. You don't even know who I am.' He shook his head. 'I lied to you! I even *betrayed* you! You can't call me brave and loyal . . .'

White stared at him. 'Whatever can you mean, Kit?' he asked, puzzled.

And so, all in a rush, the words pouring out of him, Kit told White about Walsingham and Gabriel and how he had spied on White during their time in London.

He told his master how his father had died a traitor's death at Tower Hill and how he had kept it a secret.

He told him about the nightmare and the man with the devil mask and about Gabriel's death and his revelation that Kit's father had not been a traitor at all; that the letters that took him to the gallows were forgeries.

White listened intently, nodding and occasionally encouraging Kit with a hand laid gently on his shoulder. 'You cannot be blamed for keeping your identity a secret in times like these,' he said gently. 'As for Walsingham

— well, he has the life of our Queen in his hands and so we must all understand the lengths to which he must sometimes be driven — but even so, to threaten children . . .' White shook his head and sighed. 'Never fear, Kit,' he added, 'for no one near the court does *not* suffer the attentions of Walsingham's intelligencers at times. I am sure he had others to report on my activities too, so do not blame yourself.' He paused, glancing over his shoulder as though he had seen someone close by, then spoke only when he felt sure they were alone again. 'You know, Kit,' he said, 'I met your father on several occasions.'

'You did?'

'Aye, lad. Met him and liked him. He was a good man and many of us were shocked by the news of his arrest and execution. I was on the expedition to Newfoundland and did not learn of it until I returned. It comes as no surprise to me to hear that he was an innocent man.'

Tears once again sprang to Kit's eyes. 'I thought . . . I feared you might hate me, sir,' he said. 'Hate me for being a liar and the son of Catholics . . .'

'I am so very pleased to have met you, Kit,' said White, placing a comforting hand on his shoulder. 'And right proud to know you. When we get back to London, I promise with all my heart that I will intercede on your behalf with Walsingham. I shall see things put right, Kit. You have my word.'

Kit wiped his tears with one hand, his nose with the other. 'Thank you, sir,' he said, aware that he felt a real sense of relief at finally owning up to White. But he was also certain that this feeling was tempered by the realization that the events of his childhood could never be over until he had discovered the identity of the masked man and seen him breathe his last breath.

A few days later, word came from the men Lane had sent to the island of Croatoan in the Outer Banks: a fleet had been spotted on the horizon, flying the cross of St George.

'Sir Richard has come!' said White with rather forced excitement, trying to raise Kit's spirits. 'Our supplies have come, Kit. We are saved.' His voice sounded distant and thin, but Kit nodded and smiled weakly.

The following day White persuaded his reluctant assistant to accompany him to see the fleet arrive. They climbed to the top of the dunes and Kit looked into the sky, where the clouds seemed to pulse as if they were alive, throbbing in the duck-egg blueness of the morning. A seabird passed overhead, trailing its shadow across his face, and he closed his eyes.

'Look, Kit!' said White.

Kit opened his eyes once more, dazzled by the light at first. Sailing towards them from the south was a huge fleet of ships, their white sails catching the bright sunlight. Even Kit in his dazed and half-starved state raised a smile at the sight. A tear welled in his eye and trickled down his cheek. White put his arm round his shoulder and squeezed.

'It is going to be all right, Kit,' he said. 'I know it is.'

The ships anchored and boats were launched. Kit ran down to meet them as they neared the beach and surged forward on the breaking waves. Some men ran forward to grab the prows and guide them in. Kit watched as one of the men leaped from the boat into the sea, striding through water up to his thighs, seemingly oblivious.

But as the figure approached, he saw that it was clearly not Grenville, and the men who were with him looked like an army from the Apocalypse, dressed like men of all nations, bristling with weapons. Their faces were dark and scarred and gold earrings sparkled under their long hair. They did not have the look of saviours about them. 'Well, well!' the leader shouted as he began to stomp at speed up the beach towards Kit. 'What have we here? Are you English or savage, lad?' he said, ruffling his hair.

'English, sir,' Kit replied.

'Excellent!' he said with a loud laugh, slapping Kit's shoulder so hard he nearly knocked him over. 'Well, do you not know me, lad?'

Kit peered at the man. His face was tanned like leather, rosy at the cheeks; his beard bleached by the sun. His red hair was curly and unkempt. There did seem to be something familiar about him . . . 'No, sir,' he said eventually. 'I don't think so.'

The man smiled, seemingly surprised that there was anyone who could fail to recognize him. 'Are you sure you are a son of England?' he asked.

'Well, yes,' said Kit. 'I suppose.'

'You suppose?' said the man with a chuckle. 'You either are or you are not.'

'Then I am.'

'Then I dare say that you have heard mention of the name Drake.'

'Of course,' said Kit.

'Well, then! 'Tis he that stands before you!'

'Sir Francis Drake!' said Kit in amazement.

'None other!' said Drake.

He marched up the dunes and introduced himself to White, who could not have looked more terrified if the Spanish army had been advancing towards him with swords drawn. Kit caught up with him and found him ashen.

'So this is Sir Francis Drake,' said White. 'I have not met him before.'

'No,' said Kit. 'I have seen him before but from a long way away. He is more frightening close up.'

'Yes. And these men. They look more like pirates than English sailors.'

'We *are* more like pirates than English sailors,' said one of the men walking past. He chuckled and was joined by two of his comrades. White smiled and nodded and they followed Drake up the track to Roanoke.

Lane was clearly intimidated by the presence of this famous sea dog but there was little he could do but follow him around, with Nugent trotting along behind.

Kit was surprised to find that even the grown men of

the colony were as excited as children to hear that Drake had arrived in their midst, and Drake for his part was happy to tell them all about his recent adventures in the Caribbean.

He had launched an audacious attack on the Spanish city of Santo Domingo on Hispaniola, had taken it with barely a fight and then blasted the city apart until the citizens agreed to pay him a huge pile of cash to leave them alone. He freed the slaves there, who eagerly climbed aboard his ships to escape the Spanish.

Kit remembered how he and Hugh had strained to catch even the merest glimpse of Drake when he was knighted. He had dreamed of one day meeting this great man, yet now – wearied beyond belief by the past year's events – he could not have cared less about what the Queen's Pirate had been up to for the last few months. He was about to turn away when something struck him on the back of the head and the world turned black as night . . .

Chapter 45

Kit stood in the hallway of his parents' house, a young boy once more. There was noise and laughter coming from the hall, and guests walked by, wearing and holding masks to their faces.

'Christopher,' said a man whose mask took the form of a raven's beak, 'are you not playing with your cousins?' He lifted his mask to show his father's smiling face.

'They are playing hide-and-seek, Father.'

'Well, hide then,' said his father.

'I don't know where, Father,' said Kit.

A woman in a white gown crouched down beside him, holding a mask of white feathers on a stick. His mother moved her mask aside and kissed his cheek. His father leaned forward and whispered in his ear. 'The linen chest,' he suggested. 'You know the one.'

Kit chuckled and moved towards the stairs, past the newel post with its carving of Adam and Eve. He let his finger move slowly across the apple that Eve held out and felt the smoothness of the wood, polished by the passage of years.

He climbed the stairs and saw the small painting of St Sebastian that had always troubled him, and he flinched again at the arrows piercing the saint's naked flesh as he stood tied to a stake, looking up to Heaven.

Once again he opened the linen chest and once again he climbed in, but now he did not fear the coming of the devil-faced man. This time, when he saw him hiding the letters, he simply stared at him with a murderous anger, remembering the smiling faces of his parents. Then he saw it, catching the light and twinkling; the devil-man had a ring on his little finger – a ring of twisted silver. The lid to the chest was suddenly yanked open and Kit looked up to see the medicine man staring down at him.

'Open your eyes,' he said in perfect English.

Kit opened his eyes and slowly focused on the ring he had just been dreaming about, and from the ring to its familiar owner.

'Wylam!'

'Kit,' he said with a grin. 'Pity. I had hoped you might sleep on. Ah well. But what a strange quirk of fate, eh, Kit? Imagine my surprise when I heard you telling your life story to Master White. I had never suspected your true identity until that moment.'

'You killed my parents!' shouted Kit.

Wylam held a dagger towards him. 'I will have to ask you to speak more softly, Kit,' he said. 'And I shall only ask once.'

'You killed my parents!' hissed Kit.

'Come now,' said Wylam. 'I could not have known your mother would die. She never seemed that weak when I knew her, but you can never tell.'

'Why?' Kit demanded. 'Why?' But as he asked the question, he realized that he knew the answer: Wylam must have been working for the Spanish . . .

'White knows who I am,' said Kit, but as soon as he said the words he realized the implication.

Wylam smiled. 'Yes,' he said. 'Master White knows little that could incriminate me, but I cannot afford to take the risk for I heard him promise you he would look into the matter, and Master White is a man of his word. Master White will sadly be lost at sea, I fear.'

'I'll kill you!' hissed Kit.

Wylam smiled his wide, handsome smile. 'No,' he said, showing Kit an arrow. 'I think not. This is rather beautifully made actually, though a tip of shell and shaft of reed will barely dent a breastplate. These folk are done for, but that is by the by. It will look like the savage there attacked you, do you see?' Kit realized for the first time that they were deeper in the surrounding woods than when he had collapsed, and that there was a body lying next to him; the body of an Indian. He recognized him as one of Wanchese's friends and cursed.

'Friend of yours, was he?' said Wylam with a grin. 'I will be the hero when I return with the news of your death — and the body of your murderer.'

Kit tried to move and realized his hands were bound together at the wrists. 'It's been you all along, hasn't it?' he said. 'You were the spy that Gabriel was hunting for and you killed him, didn't you?' Kit closed his eyes as he realized his own stupidity: Gabriel had not being saying 'Why?' when he died; he had been trying to say 'Wylam'. When Kit had told him of the devil mask, he must have worked out who had framed Kit's father.

'Was that his name? The intelligencer?' said Wylam absent-mindedly, playing with the arrow. 'I saw him hanging around outside White's house. I do not think he was watching me, but it seemed safer to kill him.'

Slowly Wylam's part in the events of the last months seeped into Kit's consciousness.

'And it's been you trying to ruin things here, hasn't it? Ruin it for the English? I bet you even stole Grenville's cup.'

Wylam smiled in acknowledgement. 'I tossed it in the river as we rowed to the next village,' he said, clearly enjoying the confession.

Kit closed his eyes tightly as if in pain, seeing everything clearly now. 'And you didn't try and talk Grenville out of retaliating, did you? You persuaded him to attack!'

'He didn't need much persuading to be honest,' said Wylam. 'But I did give him a push. It all helped to ruin relations between the English and your shaven-headed friends.'

'But why?' said Kit. 'Why would you trick my father

to the gallows? Why would you turn on your own kind to help the Spanish?'

Wylam looked taken aback by the question. 'Because I am a *true* Catholic!' he said. 'Not some ridiculous half-breed like your father, who thought he could show allegiance to that faithless whore Elizabeth and stay true to the Holy Father in Rome who had excommunicated her. Your father was even financing this venture,' he said, waving the arrow around. 'He actually backed an English Catholic colony in America. He was told that he would be excommunicated if he carried on, but he would not listen. He had to be stopped, Kit.'

Kit winced from the pain of the blow to his head and the sharp sting of what he was hearing.

'He was planning to bring you here himself,' continued Wylam. 'It's ironic, don't you think?'

Kit could think of nothing to say. His whole mind was now fixed on how he might get away.

'Soon the Spanish will come to England with a force never dreamed of,' Wylam told him. 'Do you think pirates like Drake and Grenville will be able to pit themselves against the might of Spain?'

'Yes!' said Kit with more confidence than he felt.

Wylam smiled and shook his head. 'Spain will rule the world, Kit,' he said. 'It will crush England and it will drive northwards in the Americas until this land too is claimed for the one true church.'

'And what about the English?' said Kit, surreptitiously

testing the bonds that tied his wrists. 'What about your own people?'

'The English people will rejoice,' said Wylam. 'And they shall embrace their true Queen.'

'Their true Queen?'

'Mary, Queen of Scots,' said Wylam. 'She who is forced to be a prisoner shall yet be free and shall rule a reborn, Catholic England. Even now, plans are afoot to assassinate Elizabeth and free the true Queen, Mary. Then we shall have revenge for the Catholic martyrs, for the rape of Ireland, for the massacre at Smerwick!'

'Shut up!' said Kit. 'I'm sick of hearing about the past. You don't care about the dead, you just care about the excuse it gives to kill! Walsingham, Lane, Raleigh, you . . . You all think God's on your side, but what kind of God wants men tortured and women and children butchered? You're all mad!'

Wylam did indeed look fanatical now; he put his hand to his temple, closing his eyes and taking a deep breath. 'I rather think we will never agree,' he said finally, opening his eyes once more and taking up the arrow. 'I shall kill you quickly, Kit, for friendship's sake; that I promise.'

'At least let me stand,' said Kit pitifully. 'Don't kill me on the ground like I was a dog.'

Wylam nodded wearily and, smiling, helped him to his feet. As he did so, Kit kicked Wylam as hard as he could between the legs. Wylam gasped and groaned, doubling up in pain. Kit grabbed an arrow from the dead Indian's quiver and ran as fast as his legs would take him, deeper into the woods. He ran with his head down, holding the arrow up in front of his face as protection against the twigs and brambles that arced in front of him.

He saw a group of Indians in the distance and thought about running to them for assistance, but they were hardly likely to come to his aid after what the English had done to Wingina. He looked back towards Wylam, but the spy had gone.

Kit crept through the woods, trying to remember everything Wanchese had taught him. He avoided every rotten twig, every branch; walking on moss, trying to take quiet, easy breaths despite his fear. He attempted to undo the binds around his wrists but they were too tight so he simply moved as fluidly as he could, looking about him for any sign of Wylam. He could see nothing at all. Then suddenly, a bird took flight some yards away and Kit dropped to the ground.

In a tree opposite, a racoon looked down at him quizzically as it sat on a branch and polished a crab apple on its furry belly. Kit heard a noise behind him and crawled on his hands and knees behind a fallen tree, trying to calm his breathing when his body wanted to pant. He sat and held the arrow between his knees, using the point to saw through the cord around his wrists.

Again there was a noise beyond the fallen tree and Kit put his face nervously to the roots and peered through, but he could still see nothing. The noise had sounded closer this time, but there was no sign of Wylam. Kit strained his eyes, but nothing moved.

'Kit, Kit,' said a voice behind him.

His hands were finally free, but he turned to see Wylam standing over him holding an arrow in one hand and a twig in the other. Smiling, he threw the twig into the undergrowth beyond the tree. That was the noise Kit had heard, and he closed his eyes and cursed.

A raven croaked in a tree high above their heads and Kit saw its wings beating through the branches. Wylam smiled and stepped forward. But before he had a chance to do anything, Kit rammed the arrow into his thigh and scrambled away. Roaring like a wounded animal, Wylam set off after him.

Kit tripped. He could hear Wylam closing in on him – as well as the swish of his sword being unsheathed. He tried to get to his feet and winced with pain, realizing he had twisted his ankle. Then he saw that he had run round in a wide circle and was now back by the dead Indian.

Kit made one last effort and, despite the pain, managed to throw himself forward, grabbing the Indian's bow and rolling onto his back, an arrow aimed at Wylam as he staggered towards him. 'No!' he screamed.

Wylam grinned and looked at Kit as though he had never truly seen him before. Then, as quickly as it had come, the smile disappeared and Wylam lurched forward. Before he had taken half a step, there was an arrow jutting out of his chest and he staggered back.

Wylam looked from Kit to the arrow and back again with an expression of confusion. Kit already had another arrow trained on him. Wylam lurched forward again;

again Kit fired, and another arrow joined the first. This time Wylam fell backwards, sitting at the base of a tree, eyes open, lips parted as if about to speak.

Kit got painfully to his feet, another arrow trained on Wylam. There was a sound of thrashing through the undergrowth and – alerted by Kit's scream – White arrived, Lane and Nugent close behind. Kit was still aiming his bow at the fallen Wylam.

White put his hand on his shoulder and Kit let out a gasp and looked about him as if coming out of a trance.

'Kit?' said White. 'What has happened? Master Lane and I heard your cry.'

Lane lifted his pistol and pointed it at Kit's head.

'Lane!' shouted White. 'No!'

'I warned you, boy!' he said. 'You'll hang for this. Nugent, take him to the jail.'

'He was a spy!' cried Kit. 'Wylam was an agent of the Spanish!'

'Truly?' said Lane. 'And how do we not know that you are an agent of the Spanish? There has always been something about you I didn't like; too damned friendly with the savages for one thing.'

'The boy is telling the truth, sir,' said White. 'I am sure of it.'

'I will be the judge of that, mapmaker,' snarled Lane. 'Stay out of this or you'll end up in the jailhouse with the boy.'

'He was a spy!' repeated Kit. 'He killed my father!'

White stared at him, startled.

'What nonsense is this?' said Lane. 'What cause could a man like that have to kill your father? He could scarcely have even known him, lest he was in his service . . .'

'My father was Sir Richard Fulbourn,' shouted Kit, turning to White, who was still shaking his head in disbelief at Kit's denouncement of Wylam.

'Did you hear that?' said Lane. 'Fulbourn was executed for treason! We have the son of a Catholic spy among us, standing over the body of a man he has murdered. What do you say now, Master White?'

'Be still, Lane,' said a voice behind them, and Drake and two of his men appeared with a black man – one of the freed slaves from Hispaniola. 'Is this the man?' asked Drake.

The black man crouched down and lifted Wylam's hand, looking at the ring. He turned to Drake, nodded vigorously and fired off a volley of Spanish.

'This man was heard talking to Angulo in Hispaniola,' said Drake. 'He was passing on information about your plans and the position of the colony.'

'And you would take this Negro's word?' said Lane. 'How can he be sure that this was the man?'

'Well,' said Drake with a chuckle, 'he says you all look the same, but with this one, he remembers—'

'The ring,' interrupted Kit.

'Aye,' said Drake, nodding. 'He recognized the ring.'

'Enough of this nonsense!' shouted Lane. 'Take the boy, Nugent, and we'll see what else he knows!'

'Don't be stupid, Lane,' said Drake. 'The man there was an enemy of the Queen. The boy has done you a service. You should be thanking him, not clapping him in irons.'

'Well, I am governor here,' said Lane. 'And I will impose discipline as I see fit. This boy is the son of an enemy of England.'

Drake took a step forward. 'You will release him this instant or I will have it done,' he said, looking at Nugent and the two men who had come to stand next to him. 'If you think your gang of bully boys is a match for my men, then let's have at it now, sir, and be done. Come,' he said, grabbing his sword hilt. 'You and I shall start the dance.'

Lane looked as though he were thinking about taking Drake up on the offer, but he looked past the general to his men, who were forming up behind him. They had struck fear into Spaniards up and down the Americas. Lane's men were no match for them and he knew it. He bowed to Drake and walked away, a beaten man.

Lane asked Drake if he would take some of the sick and injured men into his care, but he steadfastly refused to close down the colony and return to England a failure.

Drake readily agreed to take the invalids home and offered Lane a ship, the *Francis* – which several of the gentlemen went aboard to inspect. He also unloaded two pinnaces and several small boats to enable Lane to explore the coast still further. Lane seemed to recover some of his old fire, as – to White's dismay – he announced that he would be able to renew his search for the copper mines at Chaunis Temoatan.

Kit was with White one day when he took the opportunity to have a quiet word with Drake. He asked him if he could not relieve Lane of his command and put another in charge in his place, but Drake said that he did not have the authority to do such a thing.

'Understand, Master White,' he said, 'that this is Raleigh's project; see how it would appear if I were to interfere. I have offered to take the colony back to England, but Lane won't hear of it.'

Kit heard a noise and saw Nugent walking away. He had been listening for sure. His heart sank at the thought of Lane hearing that White was trying to have him stripped of his authority.

Suddenly he saw the medicine man appear at the edge of the wood, his cloak fringed with black feathers, dancing his weird twitching dance and squawking like a bird. A sudden gust of wind swirled around them, hurling sand into their faces. Kit closed his eyes to shield them, and when he opened them again, the medicine man was gone and the wind was blowing wildly, tugging at the thatched roofs and hurdle fences.

'Come on,' said Drake to his commanders. 'Back to the ships! There's a storm brewing.'

White and Kit went over the lagoon to the Outer Banks and it was clear that Drake would not be able to get out to his ship now. The sky above the sea was a blanket of black cloud, passing like a great shadow across the face of the sun: night was leaking into day. The sea was darkening too; darkening and churning as if monsters were stirring beneath its surface.

Then, all at once, a strange shimmering giant snake appeared, joining sea to sky. It seemed to dance upon the water with its head in the clouds. Kit was filled with an ice-cold fear that gripped his guts and made him weak. At first he thought he must be seeing a vision of some kind, some sort of waking nightmare, but he could tell by the faces of those around him that they saw it too. Some of the mariners had witnessed waterspouts before, but they feared them all the more.

Sailors struggled to row back to the ships. One of the boats was pushed up by an incoming wave until it stood on its rudder, then it tipped over completely, spilling its crew into the churning sea. Kit could just make out men clambering up the sides of the ships as the storm slammed into them, sending the vessels spinning and dipping. Anchors were hurriedly hauled aboard before the ships could be dragged onto the shore, where they would be smashed. As bad as the storm was, the sailors knew they stood more chance fighting it in open water than with their backs to this treacherous coast.

Then, as Kit watched, something fell from the sky and landed on the sand nearby. He was just trying to work out what it was when another landed at his feet and a third struck a soldier, clanging against his helmet and knocking him unconscious.

As another soldier went to help his comrade, there was a mighty roar and hundreds more of the missiles rained down. Kit dashed for cover with his hands over his head. They were hailstones – bigger than he had ever seen in his life.

The storm raged for hours, with a spiteful violence as if the heavens were having a tantrum. It ripped the roof off two of the houses and threw empty barrels about as if they were corks. When the tempest had passed, the Indians emerged from the forest and stood at the edge of the trees looking at the English fort. Kit had the impression that they hoped the foreigners might have been blown away. The ships gradually returned to anchor offshore, though Kit could see straight away that one was missing.

'The *Francis* has not returned,' Lane said as he called the gentlemen to a meeting.

'Good heavens,' said White. 'It has been lost? With all our fellows aboard? This is terrible.'

'Possibly.' Drake nodded and stroked his beard. 'Possibly.' He looked at Lane.

'Possibly?' said White, raising his eyebrows. 'Is there yet hope then?'

'The *Francis* is a good ship. It would take more than a storm like that to sink her in open water.'

'I don't understand,' said White.

Drake sighed and explained that the most probable explanation was that the gentlemen on board the *Francis* had decided they had had enough of the New World and were heading back to the old one.

'Deserted us?' said White. 'No!'

'Come now, Master White,' said Lane. 'After all you have gone through, you still seem surprised by the actions of your fellow men; particularly the spineless ones we have been cursed with on this venture.'

'I hope I shall always be surprised by treachery.'

'I find it better to expect it, I must say,' said Drake with a chuckle.

'You seem to find the matter amusing, Sir Francis,' said Lane.

'No. Desertion is a serious business, Master Lane,' said Drake. 'It speaks badly of those who serve – and those who command.'

'It is my fault, then?' said Lane angrily.

'I cannot judge,' said Drake coldly. 'I will leave that to your sponsors. And to the Queen.'

Lane opened his mouth to reply, but whatever he was going to say remained unsaid as he looked from face to face among the gentlemen of the colony, none of whom would hold his gaze. He realized that there would be none who would speak in his defence. Kit saw that even the normally dog-loyal Nugent was staring at his feet. With his dreams of finding the Indian mines in tatters, and no support around him, Lane looked as if something had broken inside him. When the remaining gentlemen began to press for the colony to be taken home with Drake, he offered little resistance.

Chapter 46

Kit stood watching as the colony was packed up around him. Soon only the tattered houses and the rubbish heaps remained to show they had ever been there. A couple of storms and there would be barely a sign of their presence.

The Indians stood and watched from a distance as the ghosts prepared to leave their country as suddenly as they had arrived. Suddenly Kit found Wanchese standing beside him; they embraced like long-lost brothers.

'Are you coming back to England?' Kit asked.

'No,' said Wanchese. 'I stay here.'

'But Manteo . . .'

'Manteo will go with English.'

'I'm sorry,' said Kit. 'Sorry for what they – we – have done. I was there when Wingina . . .'

Wanchese put his hand up. 'Wingina was fool,' he said. 'He had no right to bring Mondoag enemy into Secota. And what point to anger these English? Kill and more will come from the sea.' He looked towards the dunes and Drake's fleet at anchor beyond. 'All life came from the sea,' he said. 'Now death will come from the sea also.'

Kit felt suddenly overwhelmed by a sadness he could see mirrored in Wanchese's face.

'I go now,' the Indian continued. 'But someone else . . .' He pointed away to his left and Kit saw, standing in the shadow of a myrtle tree, the beautiful Acaunque. Wanchese patted Kit's arm and, as he and his friends left the colony, Acaunque walked towards him.

Tears now came to Kit's eyes. He could think of nothing to say or do, and stood motionless, aware of the slightest of breezes brushing against his face.

Acaunque sat and Kit sat with her. She began to talk in her soft lilting voice. She spoke for a long time without pause and Kit made no attempt to interrupt. Occasionally he would hear a word he recognized, but it would be carried away on a torrent of words he did not. But he understood that she was telling him about herself; that she was trying to give something of herself to him before they left.

When Acaunque stopped, Kit began to speak. He too spoke without pause while she listened. He told her about his family and how that life had been snatched away, and how he had lived on the streets and met Hugh and become a thief. He told her how a chance meeting with White had changed his life and set in train a course of events that led to America, to Roanoke and to her.

When he finished, she stood and looked towards the Outer Banks and the ships beyond. When she turned back to Kit there were tears in her eyes. He reached out a hand and gently brushed her face. Acaunque put her fingers to her lips and pressed them against his chest. Then she turned and walked away.

Kit stared at her back as she left, willing her to turn round, but she did not. He closed his eyes tightly, the sounds of the departing colonists fading away as his mind focused on a bird singing somewhere in the trees nearby. And then he made his decision.

He was going to stay.

There was nothing for him to go back to. White was a good man, but Kit was never going to be able to return to that life in Cheapside, or any life that London had to offer. Hugh was his only friend there, and he had moved on to another life. Kit was going to do the same. He was going to stay in Virginia and take his chances with these people; with Wanchese, with Acaunque.

White was among the last to leave. He instructed Drake's men to load his bags and equipment and all the specimens he and Harriot had collected onto a waiting boat. He then climbed aboard another to be rowed out to Drake's flagship, the *Elizabeth Bonaventure*. Kit said that he would go across in the pinnace with the bags to make sure the sailors looked after them and White nodded his approval.

But as soon as White's back was turned and his boat set off, and while the sailors were occupied with loading

349

the pinnace, Kit slipped away and into the dunes, hiding behind a clump of grass as White's boat bucked across the breakers on its way to the ship.

He had a momentary pang of remorse as he thought of the sadness his disappearance would cause to White; of how his master would worry and assume that some terrible accident had befallen him. But if he was going to stay, this was the only way. White would never have allowed it.

White arrived at the *Elizabeth Bonaventure* and was helped aboard, disappearing from view. Kit was about to turn away when he noticed a commotion aboard the pinnace. The sailors were arguing. The pinnace had barely left the shore when it became obvious that it was overloaded and sinking. In desperation, the sailors began to throw random items of baggage overboard. Kit could not believe his eyes as he saw White's bags with his precious drawings and maps being tossed into the water.

'No!' he shouted, already running as fast as his legs would carry him towards the shore.

He ran headlong into the waves. A chest containing pigments had cracked open and the bottles were releasing their contents in multi-coloured clouds as Kit waded forward, desperately grabbing at a bag ahead of him and clambering aboard the pinnace.

'Nearly left you behind, son,' said one of the sailors, tossing another chest overboard.

'Stop!' shouted Kit. 'They're valuable!'

'I told you they might be gold!' said one of the sailors angrily.

'No,' said Kit. 'Not gold. Drawings. Maps. Seeds.'

'Oh,' said the sailor and continued throwing things over.

Kit tried to stop him, but the sailor shoved him away and he fell heavily to the deck, clutching the bag he had saved and watching the shoreline recede. If he left the pinnace, the sailors would once again throw the bag away and he could not bear to see all White's hard work destroyed so casually. Fate, it appeared, had decided for him: he would have to return to England now . . .

Indians slowly began to appear on the sandbanks to watch the English leave. Kit wondered if Acaunquewas among them, but he was too far away to tell. Looking at them standing there, he felt a terrible sadness come over him again. He would miss this land so much. To his surprise, however, he saw another pinnace – *off* loading dozens of men onto the beach.

'Who are they?' asked Kit.

'They're African slaves we picked up in Hispaniola,' said a sailor. 'We thought you could do with the help. They're worth a fair bit of money, but with all you lot on board now there's no room for 'em. Still – they're better off landed here than they were with the Spaniards.' Kit looked at the forlorn figures stranded on the Outer Banks and doubted it. Without the strength to stop himself, he began to cry.

When he climbed aboard the *Elizabeth Bonaventure*,

White was waiting for him and stepped forward concernedly, seeing Kit's soaking clothes and tear-filled eyes.

'It's all ruined, sir,' said Kit. 'We've ruined it.'

'Not ruined, Kit. Not yet ruined surely.'

'They would have been better off if we'd never come!'

White became aware of a commotion behind them. Lane was shouting at two sailors who had returned with the pinnace Kit had boarded.

'Well, go back and get them, then!' Lane was shouting.

'We take our orders from Sir Francis,' said one of the sailors.

Lane pulled a pistol and pointed it at the man's face. The sailor did not flinch.

'Lane,' said White, 'put the pistol down.'

Lane did not move. 'This man was instructed to fetch our things,' he said. 'Yet he has returned with an empty pinnace.'

'Empty?' queried Harriot, walking forward.

'Do as Master White instructed, Lane,' said Drake from behind them. 'Put the pistol down.' He was holding a pistol himself and sounded very bored at having to threaten Lane again. 'Put it down or I'll blast your silly head off.'

Lane dropped his pistol and Drake stepped forward and took it from him.

'And rest assured, Master Lane, if there is any repeat of this behaviour, I will have you hanged for a mutineer,' Drake added.

'A mutineer?' said Lane. 'You call me a mutineer! This man has disobeyed my orders and refuses to return to shore to retrieve our possessions.'

'Is this true?' said Drake.

'There would be no point, Captain,' said the sailor. 'We threw the stuff overboard.'

'What?' cried White. 'Do you realize what you've done? There were all manner of seeds and plants for the Queen in those boxes, damn you. The work of months has been destroyed.'

Drake smiled. 'Seeds?' he said. 'I had thought these fools might have discarded treasure, with all your fuss!'

The crew laughed and White's face reddened.

'There were maps and charts too,' said Harriot. 'Even you might see the importance of them.'

Drake's smile disappeared. 'Mind your tongue, wizard,' he said. 'Unless you want to join them.'

'*I – am – not – a – wizard!*' yelled Harriot.

'The pinnace was too heavily laden, sir,' said the sailor. 'We could not get it off the beach. With the storm looking like to return, we did not see another trip being made.'

'You did right,' said Drake.

'They did right?' said Lane. 'Right? I had a string of pearls among my things. They were so fine I planned to give them to the Queen.'

After a moment's pause Drake began to laugh and was joined by the entire crew, so that the laughter echoed round the deck and up the rigging.

'A string of pearls?'

'Yes,' said Lane. 'What of it, sir. I see no cause for merriment.'

Drake shook his head. 'When I returned from travelling around this entire globe,' he said, loudly so that his crew could hear, 'I delivered to the Queen holds filled to bursting with silver and jewels. I think it better that your string of pearls amuses the fishes. Our Queen requires greater excitement.'

The crew erupted into cheers of 'God Bless Queen Elizabeth!' and Kit could see that Lane wanted to strike Drake, but knew that such a move would be fatal. Lane seemed to visibly shrink.

'Look lively, lads,' said Drake. 'We sail for England.' Again the crew cheered before swarming over the ship, attending to their various tasks.

'All my drawings!' muttered White, looking forlornly back to shore.

'Not all,' said Kit, holding a bag out towards White, whose face lit up like a burst of sunshine.

'Bless you, Kit,' he said, tears in his eyes. 'Bless you, lad.'

Kit felt the wind fill the sails with the same punch that now struck his stomach as the full realization that he was leaving Roanoke hit home. He stared longingly away to shore like a cabin boy on his first voyage; he was still staring two hours later when the shoreline had disappeared beyond the cold grey horizon.

Part Three
England, 1586

Chapter 47

At the end of July 1586, a month after leaving Virginia, Kit was watching the cheering crowds on the quaysides at Portsmouth, and the heaviness of heart that had plagued him for much of the journey momentarily left him as he smiled back at the people and waved along with the crew.

'England,' said White.

'Yes,' said Kit. 'I never thought I'd be so glad to see her again.'

'Absence will do that.'

'They seem glad to have us return,' said Kit, waving more vigorously. 'Look at them all.'

'They care not one jot about us, Kit,' said Harriot, nodding towards Drake, who was ostentatiously bowing to the crowd. 'It is Sir Francis they are cheering.'

White nodded and sighed. 'It seems that the people are more interested in tales of destruction than of colonization,' he said wryly. 'The English like a simple tale. Adventure. Gold. Routing Spaniards. Drake gives them what they want.'

Kit nodded, watching Drake clown for the crowds, grinning and bowing. It was not so long since he too had hungered for just that kind of tale, but it felt like a thousand years ago.

After a few days' rest in Portsmouth, they set out for London and Kit stood at the forecastle as they sailed up the Thames. He was surprised to realize how elated he felt when they rounded the final bend in the river and saw the silhouette of London, jagged with church spires jabbing at the sky like the teeth in a jawbone.

Why was he so pleased to return to a place that had never treated him kindly? There would be a meeting with Walsingham – and who could tell how that might end? He remembered Wanchese picking up the soil of Roanoke. Maybe home was home whether you loved it or not. It was a mark on your back, whether you knew it was there or not.

It was not until they reached White's house and saw their dishevelled state reflected in the expressions on the faces of Mrs Fisher and Annie, that Kit realized what they must look like after their adventures. When he looked in the glass later, he hardly recognized the boy who looked back.

'So,' said Annie later, when they were alone in the kitchen, 'you're a Catholic then, Master White says?'

'My parents were, at any rate.'

'You don't look like a Catholic,' said Annie.

Kit laughed. 'And what do Catholics look like?'

'I don't know,' said Annie with a chuckle. 'Not like you.'

'You don't hate me then?' said Kit.

'Not any more than I did before,' she said with a grin.

'Thank you,' said Kit. 'And I promise I won't poison the water.'

Annie blushed, remembering what she had said outside the church all those months ago. Kit laughed at her embarrassment and ducked just in time to miss the slap she aimed at him.

They washed and changed their clothes. White's daughter, Eleanora, and her husband, Ananais, came by and Kit was touched to see how happy Eleanora seemed to be to see him – as genuinely pleased as if he had been her own brother. They ate well and tried as best they could to tell their eager listeners something of what had happened while they were away; but there was too much that could not be said, too much that would not be understood. Several times, White and Kit would exchange glances when a subject was skirted round. They were bound together now by their experience.

Ananais slapped Kit heartily on the back. 'I knew you were hiding something,' he said. 'I just knew it.' But it was the secrecy he seemed to hold against Kit, not the secret itself. He appeared to be no more concerned by Kit's Catholic background than his wife.

Eleanora hung on every word that Kit and White spoke about Roanoke, her eyes wide and sparkling with excitement. No detail was too small, no incident too trivial. When they could think of no more to tell her, she groaned and swore that had she been a man, she would have sailed with them. Kit saw Ananais smile at his wife; not in a mocking way, but with pride at her spirit.

Tiredness began to overtake Kit long before White insisted that he go to bed. He sank into sleep, putting up no resistance, letting no thought keep him awake. He slept and dreamed; dreamed of his parents and the house he had shared with them. It was a happy dream, filled with laughter, and he would gladly have exchanged it for his waking life. He awoke as usual, but with the laughter still inside his head, and he felt strengthened by it.

A few days later, Annie was in the kitchen helping Mrs Fisher prepare breakfast.

'Oh, you're with us then?' said Annie as Kit stretched.

'Oh leave him be,' said Mrs Fisher. 'He's still dog tired, poor lamb.'

'Poor lamb?' snorted Annie. 'Him?'

Kit frowned.

'Don't listen to her,' said Mrs Fisher. 'She was that worried while you was away. She was always asking whether I thought you were well.'

'No I wasn't!' said Annie, her face flushing red. Mrs Fisher laughed derisively and flounced out, heading for the larder. Annie leaned conspiratorially towards Kit as he stood up. 'Those native girls don't wear barely a thing,' she whispered. 'I seen those drawings Mister White did. You can see their paps. Ain't they got no shame?'

'Yes,' said Kit. 'Well, no. I don't know.'

'Well I think it's . . . it's . . .' Annie struggled for the right word, but it seemed to flit away before she could catch it. In the end she turned on her heels and left the room sobbing, crashing into White as she was leaving.

'What on earth is the matter with Annie?' he said, staring after her.

'I don't know,' said Kit with a baffled shrug.

White shook his head. 'I need to make my report to Sir Walter,' he said. 'Will you come with me to Durham House?'

'Aye, sir,' said Kit. He had never been to Raleigh's house, and he was intrigued to see what lay behind those walls.

He carried White's bags as he had done so many times before, though this time they were catching a boat along the Thames rather than crossing the lagoon in Virginia, or following some mossy forest track to a native village. Kit felt so changed, and yet London seemed so unchanged. It was as though he had left some part of himself on Roanoke; some part of himself that was lost for ever. It was more than the vague homesickness he had felt on leaving London – it was a constant sense that he had misplaced something vitally important; that he was looking for something he would never find.

Durham House stood on a bend in the Thames, stretched out along the river, its roofline bristling with chimneys, towers and leaded turrets topped with glittering weather vanes.

The ferryman steered their boat towards the watergate and they slipped through from the choppy waters of the river into the quay built below the house. Torches burned on the walls of the vaulted chamber, and light rippled across the dank walls and ceiling, reflected up from the water below as the boat was moored and Kit and White got out.

Sullen guards dressed in black stood nearby, their shimmering breastplates and metal-crested helmets picking up the warm glow of the torches and looking as if they were fresh from the blacksmith's forge.

They clearly knew White as a frequent visitor, but Kit felt less welcome. There was something ominous about the place and he could see that the ferryman was eager to take his money and leave, letting go of one oar in his haste to row away.

White saw the unease on Kit's face. 'Come now, lad,' he said, seemingly reading Kit's mind. 'We are in London still. That was the Thames, not the Styx.'

'The sticks?' said Kit. 'What sticks?'

'Not "sticks",' said White with a chuckle. 'The River Styx. It is the river the Greeks thought men were ferried across on their way to the land of the dead. We still need to do something about your education.'

'I know plenty of things,' said Kit, looking a little hurt.

'Of course you do,' said White with a smile, and he

led the way up a well-worn flight of steps, the stone getting progressively less green as they climbed, until they emerged through an arched doorway, past another guard and on into a hall.

'The Queen herself once lived here, you know, Kit,' said White as they walked. 'And two of her father's wives. These walls could tell some tales.'

The first face Kit saw when he walked into the hall, however, was that of Joachim Ganz.

'Young Master Kit,' he said. 'Good to see you.'

'And you, sir,' said Kit.

'Sir Richard,' said White. 'I did not see you there.'

'Master White,' said Grenville, shaking his hand. 'And your boy.'

'Kit, sir,' said Kit. 'Kit Milton.'

Grenville nodded disinterestedly and White went up to see Raleigh. Ganz and Kit talked while Grenville paced about awkwardly. Kit saw him looking out of the window, his fingers flexing as if he longed to be away, down at the quayside boarding a ship. After about half an hour, White appeared at the foot of the stairs leading to Raleigh's study.

'Sir Walter wants to see you, Kit,' he said.

'Wants to see the boy?' said Grenville. 'Has the world gone insane? I have been waiting here for an hour.'

White shrugged and Ganz smirked. Kit looked from face to face, then White flicked his finger towards the stairs. Kit gulped and set off towards them.

He climbed the spiral staircase to Raleigh's study

in the turret and knocked on the door; a voice asked him to enter. As he opened the door, he saw Raleigh standing at a window looking out over the river.

Raleigh turned to face him and walked over to the fire. He invited Kit to sit and sat down himself on the other side of the hearth.

Raleigh's hair was long and curly, swept back from his face to show a high, pale forehead. From his ears hung huge pearls, and pearl buttons shimmered down the front of his white jerkin. His beard tapered to a sharp point and his moustache curled up mischievously at the ends.

'Ah, Christopher,' he said in the West Country burr with which Kit had become so familiar in his time in Virginia.

'My name is Kit, sir.'

'Kit it is then,' said Raleigh. 'I see your mother's eyes in yours.' Kit said nothing, and Raleigh continued. 'I was at Oxford with your father, you know. It was a great shock to me when I heard he was accused of being involved in a plot against the Queen.'

'Falsely accused,' said Kit.

Raleigh smiled. 'So I have always believed,' he said. Kit looked away. 'I was proud to call him a friend,' Raleigh continued.

'Even though he was a Catholic?' said Kit bitterly.

'Even though he was a Catholic. I have had many friends who are Catholics, Kit. Do not take me for one of those creatures who would have you all burned at the stake. Your father knew that I could separate the religion from the man; your mother too. I do not despise you for being Catholic.'

'I'm not a Catholic, sir,' said Kit.

'You have changed your religion?'

'I think I've lost it, sir.'

Raleigh nodded slowly. 'I see. You have suffered much. Suffering spawns zealots and atheists in equal measure.'

'But you didn't try and help him, then?' said Kit, his lip trembling. 'My father? When he was arrested? What with him being your friend and everything, sir.'

Raleigh closed his eyes. 'I was not the man I am now, Kit,' he said. 'I did not have the position I do now. I was in Ireland when your father was executed.'

'I hear you were at Smerwick, sir.'

Raleigh shifted uneasily in his chair and seemed momentarily to have lost his normal composure. 'War is a different world, Kit. Ireland is a different world. Those people . . .' Seeming lost in his thoughts for a moment, Raleigh looked down, and for an instant did not see his pearl-studded jerkin but the blood-splattered one he had worn that day at Smerwick. 'Those people needed a show of force,' he said, looking up. 'The Italians should never have been there.' His voice seemed to peter away as the memories came back.

'May I go now, sir?' said Kit.

'Of course, of course,' said Raleigh, getting to his feet. As Kit reached the door, he said, 'Once again, Kit – I am so sorry about your parents; so very sorry.'

Kit stopped in the doorway and looked back into the room. Raleigh was already back at the window. Kit wanted to hate this man who seemed to float so easily on the dark waters in which his parents had drowned, but he could not. He simply had no feelings for him at all. And as he descended the stairs, he looked back again – up the steps winding their way to the study – and thought of Raleigh looking out of the window towards the sea. How like a prisoner he was.

Chapter 48

Barn Elms looked very different under a bright August sky than it had on the chill winter's day on which Kit had last visited Sir Francis Walsingham. He and White were shown to the garden, where Walsingham was at work among the immaculately clipped hedges, wearing his customary black but with a rather battered straw sun hat on his head instead of his usual skullcap.

He stopped work when they arrived and led them over to some chairs the servants had placed in the shade of a walnut tree. Walsingham seemed to notice his hat for the first time and took it off immediately.

'Sir Francis,' said White. 'I trust you are well.'

'I am not too bad, thank you, Master White,' said Walsingham wearily. 'Though my health has been poor of late. I swear I spend more money on doctors than I do on food.'

'I am sorry to hear it, sir. How is Dame Ursula?'

'She is worried about our daughter Frances, who worries about her husband.'

'Sir Philip is in the Netherlands, sir?'

'He is,' said Walsingham. 'The Earl of Leicester is in command; the boy Essex with him. Would that he were back in England – with "Sweet Robin", the Earl, away from court, the Queen is surrounded by all manner of fawning favourites. It makes me bilious to see it.' Walsingham dropped his voice, though there was no one but the three of them in the garden. 'But there are more pressing matters. We need Her Majesty to make a decision about Our Lady of Staffordshire.' Kit's ears pricked up. Walsingham was talking about Mary, Queen of Scots. 'We have her, Master White. We have her accomplices and we have the proof of her own involvement. This time she must pay the full price. We need the Earl back in England. The Queen will listen to Leicester.' Walsingham glanced at Kit. 'But we will talk of this another time.'

'Of course, sir,' said White. 'In the meantime, let us hope that Sir Philip and Leicester fare well.'

'They do God's work. I pray daily for their swift and safe return.'

'Aye, sir,' said White.

'I read your report on Virginia, Master White,' said Walsingham. 'It was very thorough. A rather different story will come from the hand of Master Harriot, of course. We do not want to frighten the sponsors – especially the Queen.'

'And Master Lane, sir?'

Walsingham sighed. 'You have no idea how many

letters I have had from that awful man,' he said. 'I think we shall send him back to Ireland. His enthusiasms will be of greater use there.'

White had already warned Kit to be careful how he spoke to Walsingham, but as usual Kit forgot himself almost instantly. As soon as the opportunity presented itself, he jumped straight in.

'My parents, sir,' he said. 'You know now that my father was not a spy,' said Kit.

'So it would appear, Master Fulbourn,' said Walsingham.

'What do you mean, "So it would appear"?' said Kit angrily.

'Steady, Kit,' said White.

Walsingham smiled. 'It was a figure of speech, lad, nothing more,' he said. 'I am convinced of your parents' innocence, I assure you.'

'Then you will tell the Queen, sir?'

'Ah,' said Walsingham with a sigh. 'That is something else altogether.'

'But you have to tell her!'

'I am not aware of having to do anything of the sort.' Walsingham turned away to admire his garden. 'Queen Elizabeth is a very astute and intelligent woman. She may ask what proof I have of their innocence. Gabriel is dead. Wylam is dead, and so—'

'No!' yelled Kit.

'Kit!' hissed White.

'Have a care, young Fulbourn,' said Walsingham.

'Not many are given the luxury of raising their voices to me once, and I have let you do it twice. I will not let it happen a third time.' He cocked his head and his neck clicked. He took a deep breath. 'Do you love your Queen, boy?' he asked suddenly, peering into Kit's eyes.

Kit frowned and curled his lip. 'You ask me to love a person who killed my father for a lie?' Beside him, White sucked in his breath sharply at this near treasonous outburst . . .

'The Queen did not kill your father, lad,' said Walsingham. 'If he was guilty, he killed himself. If he was innocent, then our friend Wylam killed him.'

'He was innocent,' said Kit quietly. 'You know he was. It's not fair.'

There was a tense silence in which a white butterfly flitted past like a miniature flag of truce. Walsingham took a deep breath before speaking again.

'Now listen to me. Gabriel spoke well of you and I valued his opinion more than most. Master White clearly holds you in high esteem. Master Ganz speaks well of you, and he speaks well of almost no one.'

'Master Ganz works for you?' said Kit.

Walsingham shook his head. 'Master Ganz is not an intelligencer, if that is what you mean. But he is a very clever man, Master Fulbourn, and I will always listen to a clever man.' Walsingham winced and clutched at his side.

'Sir?' said White. 'Can I get you something?'

'No, thank you, Master White,' Walsingham said, closing his eyes. 'It will pass.' When he opened his eyes again, he looked at Kit. 'You do not have any great sympathy for my suffering, I notice.' Kit made no response, and Walsingham smiled wearily; almost apologetically. 'I work to protect the Queen,' he continued. 'I would see a hundred innocent people put to death if it preserved her life.' He smiled. 'There may be work for you if you want it.'

'You . . . you . . . you want me as an intelligencer? You want me to spy?' said Kit with a dry laugh.

Walsingham shrugged. 'There may be work,' he said. 'I do not say what it may be.'

'Why would I work for you?' asked Kit. White reached a restraining hand out towards his young servant.

'Why not?' retorted Walsingham. 'What an obstinate young man you are.'

'But a free one,' said Kit, shrugging White's hand away.

'Free?' said Walsingham with a laugh. 'Of course. Free. Yes, yes: free to scratch out a living among the fleas and rats. Free to starve; free to die like that boy – the little thief in Shoreditch? Is that what you want?'

'How . . . How could you know about that?' asked Kit.

'It is my job to know,' said Walsingham. 'You never know what might be important. Do you really mean to tell me that this life I offer you is of no interest? Look at you. You are cunning and courageous, but what good will it do you? London does not want your wits and does not need your courage.'

'I do,' said White quietly.

Walsingham looked at White for a long time before finally nodding. 'Very well, Master White,' he said. 'Very well.'

A few days later, Kit was at Hampton Court with White, but there was little of the giddy activity of their last visit. It was still busy, with courtiers and servants hurrying through the corridors, but busy with the affairs of state rather than entertainments.

It was the chosen few who milled about the Queen on this occasion: Lord Burghley, Sir Christopher Hatton and Walsingham. Raleigh was there, naturally, as were the familiar faces of Harriot and Grenville. With the Earl of Leicester away in the Netherlands, it was Raleigh who now stood beside the Queen, whispering and laughing at her jokes. Hatton looked on jealously.

Manteo was there, looking almost indistinguishable from a Londoner, though nowhere near as finely dressed as Raleigh or Hatton. Joachim Ganz rolled his eyes as Kit walked in, making him grin.

'Mr Ganz, sir,' said Kit. 'I'm pleased to see you.'

'Then you must be the only one,' sighed Ganz with a half-smile. 'A mineral man who does not find gold is like a fart, to be politely ignored or wafted away.' Kit grinned and Ganz leaned towards him. 'I gather that you kept a little secret from us, Master "Milton".'

'Yes, sir,' said Kit. 'They have told you then?'

Ganz nodded. 'I thought there was something more

than you were saying,' he said. 'But I could not tell what. We have a little something in common then, you and I. Jew and Catholic. We are the despised. Though of course we Jews are despised by everyone.'

'Not by me,' said Kit.

Ganz put a hand on Kit's shoulder and smiled. 'So you have learned something, Master Milton, have you not?' he said.

'That I should trust people equally?' ventured Kit. 'Whatever their beliefs or their homeland? Indians, Catholics, Jews . . .'

Ganz laughed and shook his head. 'No, no, no. That you should *dis*trust everyone equally!'

Harriot turned to face them and Kit was amazed to see that he was smoking a pipe, Raleigh looking on in encouragement. The Queen was telling Lord Burghley – who was backing off as far as etiquette allowed – that it was a new fashion from the Americas called *uppowoc* and she had planted some in her privy garden.

'The Spanish call it tobacco. Master Harriot tells us it is filled with goodness and is a tonic for all manner of ills,' she said. 'Mayhap we should smoke a pipe, my Lord Burghley, and we shall live to be a hundred on its health-giving properties.'

Burghley bowed and smiled. 'God willing, Majesty,' he said.

'I thought Harriot hated the stuff,' whispered Kit.

'He seems to have become bewitched by it,' said

Ganz. 'I have barely seen him without a pipe in his mouth since our return.'

White had been invited to display his drawings and maps for the Queen's amusement. She praised the draughtsmanship on his drawings of flowers and a turtle, but when it came to the sketches of natives, she picked up the paper and held it near her face for a closer inspection, then showed it to Lord Burghley. Kit could see it was White's drawing of the medicine man at Secota, the day he had first met Acaunque in the cornfields.

'Look at this fellow,' she said. 'Have you ever seen the like?'

'Never, Your Majesty,' Burghley answered.

The Queen leafed through some more drawings, pausing at one of the Indian bowmen. 'These men have pretty limbs, do they not?' she remarked.

'If you say so, Your Majesty,' said White.

'And these ladies?' she said, squinting at the drawing. 'Can this be right? Were their dugs and buttocks really visible for all the world to see? And only a piece of leather to hide their privities?'

'Yes, Majesty,' said White, blushing. 'I merely recorded what I saw.'

The Queen chuckled. 'We think we should have a masque in this style come Christmas,' she said. 'What say you, Lord Burghley?' Burghley looked as if he were about to have a heart attack at the suggestion, but the Queen slapped him on the back. 'We jest, sir,' she said. 'Fear not.'

'Of course, Your Majesty,' he said. 'I realize that.'

Kit could not contain a chuckle and the Queen turned to face him. He stopped instantly.

'Aha! We have learned that you served us well in the New World, Master . . . Fulbourn,' said Elizabeth. 'Our Pirate speaks well of you. We are very pleased to have you safely back in London.'

'Thank you, Your Majesty,' said Kit. 'I am very pleased to be back myself.' Elizabeth smiled and began to move away, but Kit spoke again. 'I need to apologize to Your Majesty,' he said. The Queen stopped but did not look back.

'Kit,' whispered White nervously as the Queen slowly turned to face him again.

'I was rude,' said Kit. 'When I was last with Your Majesty, I did not speak as a loyal subject should speak to his Queen.'

'Is this so?' said the Queen. 'Why then perhaps we ought to have you punished, Master Fulbourn.' Kit felt suddenly as though she were made of ice and he struggled to suppress a shiver. The Queen smiled. 'Be at your ease, sir; we jest. Why does no one know when we are jesting? Between the two of us, Master Fulbourn,' she continued in a loud voice, 'we believe that your father was the innocent victim of a Spanish plot. We believe that your father was no traitor to this land and a grave injustice was done to him at his trial and execution, and to your dear mother, for which all involved must answer to God.' Kit detected a slight movement in the Queen's mask-like face, and saw her swallow dryly before continuing. 'We shall remember them in our prayers. But we tell you this in confidence, Master Fulbourn, and it must go no further as our Moor informs us there is no proof. We are very sorry, Kit.'

'Thank you, Your Majesty,' said Kit. 'I understand.'

The Queen leaned forward. 'Remember, we know something of what it is to lose a parent wrongly to the axe,' she whispered.

'Yes, Your Majesty,' said Kit.

Elizabeth bowed and moved on and White put his hand on Kit's shoulder.

'Come,' he said gently. 'Let us go home.'

Chapter 49

'Well,' said Kit as he walked through the crowd of actors and hangers-on after the play was ended. 'Are you not glad to see me back?'

'Kit!' said Hugh. His initial smile faded and he stood waiting to see what Kit would do next, half-expecting his friend to run at him, fists flailing.

But Kit grinned and opened wide his arms. Hugh rushed forward in relief and the two friends embraced each other. Kit was a little embarrassed to realize that tears were welling in his eyes. When they pulled apart, though, he could see that the same was true of Hugh.

'It's been over a year! I thought you were dead.'

Kit smiled grimly. 'It wasn't a bad guess,' he said.

'I'm sorry, Kit,' said Hugh. 'I betrayed you to that . . . that . . . whatever he was.'

'Aye,' said Kit. 'You did.' Hugh looked away, biting the inside of his lip. 'But I'm glad you told him.'

'Glad?' said Hugh, frowning. 'Why?'

'Because if you hadn't told him, he would have hurt you, Hugh, be sure of that.'

Tears pricked Hugh's eyes. 'I don't care,' he said. 'I should have been braver, Kit, and next time . . .'

'There won't be a next time, Hugh. Not with Gabriel anyway. He's dead.'

'Was that his name, then?' asked Hugh. 'I can't say I'm too sorry to hear he is dead.' Something suddenly occurred to him and he backed away a little and eyed Kit quizzically. 'You didn't kill him, did you?'

Kit smiled and sat down at a table, looking over his shoulder and then back at Hugh, who sat down opposite him. 'No,' he replied. 'I didn't kill him.' Hugh waited for more, but none came. 'Actually, if you hadn't told Gabriel, I think I would never have known the truth about my father.'

'The truth?' said Hugh, raising a finger to attract the attention of a barmaid. 'Two jugs of ale here,' he called as she came over.

'He was innocent,' said Kit. 'The letters they found were a forgery – planted there by an English Catholic who was working for the Spanish. I found the man responsible,' he added softly.

'Have they arrested him?'

'He's dead,' said Kit, his mouth suddenly dry.

'Good,' said Hugh.

Kit smiled and shook his head. 'You didn't even know my parents,' he said.

'I know you, don't I?'

Kit grinned and nodded. Hugh slapped his old friend on the arm and Kit struggled to drink past the lump that now rose in his throat.

'So, does that mean you're rich again?' Hugh asked.

'No riches, I'm afraid,' said Kit. 'All my father's property was given away years ago.'

Hugh nodded, staring at the ground. 'So,' he said, looking up with raised eyebrows. 'How was . . . *Norwich*?'

'*Norwich* was very strange,' said Kit with a smile. 'I could not begin to tell you how strange.'

Kit noticed Hugh had an unusual expression on his face. 'We've got this new player in the troupe,' he said. 'He's a West Country man; you should hear his accent.' Kit smiled. 'Anyway – he says that Drake came into Plymouth the other week after giving the old Spanish what for in the West Indies.'

'Oh?' said Kit.

'Aye,' said Hugh, frowning a little. 'What's more, he says that he rescued these English colonists who'd settled in the Americas and brought them home. One of them apparently was a young London lad, travelling with his master . . .'

'Never!' said Kit.

Hugh was scowling now. 'Funny how you came back from wherever you went at the selfsame time, isn't it?'

Kit took a deep breath and sighed.

'It's true, isn't it? I can't believe you've been to America!' said Hugh, his eyes wide open. 'Did you really see Drake?'

'Aye,' said Kit. 'I did.'

Hugh whistled and took a long swig of ale, wiping the foam from his lips with the back of his hand. 'And were there savages?'

'Aye,' said Kit between his teeth. 'There were savages aplenty, Hugh.'

Hugh peppered him with questions, but Kit said that he really could not talk about the colony. Hugh protested, but Kit reminded him about Gabriel and said that the less he knew, the better. Hugh stroked his nose and readily saw the sense in what his friend was saying.

Eventually Kit asked Hugh what he had been doing since they last met, and Hugh gave a giddy description of every play he had performed and told Kit with breathless pride that he might be taken on by Leicester's Men. 'The Earl loves the theatre. Let's hope he gets back from the Low Countries in one piece.'

'Aye,' said Kit.

'It will mean better work and better costumes and' – Hugh licked his lips and took a deep breath – 'and we might even perform in front of the Queen herself. Imagine that; me and the Queen in the same room. Who'd have thought it?'

'Who indeed?' said Kit.

Kit let loose the bowstring and the arrow hit the target dead centre. All around him there were groups of archers standing in front of targets. The sun was shining, but a cool breeze turned the sails of the nearby windmill and shivered the leaves of the willows around Finsbury Fields. The air was filled with the twitter of skylarks and the twang and thud of bow and arrow.

'Do you ever wonder what is happening on Roanoke, Kit?' asked White.

'Only a few times an hour, sir,' said Kit with a grin. Though it had seemed strange at first, he had expected London to feel like home once again, and for Virginia to seem distant and other-worldly, but London now seemed foreign to him and he felt foreign in it. He felt imprisoned by its buildings and suffocated by its ceaseless activity.

'Well then, I have some rather interesting news,' said White as he prepared to shoot.

'Yes, sir?' said Kit. White released the arrow and it struck the centre of the target. 'Good shot, sir!'

'Sir Walter has asked me to be the governor of the colony in Virginia.'

Kit stared at him in disbelief. 'The colony, sir?' he said. 'There is no colony. It was abandoned. We abandoned it.'

'Ah, yes,' said White, his face all excitement now the news was out. 'But Sir Richard left some men there to hold it for England.

'But—'

White raised his hand. 'It is all agreed, Kit,' he said. 'The sponsors are all quite determined. Deeds have been drawn up. There is to be a city . . .'

'A city?' snorted Kit. 'It was all we could do to build a fort.'

'Have a little faith, Kit,' said White, refusing to let his enthusiasm for the project be dampened. 'It will be different this time, mark my words. I am to be governor and I will do things a little differently. This will be a true colony, not a military barracks. There will be families; women and children.' He smiled and licked his lips. 'I will need someone to carry my bags.'

Kit frowned. 'Me?' he said. 'Go back?' Acaunque's face flashed across his mind, her fingers to her lips and then to his chest. He reached up unconsciously to the shell necklace he still wore beneath his shirt.

'Yes,' said White. 'It will be different this time, I promise. Manteo will be with us again. And Eleanora and Ananais have volunteered to come too.'

Kit grinned at Eleanora's spirit. 'She is as brave as a lion, your daughter, sir.'

White nodded. 'She gets it from her mother,' he said.

Kit chuckled. 'You're brave, too, sir,' he said. 'In your own way.' White blushed a little as Kit continued his questions. 'So what's this city going to be called, sir?'

White coughed and seemed reluctant to answer. 'Raleigh,' he said eventually. 'It will be the city of Raleigh.'

Kit shook his head and chuckled. 'He's not shy, is he, sir?'

White looked nervously about him and then grinned. 'No, he is certainly not, lad,' he said.

'I'm not sure I envy the fellows who are holding it

for Raleigh,' said Kit, letting loose an arrow. 'How many did Drake leave?'

'Well,' said White. 'The truth of the matter is . . . that is to say . . .'

'Sir?'

'Fifteen. He left fifteen men, under the command of a Master Coffin.'

Kit stared open-mouthed.

'They have four cannons,' added White.

'Fifteen men?' said Kit, shaking his head. He burst into laughter, putting his hands to his face and wiping a tear from his eyes.

White frowned for a few moments, before chuckling himself. 'I fear we may need to make friends with those people all over again, Kit,' he said, and Kit nodded. 'But I believe it can be done with Manteo's help. I do not believe that Wingina was loved, however he met his end.'

Kit struggled to keep the image of that end at bay, looking up at the sky and blinking at its diamond brightness.

'So,' said White. 'Will you come?'

Kit took a deep breath. His life seemed to have been all about absence; of things taken from him. After so many endings, perhaps this could be a beginning for him: a New World; a new life. Could it really be different this time?

A raven flew overhead, flapping its wings lazily and croaking. Kit closed his eyes and saw Acaunque walking away to her village and disappearing into the shade of the woods. He put his hand to his heart as she had done and felt the shell necklace beneath his doublet and shirt.

'Aye, sir, I will,' said Kit, as his spirit guide loped away across the cobalt sky, flying west.

Author's Historical Note

Whilst Kit is wholly fictional, many of the events in this book actually took place and many of the characters really existed.

John White did accompany the expedition to Virginia as a mapmaker and artist, though little is known about the rest of his life. Many of his American watercolours still exist and are owned by the British Museum.

Sir Walter Raleigh was a soldier, poet, entrepreneur and sixteenth-century celebrity. Though well-connected at court, he was from a fairly modest background. His spectacular rise as one of Queen Elizabeth I's favourites did not make him popular. He was beheaded by Elizabeth's successor, James I, after years of imprisonment in the Tower of London.

Elizabeth was fifty-one years old when this story begins. She was very intelligent, spoke several languages fluently and was an accomplished musician; she played the lute and – appropriately for the Virgin Queen – the virginal (an early harpsichord). She donated a ship

– the *Tiger* – and £400 worth of gunpowder to the expedition.

Sir Christopher Hatton was another of Elizabeth's favourites, a fine dancer, Captain of the Guard, Vice-Chamberlain and a member of Elizabeth's Privy Council. He was intensely jealous of Raleigh.

The Earl of Leicester – 'Sweet Robin' – was yet another favourite. He had known Elizabeth since they were children and their relationship had been the cause of much gossip. He was fifty-two and overweight when this story begins and was as jealous of the dashing, thirty-two-year-old Raleigh as he had been of Hatton. He was a supporter of the theatre and had his own company of actors: Leicester's Men.

Sir Francis Walsingham was the voraciously anti-Catholic spymaster to Elizabeth. He was her Principal Secretary and though she was often infuriated by him, she knew how important he was to her continued safety. He was an investor in both the American and Irish settlements.

The elderly Lord Burghley was Lord Treasurer – the rough equivalent of a Prime Minister today. He was her most trusted adviser.

Sir Richard Grenville was Raleigh's cousin and an investor in the Roanoke colony. He was naval commander and pirate, with a famously unpredictable temper. There were reports of him biting pieces from glass goblets and eating them!

Ralph Lane, veteran of the Irish campaigns, was the

aggressive governor of the Roanoke colony and much of what we know about the events there is contained in his reports and letters.

Sir Francis Drake set out on the Great West Indies Raid a few months after the Roanoke colonists left Plymouth. He had a huge fleet of ships and almost 2,000 men, and blasted his way through the Carribean in an act of piracy financed by the Queen, Hatton, Leicester and Raleigh. He really did rescue the colonists (possibly also bringing back the first potatoes to England, given to him in the West Indies; they would become the staple diet in Ireland within forty years).

Thomas Harriot was one of the most brilliant minds of his age and would write a detailed account of what the English found in America, entitled *A Briefe and True Report of the New Found Land of Virginia* and featuring engravings of White's drawings. His fascination with *uppowoc* – tobacco – led to his being possibly the first recorded casualty of smoking-related illness when he died of cancer of the nose in 1621.

The site of the Roanoke colony is in present-day North Carolina, USA (Raleigh's Virginia covered a different area than the present state of that name). Manteo is commemorated in the name of its principal town, whose streets – Wingina Avenue, Grenville Street, etc. – are full of connections to this story. The state capital of North Carolina is called Raleigh – though Sir Walter himself never set foot on North American soil.

Wanchese and Manteo were actual Algonquian

natives and really did spend time in London where they were introduced to Elizabeth at court. Manteo would return to Virginia with White in 1587 to be made Lord of Roanoke and Dasamonquepeuc. A new colony was to be founded in Virginia – the legendary 'Lost Colony'. But that, as they say, is another story . . .

About the Author

Chris Priestley was born in Hull, spent his childhood in Wales and Gibraltar and his teens in Newcastle upon Tyne. He went to art college in Manchester and then lived and worked in London for many years as an illustrator and cartoonist, mainly for newspapers and magazines. He has written a range of books for children, both fiction and non-fiction. He lives in Cambridge with his wife and son.

The Tom Marlowe Adventures are inspired by his own childhood love of historical novels. *Death and the Arrow* was shortlisted for an Edgar Award by the Mystery Writers of America in 2004 and *Redwulf's Curse* was shortlisted for the 2006 Lancashire Fantastic Book Award.

Death and the Arrow

BY CHRIS PRIESTLEY

'There's devilry here and no mistake!'

London, 1715. The air is black with soot, the murky alleyways crowded with people, and rumours of a gruesome murder lurk in the shadow of St Paul's Cathedral. A body has been found 'beskewered by an arrow right through his heart'. Even in a city where crime is commonplace, this catches the attention of printing apprentice Tom Marlowe.

Soon there is news of more victims, each pierced by an arrow and found holding an odd illustrated card, and Tom is both fascinated and repelled by the strange events. When the mystery unexpectedly intrudes into his own life, he feels compelled to investigate . . .

The first Tom Marlowe Adventure
978 0 552 55475 6

The White Rider

BY CHRIS PRIESTLEY

The man – if man he was – had no face
. . . Where a face should have been there
was only the white bones of a skull!

London, 1716. The alleyways are full of spies
and buzzing with intrigue. The executioner's axe is
wet with the blood of Jacobites who oppose the
reign of King George and flickering lights have
appeared in the sky over the city.

These are strange times, and when Tom Marlowe
and his friend Dr Harker hear stories of the roads
being haunted by a mysterious white rider – a
highwayman who is rumoured to be able to kill
his victims simply by pointing at them – Tom can't
resist the chance to investigate . . .

The second Tom Marlowe Adventure
978 0 552 55474 9

Redwulf's Curse

BY CHRIS PRIESTLEY

The bones of Redwulf, an ancient warrior king, lie in barren marshland. Anyone who disturbs them will be cursed . . .

When Tom Marlowe and his wise friend, Dr Harker, visit Norfolk they are intrigued by stories of the ancient royal grave protected by a ghostly guardian. As the wind whispers across the marshy landscape, strange rumours are heard, mysterious attacks are perpetrated and horrible deaths occur. When Tom glimpses a mournful figure on the horizon he cannot help wondering if there is any truth to the legend. Surrounded by shifty-looking servants, smugglers and a black-cloaked aristocrat, anything seems possible to Tom. Can he tell legend from fact, truth from lies and solve this mystery?

The third Tom Marlowe Adventure
978 0 552 55483 1